"*A Greater Music* will grab you by the heartstrings and play you like a harp, in the best of ways. It riffs on music, language, and literature while delivering a gut-punch of an ending."
—CASSIDY FOUST, *Literary Hub*

"The experience of reading the prize-winning Korean-born writer Bae Suah is simultaneously uncanny, estranging, and spellbinding, an effect that becomes perceptible the more you read...Bae Suah offers the chance to unknow— to see the every-day afresh and be defamiliarized with what we believe we know—which is no small offering."
—SOPHIE HUGHES, *Music & Literature*

"This dulcet, contemplative novel [*A Greater Music*]...serves as an articulate and moving reflection of how life can stop 'for a time in a certain fluid place between past and future.'"
—*Publishers Weekly*

"*A Greater Music* is another addition to a growing body of literature that explores the idea that human sexuality is more pliable and fluid than the rigid labels we assign to it."
—MELISSA BECK, *World Literature Today*

"With concise, evocative prose, Bae merges the mundane with the strange in a way that leaves the reader fulfilled yet bewildered, pondering how exactly the author managed to pull this all off."
—*Korean Literature Now*

"Sparse in words, dense with multiple layers of meaning, Bae's work will surely be an international endeavor to follow closely."
—TERRY HONG, Smithsonian Asian Pacific American Center

RECITATION

—

Bae Suah

TRANSLATED FROM THE KOREAN BY
DEBORAH SMITH

DEEP VELLUM PUBLISHING

DALLAS, TEXAS

Deep Vellum Publishing
3000 Commerce St., Dallas, Texas 75226
deepvellum.org · @deepvellum

Deep Vellum Publishing is a 501c3
nonprofit literary arts organization founded in 2013.

ISBN: 978-1-941920-46-6 (paperback) · 978-1-941920-47-3 (ebook)
LIBRARY OF CONGRESS CONTROL NUMBER: 2016959333
—

Recitation *is published under the support of*
Literature Translation Institute of Korea (LTI Korea).

—

Cover design & typesetting by Anna Zylicz · annazylicz.com

Text set in Bembo, a typeface modeled on typefaces cut by Francesco Griffo
for Aldo Manuzio's printing of *De Aetna* in 1495 in Venice.

Distributed by Consortium Book Sales & Distribution.

Printed in the United States of America on acid-free paper.

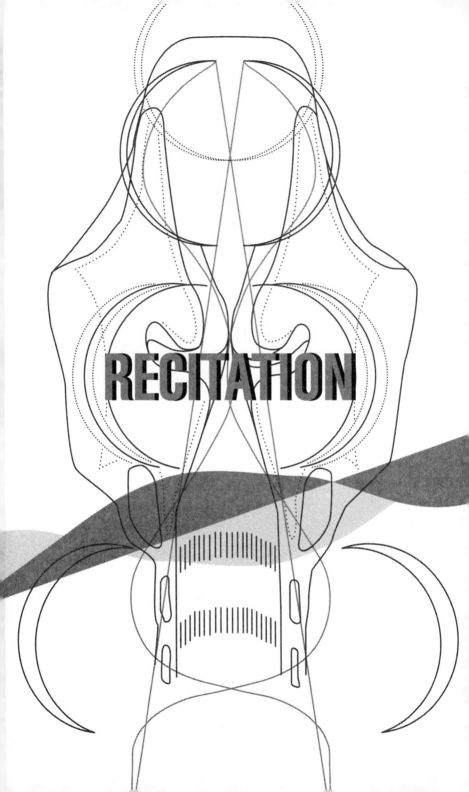

RECITATION

1. Kyung-hee said that in her hometown, she'd been a theatre actor specialising in recitation

Several times already now, she'd had the idea of visiting the houses she'd left behind. Grasshoppers spring up around her feet, transparent carapaces propelled into the air as she crosses the dirt yard and approaches the cement buildings, their desiccated structures hard and dry as stale bread, and riddled with holes. She peers through the window into the ground-floor flat, where a naked bulb casts a cold, orange light. Objects devoid of life or utility crowd the interior. A table, a cupboard. A vase, a bed. Chairs. Clothes lacking bodies to give them shape. The chill impression of those dearly missed rental houses, whose occupants were only ever passing through. In reality, though, she never once went back to any of the places she'd left behind, and there was something peculiar about the way she only drew them again and again in her imagination, like a hometown whose precise location has grown uncertain over time. Kyung-hee enjoyed talking about the various houses she'd lived in. This one was in that city and that one was in this, some days the heart of a bygone city to which no name can now be put would irrupt into a present conversation with all the suddenness of a cloud of dust whisking up into the air, some unforeseeable instant. Such cities thicken and coalesce, appearing in front of an audience in the guise of blind women. Blind women leading groups of black pigs, blind country women singing, their earlobes crudely pierced, a woman who is both a mother and a thief, a blind peddler woman standing in front of the house. Before the curtain went up, as the prima donna stepped out onto the black, sticky floorboards of the stage, the director pressed a white stick into her hand, saying: to really inhabit this role, from this moment onwards you *are* blind...

Kyung-hee told us about the groups of peddlers who wandered up and down in the square near where she lived, hawking Rolexes. Adding, but obviously they were fakes. First a tall, smartly dressed young man, then a group of bashful girls, probably students at a women's college, tried their luck with a group of travellers, asking whether they weren't perhaps in need of a watch. Because they'd broached the topic in such an off-hand manner, as if it didn't really matter to them either way, and because their introverted, extremely unbusinesslike body language managed to make them seem somehow above such things as commercial transactions, it didn't immediately occur to the travellers that these were unlicensed sellers peddling fake watches. Having just arrived in some faraway country, and feeling as though they'd finally awakened from that deep, soporific stupor known as day-to-day existence, the travellers marvel at the novel perspective they now encounter, so very other from those they'd previously known; nothing could be further from their minds than the purchase of a watch, but now their footsteps slow to a stop; the seller leans in, whispering lips brought close to the travellers' ears, seeming liable to inhale their souls.

Eight hundred for one, a thousand for two. Kyung-hee herself wasn't sure of the denomination.

We first met Kyung-hee in front of Central Station, after the last train had just pulled in. It was summer, late at night, and the taxi drivers were striking yet again. There had already been several announcements over the station's P.A. system directing passengers to the temporary bus stop nearby, but these were seemingly incomprehensible to Kyung-hee, as she was still sitting on her big suitcase when all the other passengers had disappeared. She was wearing a long-sleeved denim jacket over a pigeon-grey dress; she looked exhausted, but not to the point of having lost that tension or agitation peculiar to travellers. Feeling unaccountably friendly, we offered to accompany her to whichever hotel or hostel she was planning to stay at. But Kyung-hee's answer was that she didn't have a reservation at any hotel or hostel in this city; she'd merely arranged to meet someone at the station, but he seemed to have forgotten their appointment, or else something had come up to prevent him from keeping it. He wasn't someone Kyung-hee knew directly; they'd been introduced through a mutual friend who lived in Vienna, and he'd agreed to let Kyung-hee use his living room for a few days, though now of course he hadn't shown up. We've never seen each other in the flesh, you see, but we're both part of a community of wanderers who let out their homes free of charge, Kyung-hee explained. If someone comes to visit whichever city I happen to be living in, I give them somewhere to stay, and then when I go travelling, other people in other cities will let me use their living room, veranda, guest room, attic, or even, on the off chance that they have one, a barn. It all depends on their individual circumstances. So I know nothing about these people aside from their name and the city they live in, and if something comes up so that they can't come and meet me, well, that's unfortunate, but there's nothing to be done. I just have to spend the night at the station, then take the first train to another city the following morning.

Our curiosity had been piqued, so we stayed and talked with Kyung-hee a little further; in the end, our conversation went on for much longer than we'd initially anticipated, even after we had impulsively invited Kyung-hee to come and spend a few days with us. Of course, this had absolutely nothing to do with the fact that Kyung-hee came from the same city as we did! After all, it was such a long time ago that we'd emigrated. We'd forgotten the city we'd left behind, a forgetting that could almost be called complete, and even the threadbare skeins of faded memories, which we used to wear like sorrowful clothes, had, in time, slipped furtively from our withered shoulders. Our first impression was that Kyung-hee's travelling was entirely aimless, quite unlike our own one-off relocation, which we'd undertaken specifically in order to die in a city other than the place of our birth. We couldn't immediately tell where she came from, and like I said, we didn't care. Judging from her talk about the various cities she'd lived in, we simply pegged her as northern Chinese or Mongolian, or perhaps, though this wasn't very likely, a member of some Siberian tribe. We'd never personally met a woman from Mongolia or northern China, or, for that matter, from some Siberian tribe, but we thought we'd noticed the tell-tale traces in Kyung-hee's high cheekbones, and that characteristic northern expressionlessness which, at certain moments, crept over the upper part of her face. But we were mistaken.

Back in her hometown, Kyung-hee said, she'd been a theatre actor specialising in recitation. Despite being from the same place, we couldn't recall ever having heard of any such occupation or art form. During Kyung-hee's stay we had some other immigrants over to dinner, old-timers, and she spoke to them about her travels; intriguingly enough, at certain points her voice itself revealed her experience as a 'recitation actor', belying our shared conviction that we had never heard of such thing back in our hometown. She described herself as a traveller constrained by lack of money. One day several years ago, she'd heard the news that her old German teacher, whom she hadn't seen for a number of years, and with whom she hadn't exchanged so much as a phone call after their abrupt parting, had died, and after that everything was irresolvably vague and depressing, and neither happiness nor unhappiness could touch her anymore, and so she suddenly decided, though it was impossible, that she needed to go in search of him, she needed to travel; this, apparently, had been the initial motivation for her current roving life, an entirely unplanned development which now seemed to have been inevitable.

Kyung-hee told us that the secret salespeople all wore leather shoes buffed to a sheen, as though they had some kind of appointment to go to. On bright and sunny days their foreheads and the backs of their hands were the colour of rust, and the skin that wrapped their figures was a mixture of scurf and gooseflesh. As the afternoon declined, she said, they would shield their eyes with their hands and gaze up at the darkening sun; at such times vague shadows, black-ish splotches in the shape of leaves, would tremble on the backs of their hands. From planes passing by overhead, she explained.

Or else it was sunspots caused by seething solar flares, or eclipses, rare and invisible to the naked eye. At the time, one of them recalled how, several years ago on a flight to Japan, he'd passed over that city where Kyung-hee used to live. Muttering as if to himself, he said, "If the plane we were on had been the kind that flies really low, beneath the clouds, then the shape of that grey city would have stretched out beneath us, a wide, flat disc glinting like a sheet of beaten iron on the other side of the windows. The bone structure and flesh of a city, a long valley seemingly gashed into the land, a dried-up river bed cratered with red depressions, or the gaping mouth of a huge cement cellar. But even then, given that we would have been asleep at the time, our cricked necks jammed into the creases of our headrests, it's unlikely that we would have spotted any travellers roaming the streets, any mys-terious wandering traders in the square by the department store. Ah, I've just remembered, I was in that city another time, on an eight-hour stopover while I waited for a transfer flight to New Zealand. I paced up and down the airport corridors, trying to make sense of the hazy, distorted images visible on the far side of the windows. Why is it, I wonder, that no one ever talks about how those places known as airports, and the time spent there, feel like one of the stages of metempsychosis, a waystation on the journey from this life to the next? As the night lengthened, I huddled up on a chair in the smoking room and smoked a cigarette. And in the chair opposite, it's all coming back now, there was this enormous monkey with a chain around its neck, crouching in exactly the same pose as me." After all, the city had an airport, Kyung-hee said, or rather muttered, her words somewhat indistinct. Someone else responded that every city has an airport. Almost every city, another voice corrected, but so quietly it was practically inaudible.

"There was one girl I became friends with, a watch seller, and before I left that city she offered to share some work with me. You see, she thought I was leaving for the same reason as everyone else, because rents had doubled in the space of a few years." After a pause, Kyung-hee continued. She always spoke as though entirely oblivious to the interest which people had in that city, with its airport and aeroplanes, though perhaps she was just pretending. When the rainy season swept up the country, she said, the secret sellers all went north ahead of it, and the lonely square became the preserve of umbrella-sheltered travellers. Standing there quietly in their dark raincoats, waiting for the bus, they looked like the trees known as 'black poplars', planted at regular intervals in the asphalt.

Kyung-hee had spent two years in that city, renting a room right in the centre; towering over her lodgings was a skyscraper so tall it was difficult to judge where it ended and the sky began, while down below the pedestrian underpass stretched for several kilometres. The second-floor window had an old wooden frame, and its glass was blurred with dust and soot, but she said that if you shunted it open you could look down onto a large, square fountain, always dry, and an intersection webbed with zebra crossings, a tangle of black and white radiating out like the spokes in a bicycle wheel. Above all this hung the enormous elevated expressway, slicing through the heart of the city as though suspended in mid-air.

The fountain's stepped base recalled a ziggurat, and halfway up its obelisk was a hook on which they sometimes flew the national flag, though Kyung-hee had no idea what its original function might have been. Every time I looked out of the window, that fountain reminded me of Egon Schiele's gaunt, decapitated Venus; she smiled as she told us this. The six footbridges and eight zebra crossings converged at a narrow space in the middle of the road, between the elevated expressway's colossal pillars; here, where pedestrians waited for the lights to turn green, lurked a handful of leather goods shacks, their semi-underground rooms lit up even in broad daylight. You have to take your shoes off before entering, but every time the lights change such a maelstrom of pushing and shoving breaks out that unless you make sure to stow them securely, they'll almost certainly end up getting kicked away somewhere. Once that happens there's no way you'll find them again. After you pull open the glass door and step inside, watch your step on the loose cloth lining the stairs in lieu of a carpet. The tiny flight of stairs leads to a room where the proprietor, squatting on his haunches, offers the customer tea. The room is both his living space and a workshop-cum-store; you could also think of it as a kind of museum. You should close the door behind you as quickly as possible, to keep out the dust devils and the cacophony of swarming vehicles. While the proprietor snips away at the leather with his enormous scissors, you, the customer, sit and drink your tea, glancing uneasily up towards the door, trying to spot your shoes. Even with the door closed, the blaring car horns are every bit as deafening as they are up in the street, and the shack's entire structure threatens to collapse every time a tremor is passed down from the enormous motorway overhead—in short, the walls of the shack are almost completely ineffectual in muffling the din and vibrations from the passing traffic, so it's really no wonder you're on edge, especially since this is your first time. And look outside the door, at those callous feet trampling all over your shoes, so battered they look like an old, worn-out pair that's been dumped by the side of road! A gang of motorbikes surging this way, people scattering in all directions like a shoal of sardines, then crowding back in again! The proprietor lists the various items he is able to craft from leather: shoes, saddles, women's belts, hats, and he can even stitch on some bells if you like. A drum with bells, he says, wouldn't be a problem—if that's what the customer wants. Every now and then he breaks off from his needlework and gently works the leather with his teeth. Each time he does so, Kyung-hee said, a rank animal stench wafts up from the spit-soaked hide, heady in the narrow confines of the store.

"Those fake-watch salesmen you mentioned," a woman chimed in, "I used to see them too"; she was one of the immigrants we'd invited, but she was only stopping here temporarily, just like Kyung-hee. "I used to see them loitering in the square in front of the department store, holding rolled-up copies of the *Seoul Herald* —you know, as though they'd arranged to meet someone there, and were just killing time until they showed up. There was this one woman, sometimes she'd come up to me and try and get me to buy a watch; now I think of it, she looked an awful lot like you. At least, like you probably would have looked, twenty-odd years ago. Early one morning, we were riding the bus from the airport into the centre. Mornings often began with scattered showers, but the clouds soon dissolved in the brightening day, leaving the whole world suffused with the sun's honeyed glow. The sky's blue intensified with every passing second, and the shreds of cloud sailing away to the east were a purer white; the light sharper, more distilled. The sunlight glinted cold and smooth off every conceivable surface, as if the whole world was scintillating light, and all sharply-defined borders were being reflected in an enormous mirror—that was how it looked. I told her I didn't need a watch, that I didn't have the kind of job that went with one of those heavy, yellow-gold watches she was flogging. And then you, no, the young girl with the black hair—she couldn't have been more than twenty—gave me this bald stare, and asked if that meant I didn't have a job. I didn't answer, I just smiled. So she said in that case she would guide me up Monkey Mountain. Unfortunately, though, Monkey Mountain wasn't in our itinerary. So you, no, the young woman, I mean, gave me up for a lost cause. She waved her rolled-up newspaper and marched off to another part of the square, though she didn't actually seem all that put out. Her jet black hair, her deep, delicate eyelids, from which raindrops could have scattered at any moment, or actually, perhaps that's it, her big black umbrella, yes, it's so vivid now, as though I'm seeing it again right in front of my eyes. The square had a large flowerbed, packed full of sunflowers, right next to the bus stop for the airport shuttle, so there was always a line of people there, some standing, some sitting on their suitcases. I can see it all now, right this very moment, scene upon scene overlaid upon the present time like a painting of trembling light dappled with dark, confounding the senses. Two blind beggars shuffling from store to store, playing a Chinese fiddle, but when you got up close to them you could see that the things they held in their hands weren't the fiddles I'd seen in Shanghai, why, they were nothing but cassette players, though I suppose the long, slim antenna which extended from the recorder's round bulk might, from a distance, have resembled a fiddle's long neck. Each of the beggars had a middle-aged woman to guide them, and each of these had a small child strapped to her back, bald as a monk; men in police uniform were keeping a lookout at the level crossing; stunted youngsters loafed around in white shirts; a woman stood in the centre of the square, beating a grey quilt with a paddle; another old woman held the quilt by the corners, pulling it taut; over to one side was a makeshift stall, just a small table and chair for street peddlers to hawk souvenirs; those tourists who've decided to go to Monkey Mountain were gathered around the stall; of such elements was the scene composed. The square was bustling with life, yet with a strange undercurrent of agitation. Being tourists, our gazes snagged on every little thing. And so I can't recall exactly where she wandered off to, that young woman who was selling watches. Even with the peddlers constantly crying Monkey Mountain! to Monkey Mountain!, the sound produced by each solitary droplet of clear water as it was shaken from the woman's umbrella onto the pavement was noticeably loud and distinct, much more so than would be usual in our day-to-day reality; a sound that throws open the door of memory, which is linked to sensation, so now all of a sudden it's as though Monkey Mountain, which I never once set eyes on, which I'd never even heard of before then and never have since, really does exist, a concrete, intimately familiar location—at least, that's how it seems to me."

"But those watch sellers have nothing to do with the leather crafts shop I mentioned earlier," Kyung-hee responded curtly. "I thought a city with an airport was what you were interested in, not fake-watch sellers. Isn't that what you wanted to hear about?" Someone else who'd been there seems to have retorted that every city has an airport. Almost every city, another voice put in, but quietly, so that it didn't seem a rebuke. "A few years ago I had an accident on stage—I broke my toe in the middle of a recitation. The role didn't call for anything extreme, all I had to do was sit on a chair and read my lines, then, after a while, stand up and walk across the stage with my script in my hand, just a few paces back and forth, and tap my hand lightly against my chest as I walked; that was all the physical acting that was required of me. Aside from the chair there were no other props to clutter the stage, and it wasn't that I slipped or stumbled somehow. There was nothing about the set-up that might have been expected to lead to an accident; the stage wasn't too dark, but then it wasn't too bright either, so I wasn't in danger of being dazzled. There was overhead lighting throughout the performance, because that was best for when I was sitting in the chair and reading the script. In other words, it was just the kind of staging that I was familiar with from other performances, with nothing that might catch me off guard. I got up from the chair and walked across the stage, careful not to step on the hem of my long skirt. I had the script in my hand but I'd pretty much memorised it already, so I didn't need to keep looking down at it as I walked. Now, it's true that the script was quite intense, quite emotional. But even with the most intense script in the world, could whatever emotions I experienced really be sufficiently physical as to cause the little toe on my right foot to break, entirely of its own accord, while performing an action no more complicated than a simple step forwards? And then there was the sound it made, so loud that the audience in the front row could hear it too. *Snap!* Even more than the pain itself, the thing that really shook me was how intrusive that sound was, how definitively it seemed to have interrupted the recital. The pain only made itself felt after a couple of seconds' lapse, you see, whereas my embarrassment was entirely synchronous with that *snap.* Ah yes, I forgot to mention my shoes. Well, they weren't high heels, or the pointy kind that really pinch your toes. They were just an ordinary pair of pumps that I wore all the time. In fact, the other recitation actors used to say they made me look like some old nun shuffling about in her slippers. So it couldn't have been the fault of my shoes. What it was, was an unwitting step forward into that too intense, too excessive, too heavy, too restless, too chaotic, too aggravating, too dizzying, too much, too lacking, startlingly dramatic whirl of emotion, the kind that strips you bare and leaves you gasping out noisy sobs over every little thing, even while remaining utterly unmoved. You know, people often dismiss mental or emotional dizziness as just some abstraction, but they're wrong; it has its own concrete form, its own specific scent. And what's more, there are certain objects and places that are saturated by it. For example, sitting on the second chair in the kitchen always calls up a very specific feeling for me. As though the emotion itself lives in that chair. We step into its country quite by chance. A couple of seconds after the *snap*, when cold sweat broke out on my brow and the dizzying pain meant it was all

I could do not to just collapse where I stood, but all the same I had to grit my teeth and make the three or four steps over to the chair, a distance I only just managed; even then, finally able to sink down into the chair, I knew. I'd gone far, oh, much too far from myself. My body is a burning brand, a traffic light regulating the flow of my life. That thing, that riot of emotion, has flicked it to green: *Go.* And from that moment onwards I was set in motion, propelled into a peripatetic life. The tears streamed down, scalding my cheeks as the audience fixed me with their bright gazes, exclaiming, look at that woman, look how red her face is, like a burning lump of coal!"

So you're saying that was when you decided to go wandering—walking—halfway round the world? someone muttered diffidently. The moment your toe broke? A walking trip wouldn't exactly have been the first thing on my mind.

"It wasn't a decision," Kyung-hee replied, "more like a thought that came to me already decided. Every bit as unrealistic as my idea of walking all routes in the purest fashion. Because of course, what lay between me and my destination weren't seas, deserts, and endless, featureless steppes, but modern borders, surveillance systems, arms traffickers, soldiers, and government officials. All of this means you have to travel by train, or at least in the goods hold of a truck. And when you come to the sea, it's only natural that you have to pay for the ferry, right? Yes, it's true that I'd decided I had to go on foot, though the reasoning behind this wasn't clear even to me. But that decision came after I broke my toe. On the face of it, it's only a superficial resemblance, a chance affinity, that connects the decision with the broken toe. But the fact is that those two events both found me at a similar time in my life, sweeping in like a whirlwind and somehow taking possession of me, of my flesh. Thinking about it now, the common ground shared by a toe and trip on foot would have to be the blind sincerity of flesh. A sincerity both pure and unmediated, that's what I was hoping for, one that would be sufficient for me to be granted admittance at the border of that unidentified country I was heading for. And perhaps I would have walked all day. All day long, and then all day long the next day. But all that was something for later on; just then, my toe was in a plaster cast, and while I waited at home for it to heal I passed the time listening to Bayern 4 on the radio. For no apparent reason, I can still remember the news bulletins that were on at the time. The station had an hourly news programme, and when nothing special had occurred in the world since the last broadcast the same stories would usually be repeated again and again, more than ten times in the same day; as this is what happened with the story of the UN secretary-general's trip to Pakistan, perhaps it's not all that surprising, though it doesn't really explain it, that the soundbite about the secretary-general in his kaftan is still stuck in my head. And one day I thought yes, I have to go there on foot. Walking seemed to be the only way of acquiring a form of non-linguistic legitimacy, the highest that I myself can achieve in this day and age, a comprehensive representation of both the flesh and that which animates it. I might find my way blocked and have to turn back. Retracing my steps might take even longer, with occasional further obstacles to taking the direct route, and enough of these forced diversions could eventually lead to complete disorientation, but still nothing would prevent me from walking that lost route, the same that my feet have always taken me down at decisive moments in life. And I realised that I'd only ever lived in the city where I was born, a city which now seemed both strong as adamant and elaborately curlicued, like a besieged fortress encircled by a moat, archer's holes in its castle wall, adorned with gargoyles of pig-faced warriors. At some point, I myself had become one of the solid stones which made up that city's wall. I formed a single discrete part of that soaring battlement, from whose summit traitors were hung by their necks. I constituted and extended the city, and at the same time I was like a spear or cannon, part of that menacing bulwark defending the city against its potential deserters. And the feeling that I was a part of the city's eye. A part of that geographical entity, the physical weight of its flesh, the tangibility of its epidermal sensations. It was the first time I'd felt like that, you know. Up until then, I'd always felt that my life was lived incredibly freely. I'd never doubted that, not once.

It was probably the incident with the plaster cast that brought about that desire to detach myself from a specific location, to free my material self from being tied to a given set of coordinates, fixed in a single place. Looked at from a certain angle, perhaps it's more accurate to call my soul the author of that shriek of despair, and relegate my toe to the role of intermediary. The doctor sawed the cast off after four weeks. The serrated edge crunched into the solid cast, pain grating along my nerve endings as sensation returned to numbed bones and stiffened muscles. It hurts, I said. Of course, it's bound to be a bit sore when the cast first comes off, the doctor replied brusquely, without looking at me. I gritted my teeth and tried to bear it, but the pain's keen edge flamed through me, surely more than any doctor had a right to demand their patient endure. Every time the blade of the saw made a pass, that pain flared up inside me. It's too much, I said, I can't take it. But she told me it was nothing but the stimulation of stiffened muscles, why, even a child could put up with it. At the time I was already planning to escape my life, to get completely outside it, and to do so on foot, which made my broken toe seem especially unpropitious. My jaw clenched, mouth convulsed into a rictus, an image of perfect clarity suddenly penetrates into the heart of the pain—that of a person lying on a hospital bed. He once described hospitals as 'the home of that particular brand of physical and psychological torture which goes by the name of surgery.' Death, he said, has been reduced to nothing more than a medical formality. Though few people now remember it, the institution we know as the hospital had originally fallen under the purview of the military, functioning primarily as a facility for disposing of the city's death-row outcasts, its escapees or intruders who, according to him, were falsely accused of treachery or theft. These hangings were extremely popular, giving rise to markets and merchants trading in the necessary accoutrements of the death penalty: axes, rope, and plenty of wooden buckets for carrying away the filth. The city is the abode of the arrogant. Miniaturists and amateur anatomists transferred the corpses to the hospital. Hobbyist engineers trailed along behind, seeking a glimpse of that mysterious automaton inside each human body, wondering whether there might be a way of making it start up again once stopped. The city's condemned pass down the hospital corridors, their progress hampered by their broken necks.

Their own stench is rank in their nostrils. Their necks are bent forward at such a crazy angle that their faces are entirely hidden even to those standing directly in front of them. And so, he said, I fervently hope that nothing happens to bring you here—to this charnel house they call a hospital." This was in the letters that he wrote to me every so often.

Every time we listen to Bayern 4, we will think of you.

The toe that was encased in the cast had been sawn almost halfway through. Pain and shock had left me insensible, but I still remember the doctor's look of utter astonishment, how she practically wailed into my face: Oh I'm so sorry, I must have misjudged it, there's no way I could have known! I'm so sorry…

You must never come here.

2. Are we goshawks tumbling from this life to the next, never to meet again in our former guises?

A long time ago, when Kyung-hee saw her German teacher for the last time, she was living with a teacher couple whom he had introduced her to. She was staying in their chimney room. Rather than having the standard flat ceiling, that top-floor room, to which Kyung-hee had appended the temporary designation 'chimney room', was shaped like an upside-down funnel; the structure rose several metres up in the form of a horn, narrowing as it went, and from the point in the centre where its four sides met, a narrow, chimney-like duct stretched up in a straight line to the sky, and since there was a hole at its very end, if you stood in the centre of the room and tilted your head back to look straight up, a single point of clear sky, a wash of blue light floating in the dark void, was visible through the square duct (hole) which pierced the ceiling. The roof recalled an old-fashioned double-convex telescope, set up to point directly towards the heart of the universe, and since, rather than making distant things appear to have been pulled closer, that telescope plays the contrary role of further increasing the original distance between object and observer, anyone who experiences a night in the chimney room ends up, in their dreams, remembering that sky as having been further away from that particular point on the earth's surface than it is in all other places.

The chimney room's four walls were roughly plastered; white scabs grew tumescent on their old gray surfaces, peeling off and dropping soundlessly to the floor, and after the cleaner had done her rounds all that remained of the wall were so many sand-coloured scars. Whenever someone spoke in the chimney room, the contours of their voice would blur into an indistinct echo as they bounced off the funnel-shaped wall-cum-ceiling, ever increasing in bulk and volume as echoes bred echoes, meshing and overlapping as the voice crept up the funnel like a coiling spring until eventually, unable to pass through the hole to the sky, sinking back down again. With such a weighty amplification being also and at the same time a self-multiplication, the speaker, though alone in the chimney room, would nevertheless be seized by the feeling that there were others in there too, constantly responding to each other with exactly the same words, and with the briefest delay between each response. A cannonade of mischievous, hostile voices. Like an enormous collection of clocks, their hands all moving at slightly different speeds, the ghosts of the chimney room sit side by side on the bed, enunciating with particular emphasis, especially on the final few words, as they run through the senseless motions of their speech, but no meaning can be gleaned from these phrases, mouthed as though merely beating time like a clock's ponderous pendulum. That evening Kyung-hee made a phone call, but because of the reasons given above, neither Kyung-hee herself nor the person on the other end of the line could make head or tail of what the other was saying. It sounded like the tangled confusion of a conversation where, as when a wrong number has been dialled, two complete strangers each run on with what they have to say, entirely oblivious to the other.

The chimney room was the smallest room in the teacher couple's flat, used whenever they had friends or relatives over. Inside their front door was an entrance hall with a hatstand and several coat hooks, leading through to a second door. The chimney room and guest bathroom both adjoined the entrance hall, as did a small living room for the exclusive use of the husband, while the couple's own rooms lay behind the second door, which had to be opened with two big old-fashioned keys. And so the chimney room was originally a space for them to receive guests, so that the room's official title would have to be something like 'guest room.' Their flat was on the top floor of a four-story building, which backed on to the rubbish bins. The building was opposite a municipal gymnasium and a secondary school, which had been done up a while ago, though the school hadn't even existed back when the female teacher had still been teaching. The teacher couple, actually it wasn't both of them that were teachers, just the wife, or at least she used to be; she didn't work anymore, she had retired long ago, and in fact she was already over fifty when she first started teaching at the secondary school, so that period in her life hadn't amounted to any more than ten years, but every time Kyung-hee thought of them she habitually employed the phrase 'teacher couple.' Once they reached the age of eighty, the teacher couple abandoned their travelling lifestyle; instead, by way of substitute, they began to offer the chimney room to friends who were themselves still travelling, or else to holidaying acquaintances to whom they'd been introduced through mutual friends. And so the chimney room was also home to a band of travellers, all of whom the couple knew personally. After eighty they stopped writing letters, but they were still frequent recipients. Those who'd stayed in the chimney room would send them letters or postcards, either from the hometown they'd returned to or from the next destination in their itinerary.

The chimney room had a small television, the guest bathroom had a radio, and there was an old record player in the small living room which the couple used to listen to, but Kyung-hee never went into the living room. The chimney room's small television had a thick Braun tube coming out of the back, and the screen wasn't much bigger than that of a security camera at a bank or airport. When you pressed the button on the remote control, a thin thread of bluish-gold light extended horizontally across the gleaming black bulge of the screen, and only after several continuous seconds of an odd sound, like something coming from beyond the galaxy, would the screen flash on. It was just the same when you switched it off. There were also occasions when, even without so much as touching the remote, the screen would flicker for a brief instant, the world hemmed in by its borders would be plunged into sudden darkness, and a long, slender horizon of golden pixels was strung out across the screen before it all snapped back to normal, a single galaxy exploding into nothingness. It looked like a star going supernova, seen side-on in the form of a whirling disc. A disc with streaming saw-teeth around its edges, fire's ragged hem. Kyung-hee stared at the screen for a while, wondering what that desolate explosion might presage, but the appliance now seemed entirely inert. The radio in the bathroom, on the other hand, was shiny and new, so it switched on without a problem even when you hadn't touched it for a while.

The teacher couple gave Kyung-hee a bunch of keys. As well as the key which opened the building's ground-floor entrance, there was a small silver key for the outer of their flat's two entrance doors, and a large, broad brass key; this was for the inner entrance door, which led through from the section containing the chimney room. The couple explained to Kyung-hee that several years ago some gypsy children had robbed them, so it was imperative that the inner entrance door be locked whenever the house was empty, and at night time. But they also said that, as one of them was always up by 8 a.m. at the latest, and would then open the inner door, Kyung-hee would be able to come in and have breakfast in the kitchen. The couple called the hole in the chimney room's ceiling the 'skylight hole', and informed her that when it rained she could use the switch on the wall to plug the hole with a glass stopper; just then the heavens were restless with a shifting filigree of rainclouds. But even when it wasn't plugged with the stopper, not even a single raindrop ever made its way down through the ceiling onto her bed, which Kyung-hee found strange. Before, the chimney room must have been temporary quarters for domestic servants, or else a room for praying, or for receiving a punishment. The electronic skylight hole would have been installed more recently. The couple referred to switching it on as 'giving the room a pat on the head.'

When taking the stairs down from the fourth floor you would come face to face with a full-length, life-size photograph of John F. Kennedy, on the landing between the second and third floors. The same, of course, if you're going up. Kyung-hee had walked up those stairs many times, but it still came as a shock every time, as she momentarily mistook the photograph of the beaming president for the real thing.

That morning, there was a basket of red roses on the table; only then was Kyung-hee informed that today was the female teacher's eighty-second birthday. Her husband lit two candles, and they divided the bread between three plates. On the windowsill there was an orchid and a pot of peppermint, and the candles in the two brass candlesticks were duck-egg blue, matching the sugar bowl. The husband poured his wife and Kyung-hee a cup of coffee each, and Kyung-hee spread butter and honey on the sliced bread. Just then, they were interrupted by the bell's noisy chime. They were all surprised; there was no reason for anyone to come calling at such an early hour. Their unexpected guest turned out to be the former Lufthansa stewardess who lived next door, who'd brought a homemade birthday cake. She'd come with her daughter, who looked to be around fifteen years old; the girl announced that her cheeks were swollen because she'd had her wisdom teeth taken out just the day before, and so they all made a fuss over her, peering at her puffy cheeks and murmuring words of concern. Standing in the entrance hall, they let off tiny firecrackers and waved slender, self-igniting Yugoslavian sparklers while they sang "Happy Birthday". They each tasted a piece of the homemade cake, and the consensus was that it was delicious. Once these standard congratulations were over, the former stewardess and her daughter went back to their flat. Just before, though, the stewardess turned and looked back over her shoulder as though something had suddenly occurred to her, saying "Oh, I've only just remembered, once when I flew to Korea, Seoul was completely smothered in a yellow sand cloud, and the plane was on the point of being diverted to Japan. Luckily, we managed to touch down in Seoul after all; I remember our strongest impression of the place, stronger than that thick yellow sand suspended in the sky like a swarm of yellow dragonflies, was of the intense, peculiar scent of spices that pervaded it." It's garlic, Kyung-hee said, supplying the word that the former stewardess had forgotten, or else was deliberately leaving unsaid, and then their guests went straight home. The female teacher explained that the former stewardess' family had been their neighbours for decades, they were really quite close—so much so that, in the past, whenever the couple went on holiday and left the house empty, they would empty their postbox for them.

The teacher couple had an invitation to dinner, and were sorting through their formal clothes, trying to decide what to wear. It was an autumn dance party, hosted by a newspaper company.

It was always held on the last weekend of October, they told Kyung-hee, and it had been an annual fixture for them for over thirty years, an occasion for dancing the night away before catching the last train home. The female teacher had chosen to wear a very deep red woollen scarf over a white silk blouse. Despite the ground being muddy with rain, she'd also picked out a pair of high-heeled shoes, as these matched the rest of her outfit. Her husband was wearing a thick, soft-looking grey sweater and a grey fedora. My wife will probably be dancing on the table tonight, he told Kyung-hee. The couple begged Kyung-hee to go with them, but she had to explain that, unfortunately, she already had plans. I suppose there's nothing to be done then, the wife said. Next time, next time you'll have to come with us. She didn't have false teeth or dye her hair, her back was still straight, she had good posture and a steady stride. Aside from a little rouge on her lips, she wasn't wearing any makeup. As she was healthy and very active, only a few years ago she'd been entrusted with directing the children's theatre production of *Queen Gisella* at City Hall. *Queen Gisella* was a fairy tale. Kyung-hee knew it too. Next time, then, next time I'll have to go with you, she said. Next time, if the opportunity arises, I'll go with you to the newspaper company's ball. The couple were bent over the subway timetable, checking the times of the last trains, their heads practically touching. Last train on line 1 departs 11:45, on line 2 departs 00:05, 10:57 on line 4 but you can only take it as far as City Hall, the tram in the town centre runs until 1:20 a.m.... Why can't you just take a taxi?, Kyung-hee asked cautiously. That way it wouldn't matter about the time, you could just stay and enjoy the party for as long as you like, and it's not that far away, so the taxi fare wouldn't be too high. As Kyung-hee was aware, the couple were both very wealthy. They might well have been the wealthiest people she knew. Well, you see, the thing is that we're both awfully tight-fisted, the teacher replied. Kyung-hee couldn't decide whether she was being sarcastic or candid.

Kyung-hee came home late that night. She opened the front door with the silver key, groped about in the dark entrance hall for the light switch, flicked it on, then, after putting the bundle of keys on the table beneath the coat hooks, went into the chimney room and stood there quiet for while, her skin grazed by its chilly air. A tall elm in the back yard towered up past all four floors and above the chimney room's window, submerged in the sky's black water; only a few last leaves, already sere, still clung to its branches. As soon as Kyung-hee opened the window, a mass of cold air rushed its moist body into the room. That evening, just before she left the house, Kyung-hee had spied the soft, dark grey body of a nuthatch, sitting on a big branch near the top of the elm. As the nuthatch, its streamlined body small enough to be held in one hand, had taken up a position so close to the chimney room's window, Kyung-hee could even make out the orange and gold mix of its round belly, and the long, straight black markings that crossed over its eyes. The wind was scattering the raindrops here and there, as though they were dancing. Even when the surrounding branches shuddered violently in the wind, the nuthatch didn't move an inch, so Kyung-hee carefully reached out to check whether it was merely a beautifully-made stuffed decoration; of course, there was no way that she could reach all the way to where the nuthatch was sitting.

The nuthatch's belly was the colour of evening sunlight as autumn ripens to its zenith, but now the little bird was nowhere to be seen. A thick layer of leaf mulch carpets the streets, so the flat, worn-smooth soles of Kyung-hee's shoes were constantly slipping on the pavements' kerb stones, and everywhere was thick with the smell of rain, of the nearby river, of cobwebs festooned with moisture, of mist rising up from the leaves. Drops of rain gleaming the colour of iron tumbled soundlessly down over the bridge's metal railings. Her shoes were light summer ones, so Kyung-hee's feet were still wet. She spent a long time gazing out of the window, down into the inchoate darkness, Kyung-hee said, until eventually it seemed as though flesh, hair, and even breathing itself had all become a wriggling dream of dark green moss, a component of the night. "A spore sets down roots in an empty lung, blossoms into a pretty clump of pale yellow mould and, growing into the spokes of a wheel, bores into me, bores through my skull and flesh, stretching up towards a certain specific point in the sky, looking down on me and the world, that kind of feeling..."

The inner front door was closed like it always was at night, and on seeing the coats and shoes in the hall she guessed that the couple had returned home but were already asleep. Through the skylight hole high up in the chimney room's ceiling, a small square swatch of sky glinted black. Kyung-hee sat down on the bed, then stretched out on her side, her legs dangling to the floor. "I'm beneath the ceiling of a tent supported by pillars. The tent's walls are all flapping. Walls of fluidly shifting leather, moistened with the shaman's spit. Fire lives beneath the central pillar. They swing their bodies up on a trapeze suspended from the air, red tongues ceaselessly stretching to the sky. Actually, they know how to fall away from themselves. Restlessly scintillating their transparent flesh, they exist simultaneously at all places on the ground and in the air. In their mouths, new tongues of silence are constantly sprouting up..." As if these words, whispered while that dark grey nuthatch was perched at the top of the tree of life, had reached Kyung-hee's ears only after passing over strange mountains, after the briefest lag. "All human abodes are open to the world's core..."[1]

The next day dawned to a clear sky, and the wind couldn't stop the sun from coming into view between thick clouds, so they decided on the spur of the moment to make a trip to the lakeside. This was possible as the female teacher was still able to drive at the time, and also because a male guest, an old friend of the couple who had at one time been Kyung-hee's German teacher, was supposed to be paying a call on them. In the morning they made cheese and tomato sandwiches and filled a big thermos with hot coffee. There was still plenty of time left before the man who'd been Kyung-hee's German teacher was due to arrive when the buzzer for the ground-floor entrance went off. The intercom exchange clarified that the person who'd pressed the buzzer for the couple's flat was the niece of the Polish maid whom the couple used to employ. Their faces both clouded with perplexity at the same time. "Darling, you'll have to go down and make her understand, and send her away," the teacher said. "Though I made myself perfectly clear the last time...I can't understand it."

After the husband had gone down, Kyung-hee asked what was

---

1   from Mircea Eliade's *Shamanism*

going on. The teacher dithered, saying that she hoped Kyung-hee would understand that it wasn't as though they were turning some (foreign) stranger away without a reason. In the past, they'd employed a Polish maid, a skilled, diligent woman with whom they'd had a highly satisfactory relationship, but who, unfortunately for them, had ended up returning to Poland. Before she did, though, she introduced her niece to the couple as a potential successor. The couple had the maid's niece clean their house once as a trial, but her method of cleaning had left a lot to be desired. So the couple had decided to look for a different maid. And after they'd explained this several times to the maid's niece, who could speak the language of this place only clumsily, in simple words so that she could understand, they'd sent her away; this had happened last week, but now the young Polish girl had come back again this week, on the same day of the week, as though she had absolutely nothing else with which to occupy her time, and pressed their buzzer.

In the meantime the husband had come back up, and in answer to his wife's question of how it had gone, said that the young woman had acted as though she couldn't understand even a single word he said, and had tried to push past him up the stairs, her body language stubbornly insisting that she'd come to clean their flat. Kyung-hee kept her mouth closed for a while. Indeed, they all kept their mouths closed for a while, keeping their own counsel. Kyung-hee felt as if she had tactlessly thrust her way into the world of the couple's ethical beliefs, a world which was perfectly fair, yet private all the same. The couple's tacit determination, in spite of their perplexity, not to make any further mention of the foreign maid's niece—Kyung-hee suspected that her own presence might have something to do with this.

The male guest who'd arranged to come that day also pushed the buzzer for the couple's flat from the ground-floor entrance, just like the maid. This time the teacher called over the intercom in a cheerful voice, We'll be right down. Her husband was carrying a food hamper, the teacher had the coats, and Kyung-hee had two blankets to spread over the grass. They went down to the main entrance, each in turn encountering on the stairs the handsome young President Kennedy, his mouth open wide in laughter. The male guest presented the teacher with a bouquet of purple flowers, which he'd been awkwardly trying to conceal behind his back, and wished her a happy birthday. The teacher's hair was completely white, but groomed into an attractively rounded shape. Her husband was wearing the fedora he always put on whenever he went out; this was because his doctor had recommended that, where possible, he should not let his bald head get too much sun. His physique was robust, and the smart, achromatic clothes he always favoured, a palette of blacks and greys, suited him. After an hour of the teacher's slow driving, the four of them arrived at the lake, which was out in the suburbs. "My friend's father turned ninety this year; he never has any problem driving," the male guest said to the teacher while they were in the car. "But of course, he only drives from his house to the supermarket or the church and back, and that's all in the same area."

The sand by the lake was deep-coloured and unusually grainy, and the dirt was made up of a mix of thick gravel with conspicuous particles, pointed stone fragments, and deep black quartz.

There were several ducks by the water's edge, rummaging around among their feathers with their beaks. Two golden retrievers, accompanying some picnickers who'd arrived at almost the same time as Kyung-hee's party, bounded out of their car and down to the lake, so the ducks, their afternoon nap disturbed, yet with no indication of haste, formed a line and wandered off to another spot. Having seen the water, the dogs kept bounding about in excitement, their tongues lolling out. Kyung-hee's party found a bit of flat ground, arranged the blankets and sat down. The lake wasn't particularly big, and neither was the scenery all that impressive, but it was clean and quiet; since it was possible to park right in the vicinity, the couple explained, people liked to come here with no particular plan other than to swim or enjoy nature for a few uninterrupted hours. They ate their sandwiches, and shared a bottle of apple juice. Accompanying the dogs was a small group of teenagers, who chose a spot on the sandy earth near Kyung-hee's party and got McDonald's hamburgers and fried snacks out of their backpacks to eat. The smell of grease oscillated through the air and the paper bags rustled noisily. The sunlight, granular as the sand, streamed down onto their cheeks and foreheads, and a cold breeze sticky with sap blew over from a nearby group of Japanese cedars. Kyung-hee rubbed her face and jaw with the back of her hand. One of the golden retrievers came up to her, then, after giving her hair a good sniff, padded off again.

After finishing the last of the coffee, the teacher suggested they go for a swim. "It'll probably be the last swim of the year." The moment she finished speaking, she and her husband took off their hats and shawls at the same time and with almost the same gesture, so much so that they looked like a pair of mimes. After that, they unbuttoned their coats, and started to remove their sweaters and trousers, and the woman her blouse. Then Kyung-hee could see the swimsuits that they'd been wearing under their clothes. Lastly, they took off their shoes and socks. They tucked the socks neatly inside their shoes. They blew their noses on their handkerchiefs, each rubbing their chest and shoulders as if trying to smooth the gooseflesh down. A distinct latticework of bluish veins tracked across their bodies. For a moment, they looked not at each other's faces but at the passage of those conspicuous veins under each other's skin, their gaze intimate yet distant. As though this, too, were something they'd managed to arrange without words, they held hands and walked slowly down to the lake.

Kyung-hee described the event she'd attended the previous evening to the man who'd been her German teacher. The event had taken place at a 'theatre' which was in fact a small reconstructed fortress attached to a garden; as the 'theatre' designated as such had been situated in the very heart of a wooded park, after getting off at the subway station, the hour already late, Kyung-hee had had to walk for a while along a gloomy, narrow trail through the woods, disturbed only by the hooting of owls and the susurration of the wind. But, arriving eventually in front of the 'theatre', she walked around the fortress and discovered a long line of people queuing for tickets, stretching all the way up to the moat; people who, despite the fact that the ticket office had a clearly visible sign stating that they'd already sold out, hadn't given up hope of there being some returns, and were queuing blank-faced, their thin blouses buttoned up to the throat, their leather handbags heavy in their hands. All the women, with their scrawny, wrinkled necks, stood facing the same direction, their skin as sharp as though it would crumble into powder, and their white hair flying in all directions, more delicate than silk thread and lighter than feathers, shining in the evening dew. The oily black waters of the moat under their feet glimmered like huge dark pupils. Kyung-hee said that, brushing past them on her way into the theatre, these women had stared down at her feet, and for some unidentified reason their eyes were wet with grey tears, and their metal-encrusted handbags weighed down their withered arms, their earrings studded with purple garnets, and their chain necklaces, the pamphlets of stiff top-quality paper they clutched in their hands, and the varicose veins on their legs were all tugging their weak veins still more strongly down, down.

And when Kyung-hee went in, to her surprise she found a piece of paper with her name written on it affixed to one of the chairs in the very front row. A Belgian literature professor sat in the seat next to her, and next to him there were four young women all in black formal dress. The four blonde women all seemed to be dressed similarly and had similar hairstyles, so much so that there was nothing to distinguish between them, and their gazes, too, were all fixed in the same direction, staring straight at the stage. The women's abundant coiffures and unflinching straight-ahead stares recalled the golden retrievers, almost making Kyung-hee want to pet them. Shortly after Kyung-hee had taken her seat, the writer who was the protagonist of the day walked up to the stage. He was an elderly man, but powerfully built; he had a large grey cloak on over his brightly coloured coat. Everybody craned their necks to get a look at him, and each time he took a step their heads shifted in response, like hundreds of clams being swept along by the tide. He hadn't even opened his mouth to speak, in fact, he hadn't even got up on stage, yet already he was displaying a formidable power of command, as though the whole audience was under his spell.

After the event was over, the Belgian professor bought Kyung-hee a glass of soda water. As the four women in black formal dress, Kyung-hee, and the Belgian professor had all been invited to the writer's post-performance dinner, while waiting for a taxi in the theatre hall to take them to the restaurant they talked of this and that, and it transpired that the male guest who'd come to see the teacher and her husband that day was an acquaintance of the professor. "What a strange coincidence, I saw him at another event just two days ago, we even said hello to each other!" the Belgian professor exclaimed happily. With her glass of soda water in her hand, Kyung-hee felt the urge to tell the literature professor all about the incredibly many chance events that had come about during the course of her life, meetings and crossed paths that had hinted at something which could only then be verified after a certain amount of time had gone by. Just then the taxi arrived, and the retriever women cleaved the air like dogs diving into water.

When they arrived at the restaurant it was close on midnight; but not only were there no empty tables, the corridors and the deck were also filled with people, and as there was no room to wedge yourself inside they had to stand in front of the door, directly in the draft, and wait until a seat became available. Every time a plate-carrying waiter whisked in front of them, enthusiastic at the prospect of getting a tip, the plastic curtain covering the front door fluttered, and with so many people crammed into that narrow space, Kyung-hee said, there hadn't even been room for to her to squeeze in between the writer's tie and the retriever women's black dresses.

"There's a book I want to give you; how about you come round to mine for a bit after the meal?" the literature professor suggested to Kyung-hee as they worked their way through the asparagus, and she said she would. After one in the morning, the writer, who had to leave at noon for Beijing—Beijing, encouraged by the fact that it was hosting the Olympics, had become passionate about inviting various foreign writers and scientists—said that he hoped his guests would understand his leaving before them, but that first he wanted to smoke a cigarette. At the time, a law had already been passed banning smoking inside any and all restaurants, but the writer, untroubled by such a trivial regulation, wanted to get out a cigarette and smoke it, and none of the party could do anything to restrain him. But then the head waiter came up to him and said, "This is a no-smoking area, and we're not able to break the rules even for Nobel Prize winners like you." Anger contorted the writer's face; not because he couldn't smoke, but because he'd never won a Nobel Prize. "This guy must have me confused with Günter Grass," he grumbled, slowly raising his heavy body from the seat. One of the four women stood up with him; she had a youthful look, indeed, she was very young, perhaps still in her early twenties; she was the writer's niece, and an editor at a famous publishing house. As the young niece and the other women had sat in close formation around the writer throughout the meal, as though they were his bodyguards, Kyung-hee and the Belgian literature professor had been almost entirely unable to get a direct word with him, and were only able to greet him with glances from the other side of the table. After the writer and his niece disappeared, the three remaining women all turned in unison to face Kyung-hee, asking, so how did you come to know the writer; the question was laced with suspicion regarding her level of intimacy with the latter, which was sufficient for him to have invited her to the meal and sat her at the same table as them. And so as soon as Kyung-hee told them the name of her former German teacher, who'd come to see the teacher and her husband earlier that same day, and explained that, as something sudden had come up which prevented him from attending the event, she'd ended up coming along in his stead, the retriever women instantly lost all interest in Kyung-hee and their heads swivelled back.

Very deep into the night, Kyung-hee and the literature professor were taking a taxi home. Kyung-hee had to go to the teacher couple's flat where she was staying via the professor's guesthouse. "I'll just wait in the taxi," she said, "then you can go and fetch the book for me." The literature professor wavered a little at this talk of waiting in the taxi, saying that first he would have to go and get the key from the owner of the guesthouse, and then go to the building across the road, where the guestrooms were. So it might take quite a while, and how about they just leave the taxi and go to his room together. In that case I'll probably be able to treat you to a cup of tea. But Kyung-hee shook her head and said, "I'm grateful for the offer, but it seems easier if I just wait in the taxi. At least, easier than leaving this taxi and then having to flag down another one in this quiet neighbourhood, or else phone for one." The taxi driver parked in front of the literature professor's guesthouse, the professor got out of the car, rang the bell of the owner's house, and went inside. The literature professor seemed to have given Kyung-hee some reasonable explanation, something about how the guesthouse owner still hadn't gone to bed at this late hour, or how guests didn't keep the keys themselves, but Kyung-hee hadn't really been able to understand what he was saying. After obtaining the key, the literature professor hurried over to the building on the opposite side of the street, tottering slightly; his movements, which seemed somehow awkward and clumsy, showed that he wasn't used to the speed a situation like this demanded.

The professor returned after around five minutes with the book in his hand, and passed it to Kyung-hee through the taxi window. It was a collection of Max Frisch's lectures on literature, *Black Square*. "This book contains transcripts of two lectures that Max Frisch gave in 1981, in English, related to his own literary theory, at New York University. It was published this year. Are you wondering why the title is *Black Square*? It isn't just because the entire cover is painted black. In his lectures, Max Frisch told an anecdote about a western diplomat who visited a St Petersburg art gallery during the Cold War, where he'd been able to see 'Black Square' by Malevich, who led the Russian avant-garde in the early twentieth century and who critics called the founder of Suprematism. That painting wasn't hung in one of those display cabinets designed to keep the general public at a distance, but concealed in a secret warehouse. The diplomat said to the gallery director:

'I don't understand why this painting isn't shown to the public. As you can see, it's no more than a simple black square. I mean, even if it had been hung with other paintings in the social-realist category, people wouldn't have been able to guess its meaning. Perhaps they would think it's simply black wallpaper.' At that, the director replied: 'What you say is correct. People wouldn't be able to understand why a painter might paint a black square, of all things. But even so, the moment they see this painting they would become aware that there are things of value existing in this world other than society and the people. And so this painting can't be displayed.' I hope you read this book and also attend the forum on Max Frisch, which will be held next year in Brussels. You see, our hope is that this book will be published in translation in all the civilised countries of the world by 2011, which is Max Frisch's centenary." Kyung-hee didn't actually like Max Frisch all that much, she wasn't particularly interested in him. But she promised the literature professor that she would read the book. "It's a real stroke of luck that I met you today," the literature professor said, sounding deeply grateful. There wouldn't have been another opportunity for him to give the book to Kyung-hee; he had to take the train back to Belgium in the afternoon of the next day (technically the same day, as it was past midnight). His daughter had given birth to her third child. As he said this, the literature professor grinned broadly, not bothering to hide his obvious delight.

The teacher couple's heads bobbed up on the surface of the lake side by side, like two balls. They were swimming skilfully, moving their limbs leisurely; as they pulled further away from the lakeside

BAE SUAH

their figures gradually diminished, so that eventually they looked like two grey nuthatches sliding along the surface of the water. The male guest who had been Kyung-hee's German teacher had known the couple since he was a boy, but he said that their wild temperament absolutely hadn't altered with age, in fact if anything they seemed to be growing gradually more feral. Kyung-hee had first come to know the teacher couple only a few days previously, but it suddenly occurred to her that she'd seen a photo of the teacher in her younger days somewhere. Now it came back to her, she remembered that she had also heard a certain anecdote about the wife.

"A couple of years ago when I was staying in a boarding house in München, I remember chancing upon a photo of the female teacher. One day the proprietress showed me an old album. Among the photos she spread in front of me then, of München in the sixties and seventies, there was a small picture of a young blonde woman, which seemed as though it had been included by mistake. The woman in that photo was an old friend of mine, the proprietress said quickly, we met while I was studying French literature. And our friendship was ruined because she and my ex-husband fell in love. I made it up with my ex afterwards, but things between my friend and I were never the same. I didn't ask any questions at the time, because I didn't want to pry into past affairs and stir up painful memories for the proprietress. And so I don't know the ins and outs. But it's strange, after I came to the teacher couple's house, according to what the wife herself told me one morning, a long time ago she had broken with a female friend, a complete rupture; she also said that friend was now living in München.

That they'd become friendly while they were studying French together, and that things had turned out the way they had because they'd loved the same man. That's how it is, the wife's current appearance is certainly far removed from that of the cute young woman I saw in the photo, but even so, trivial events that seem to me like nothing but chance—you introducing the teacher couple to me as old friends of yours, and the fact that you used to cohabit with the guest-house proprietress in München without being legally married—end up spontaneously forming a particular pattern and taking on a given form. I don't spy on the past. But because I have an instinctive preference for stepping unhesitatingly out into a whirlpool of invisible stories which evoke an individual life as one long, unbroken thread, and because for some time now I've been aware that such lives are all around me, addressing me in desolate voices—ah, there are times when I regret that I didn't think of studying a discipline like archaeology or ancient history, then I would be able to clearly make out these whisperings of countless bones and stones—regardless of whether or not my conjectures have any basis in fact, I'm actually growing even closer to this house, this couple, and to the sleep I experience in the chimney room, the dreams I have then, the dream of the ceiling facing the sky. For example, the long, deep sleep of the teacher wife which goes on behind the locked front door."

As though it were actually my own, an unfamiliar self from the distant future, Kyung-hee added. And said that it was similar to the intense vertigo she was faced with when travelling around some country villages. "Photographs of unknown faces hang at the threshold. Photographs containing expressions which, while solemn and sincere, cannot conceal their discomfiture.

Old photographs like sere leaves. Faces generally guessing that
they would soon die. Photographs in which the sitter wears
a uniform, like a school uniform or an army uniform from some
long-forgotten battlefield. A few years ago when I went for a walking tour along Korea's southern coast, I encountered such photos
and thresholds countless times; when I stood there in silence and
peered deeply into them, although admittedly I was apart from
them, although on the surface I had lived a life quite unlike theirs,
in spite of that, and for no reason I can comprehend, I felt that
they were me, that these were photographs of an obscure self that
I didn't know, my own figure that was strange to me, that although
it was actually the face not of a past or future 'I' but of the 'I' of now,
it was entirely unrecognisable to me because such a thing is simply
a certain kind of eternal reverse image. This explanation of mine
is long and tedious, but in fact people can usually express it in
one simple phrase, "the reiteration of existence". Or else, to give
a more precise explanation, when the being that is a given person
crosses countless mountains and rivers and arrives at a temporal
and geographic limit of whatever degree, then at that point those
countless mountains are already a single world mountain, and the
waters of countless rivers are all flowing as a single world river,
and I am therefore inside that mountain and that river; inside the
temporal totality of this universe, where millions of stars are simultaneously self-annihilating in a great flash of light, this universe
which is dying with a mad frenzy, I felt the fact that, at that time,
a certain entity is not me, the fact that I am not that particular
entity, the fact that I am the self of precisely now, could no longer
be as definitive an explanation of certain phenomena."

While Kyung-hee was saying all this, the teacher couple, who had been moving further towards the centre of the lake, creating a calm wake, had become very tiny splotches, and it was as such splotches that they briefly turned back to the shore and waved. An aeroplane flew by overhead. An aeroplane strangely small and close to the ground. It seemed to be not so much flying as staggering through the sky. As though attempting to reconnoiter the holiday-making down on the ground, it was turning clumsy circles in the air, like a newly-fledged hawk. In a movement describing a question mark. I always think of it when I see a plane, Kyung-hee said. A couple are making love on the roof of a building; a plane passes by overhead, casting a huge shadow over their bodies. While they are looking up at the plane, a dog falls out of the sky. It crashes into the roof, a bloodied wreck. A dog that someone had pushed out of the plane. The couple are also bloodied. The couple who had been making love.

"It's a scene from the novel *Eyeless in Gaza*. Aldous Huxley. A scene that really makes an impression, you know, one you can't forget. I found that book every bit as interesting as *Crime and Punishment*. What about you?"

That was a goshawk in the sky just now, the male guest who had been Kyung-hee's German teacher said abruptly. "I don't remember anything apart from the title, which is one of the most memorable of all the book titles I know. As for the content, I've forgotten it all, so there's nothing to say, but perhaps the reason I can't remember it is because the impression it left was of little importance." He added, "As for what happened to the couple making love, it didn't make much of an impression on me at the time but, strangely enough, right now it's coming back to me. The couple who met during the war are making love; a German army shell drops onto the house. The war is still going on, you see. The man sustains a head injury, collapses and loses consciousness. The female protagonist, thinking he's dead, automatically offers up a prayer to God, if you bring him back to life I'll do anything, even if it means never seeing him again. And then, unbelievably, he's alive again. Rather than being dead, the man had simply fainted. And so, after getting dressed and putting on her hat, and without any explanation whatsoever, the woman simply leaves the man, only making the excuse that she's remembered something urgent she has to do. It was probably chance, but even so, she'd promised her god that she wouldn't see the man again if he brought him back to life. But the man knows nothing of this. They spend the rest of their lives living practically next door to each other, never able to return to their previous relationship, and they end up wandering the foggy streets of nighttime London. But that's *The End of the Affair*." And he muttered again, as though to himself, as though seized by something, " it was a goshawk, not a plane."

At that, Kyung-hee confessed that she could never distinguish precisely between one type of hawk and another; the very fact of having made such a response seemed to stake a claim for its having at least some degree of significance, but in fact it was made almost without thinking, and Kyung-hee couldn't help but feel that it was somewhat untimely in nature. Or else, perhaps it was timely enough as a confession, but the vocabulary used to construct it was altogether wrong. Still, Kyung-hee felt duty bound to carry it to a conclusion now that she'd begun, and so carried on speaking. A confession on the subject of natural history, specifically her inability to tell the difference between goshawks and black kites, peregrine falcons and the general kind of hawks, mountain eagles and sparrowhawks, and the difficulties she had in forming a clear picture of a 'kestrel' or 'buzzard', despite the fact that these names appeared in books as frequently as our everyday encounters with sparrows and pigeons. Saying that also, just briefly, although she wasn't religious, when she thought about death its inevitability was sufficient to provoke a sense of respect in her, and that she felt as though that mysterious, unknowable death had already triumphed over each of us long ago, something that we ourselves were the only ones unable to grasp. And that she therefore thought of life and love, of death, which are more commonplace than miraculous, as they appear in *The End of the Affair*, as the avatars of a sincere god.

The clothes that the teacher couple had stripped off and left on the sand, including the husband's hat, were slowly losing their animation. They still had shape and colour, but unless you examined them closely their original character could no longer be discerned, they had become nothing but anonymous flotsam. The couple had been wild in their younger days, and it was only a few years ago that the wife had danced on the table at the newspaper company's party, and the man had been a long-haired liberal, the male guest who had been Kyung-hee's German teacher insisted once more. Or had that been a story about the man himself, or even about Kyung-hee? The man kept talking. About how, when he was young and living in the Middle East, he lost his way for two hours by the Mediterranean, had his watch stolen by a Jordanian soldier, was treated to a glass of liquor by someone referred to as 'Captain', and about how, on the way back to his home in Europe, he bought two yellow fur hats, one for each of his women. But as soon as the woman who'd had the right to open his bag first discovered the two hats, she went into the other room and cried, loudly and pitifully, and so there was nothing else for it but to say that he'd bought both of them for her. Kyung-hee recalled once again the anonymous lovers trapped in the shadow of whirling time.

All their lives, they could never revive their former relationship. When, after having crossed countless mountains and rivers, I end up arriving at somewhere beyond temporal and geographic limits, perhaps the fact that I am my self of right now, that my thoughts are bounded by my own consciousness, can, amid the totality of all the light that this universe has ever produced or has yet to, no longer be unique and exclusive, Kyung-hee thought to herself once again. In that case, what is the nature of this desire, which persists though I know it to be futile? The desire to be myself, this pitiful desire to want what this so-called self wants. Like a personality which endures eternally through repeatedly changing its form, like another sky situated at the same time both above and below the clouds. Yes, that was a goshawk flying through the air. And she opened her mouth and inadvertently let slip the thought that had flashed into her mind. "In that case, are we goshawks tumbling from this life to the next, never to meet again in the same form as before?"

3. I will long for you

The healer removed his shoes by the front door and ushered Kyung-hee inside. The house's interior, flooded with sunlight, had no scent of burning incense, no stone statue of Buddha, no eagle's head, no eastern-style silk cloth patterned with gold leaf, or anything of the kind. Everything was radically spartan, redolent of twenty-first century proletarianism, with every available surface covered in plain white square tiles. The door to the kitchen stood open, letting out the strong aroma of frying sausages. The healer was a plump man who only came up to Kyung-hee's shoulders, his hair as black as squid ink. He was the very first person to respond to Kyung-hee's ad seeking a room in Berlin for a stay of several months, which was why she was here now. No conditions at all, the healer had said, all I need is two hundred euros per month. There's no deposit, and no additional charges. Your room is furnished, including a desk and a bed, there's central heating, and you can also use the kitchen. Quilt and blanket goes without saying. But there's no internet or washing machine. You can access the internet at the library, and I'll let you know where the local launderette is. There's a radio, and a coffee maker. You can even borrow the television in my room, if you so desire. Only during the week, that is, I'll be using it myself at the weekends. But the bathroom and kitchen have to be cleaned every day, and that falls upon the residents. You have to wash up as soon as you're done cooking; there's only one frying pan, one plate, one saucepan and bowl, so no one else will be able to eat otherwise. All the same, you won't lack for anything. There will be three of us living here, but since there are four beds, in cases where, by some chance, there happens to be an unexpected visitor, you can use the spare bed. When I bought the beds they were being sold as a bundle, on special offer, you see.

"In that case, would it be okay if a friend came to stay?" Kyung-hee asked cautiously, making an effort not to give the impression of cutting the healer off mid-conversation. He didn't answer straight away. He examined Kyung-hee doubtfully, a deep furrow creasing his forehead. "If this visitor needed to use the shower every morning, well, I'm sure you can see that that wouldn't exactly be ideal." This reply was made in the manner of someone at a loss for what else to say, though the hint of dissatisfaction was ever-present in his voice. Even so, his face was soundlessly insisting, the ideal guest would be the one who never actually arrived.

As the healer always left the door to his room wide open, Kyung-hee was able to see that, alongside a passage in Tibetan taken from a sacred text—not that she'd been able to recognise the alphabet, but this was something he'd explained to her at a later date—he had on his wall a sheet of white paper on which 'homo spiritus' had been written using brush and ink. His official profession was that of healer-cum-philosopher, and he spent every weekday at the library studying Nietzsche, only returning home late at night. There was one other lodger in the healer's house. This was an engineering student, a tall young man named Eun-hwan; Eun-hwan had fallen out with the healer, his landlord, but was apparently planning to move to another city soon anyway, as he had to change schools. The sunlight streamed in through the bright window under which Kyung-hee was sitting. Her obtaining a room in the healer's house had been all because of a certain man, a man who, for the sake of convenience more than anything else, she had known as 'Mr. Nobody'—no one had been able to tell her his original name, since there was no one who could remember it exactly, or remember how to pronounce it. Kyung-hee had needed a Berlin address, somewhere she would be able to receive a letter from Mr. Nobody. Though the two of them had met for the first time at a restaurant in Europe, both in the capacity of travellers, they had in fact already been aware of each other's existence.

They had sat at opposite sides of the large table, like perfect strangers. The gathering had been arranged for some people from Mr. Nobody's hometown—thinking about it, they had all immigrated in the distant past—and Kyung-hee had been invited with her friend Maria. Maria was one of Mr. Nobody's readers, who had gone into raptures over his book. Mr. Nobody's face was so utterly devoid of expression it was as though he was wearing a flat mask. But Kyung-hee knew that he was aware of her, and in a slightly more particular way than ordinary people 'knew' her. And so it wasn't that Mr. Nobody was a stranger to Kyung-hee. With his body half turned away, Mr. Nobody asked Kyung-hee where she lived. "In Berlin," she answered casually, not giving it any particular thought. That wasn't even half true. At the time, it hadn't been long since Kyung-hee had begun that travelling which consisted of leaving all familiar objects and streets behind, and she had chosen to extend her stay a little even after a television crew who had come to Berlin to produce a radio play had finished filming and gone home, staying behind on her own.

And she had been planning to return to Seoul in the near future, which had at that point become the central transfer station of her travels.

"Around Berlin Templehof airport, you know." At that, Mr. Nobody had blurted out, "What a lucky coincidence! I stay in Berlin at least one month a year; perhaps I'll be able to get in touch with you when I'm next here, if that's possible. If I knew the address, I'd be able to drop you a postcard." And so Kyung-hee promised to send Mr. Nobody an email with her Berlin address. When they went outside the restaurant to get a taxi, a soldier in dappled camouflage gear, on his way home, made Mr. Nobody's body disappear obliquely from Kyung-hee's field of vision. The external world flitting darkly past. As soon as they stepped outside, they choked on the smell of the road and invisible air which came from the shoes of the travellers that filled the street. When Kyung-hee, who had been walking along the pavement, happened to move close enough to the road for his speech to be audible, Mr. Nobody repeated the phrase "your Berlin address," though without looking at Kyung-hee. From that day on, the word 'Berlin' was never absent from her mind.

"I'm travelling at the moment," Kyung-hee explained her position to the healer. "And I need an address in Berlin where I can receive post. I'm planning to be here for a while, you see. It just happened to turn out that way, it looks like I'll be without work for a while. And so I've been left with this stretch of free time."

"Getting work, the need to get work, the need to be occupied with work, being engaged in work, is a reality which weighs heavily on us all." The healer accompanied his answer with a sigh. He and Kyung-hee were sitting facing each other at the kitchen table, each with a mug of tea in front of them. "After all, though this business of 'work' certainly has various shades of meaning, the most definitive of its attributes is that it prevents us from travelling. I'm not talking about the couple of weeks here and there that you spend on a business trip or in a hotel. I'm talking about wandering in the true sense of the word. Crops grab hold of you by the ankles. After planting the seeds you have to tend the patch constantly until the grain ripens, and by the time the harvest is over and you've piled up the grain in the warehouse, winter's gusting snowstorms are already on the horizon. And then what about livestock? You're responsible for giving them food and water, every single day without fail. My father was a farmer, so I'm only too aware of what that kind of life is like. Even if he'd won the lottery, he couldn't even have dreamed of a trip to Venice, you know. None of the farm-hands would have known the livestock as well as he did, would have looked after them as though they were a part of their own body. It isn't revolution that liberates farmers, is it, only ageing and senility, which mean death isn't far away. That's right, for a farmer 'work' and their 'address' are one and the same. Work is a kind of ID card that shows how much money they have, and how much freedom. And so for my father, anything surplus to his needs, a luxury along the lines of 'my Berlin address', was impossible. There was a period in my life, too, when I used to dream of filling my days with nothing but endless travel. Of wandering from place to place, that is, getting by on whatever I could earn from my writing. Though now, to almost all adult members of society it will appear self-evident that my dream has been frustrated..." The healer gave another exaggerated sigh. "Even so, if you look at it from a certain angle there are also times when, irrespective of whether or not that dream is realised, at least one thing is clear; that I'm living a completely different life from that of my father. Of course from your point of view, someone who's always been a city-dweller, the difference probably won't seem all that great, but..." The healer trailed off and glanced at Kyung-hee. Kyung-hee told the healer that she might be having a visitor, that he might stay in her room for a day or two, and asked cautiously if such a thing would be possible. The healer made no reply other than an unenthusiastic 'huh.' Narrowing his eyes peevishly, he seemed to be asking whether Kyung-hee's visitor was the kind who absolutely had to turn up, but Kyung-hee interpreted his non-response as something that could be taken, if not as a positive sign of assent, then at least not as a flat-out refusal.

In the daytime, when the healer landlord was out of the house, Eun-hwan talked to Kyung-hee about how he'd ended up falling out with the healer; here, too, the subject of visitors came up. Eun-hwan was dating a Japanese girl called Yoko. Yoko had a fairly nice flat in the city centre, not far from the university, and so they generally spent time at hers. "And I still paid up in full every month, you know, even when I spent more time there than I did here." But then, around six months ago, there was a fire in Yoko's building. Not some huge conflagration, just someone chucking burning newspaper into the rubbish chute as a practical joke. The fire engine came, Eun-hwan said, and they put out the fire pretty much straight away, but the building had become filled with smoke in the meantime, and the smell lingered stubbornly afterwards.

"Even opening the windows was no good. You could still smell burning newspaper, in the corridors, in the lift, in the passage leading to the main door. People chuck all kinds of things into the rubbish chute, you know, even though they know they're not supposed to. Everything; plastic, toys, rubber gloves, food waste. So the smell was worse than if it had been just newspaper that burned; somehow even nastier because you couldn't tell what it was. Yoko and I decided there was nothing else for it but to come and stay here, just for a few days, until the smell had completely faded. Even then, I was still a bit uneasy about the whole thing. I was well aware that, for whatever reason, my stingy landlord had an unshakable dislike for the beings known as visitors. Of course, it was to be expected that he wouldn't welcome the prospect of a stranger encroaching on his privacy, but he himself frequently put up female shamans from Korea, and I never said so much as a word about it. Anyhow, I was practically never here since I'd got together with Yoko, but still paid the rent on time, so I didn't think that it would be such a huge problem for Yoko to come and stay for a few days. But I didn't want to give him an excuse to make trouble, so I didn't actually let him know that Yoko was here, just in case. She brought her stuff over in the daytime, when the land-lord was out, and since he never got back until late at night I told Yoko that in the evenings she should just keep to the bedroom, as far as possible. I mean, thinking about it now, it wasn't as though we absolutely needed to behave like that. You know, it would have been better if I'd kept it all above board from the beginning.

Anyhow, I explained to Yoko that she had to sneak around like that because the landlord was a bit of stickler. And then he goes and chooses that day of all days to knock on my door, something he never did ordinarily. The reason being that he had the sudden, irrepressible urge to borrow a mirror. My room's the only one with a mirror, you see. Well, I opened the door just a crack and tried to pass the mirror through to him, but he still managed to spot Yoko. Yoko lying on the bed. That threw me for a moment, but then I blew up in a rage at having to explain myself over such a private situation. I thought to myself, what on earth is the problem? What's wrong with someone having their girlfriend over? She hadn't even been there a single night, and she hadn't caused either the landlord or the other lodger the slightest inconvenience, just kept herself to herself; was it really on me to start apologising? So I didn't say anything, just closed the door in his face. Without any explanation, that is. The next morning, just before he went out, he pushed a piece of paper under my door. On the paper he'd written the question, how much longer is that Japanese woman planning to stay here for? The phrase 'that Japanese woman' was odd and offensive. Because he'd met Yoko before and I'd introduced them, so he knew her name perfectly well. And she'd never wronged him in any way. On the contrary, she even helped clean the kitchen before she went back to her own flat. And still the landlord has been giving me the cold shoulder ever since! I explained it all to him the next day, right, about the fire in Yoko's building, how she'd been planning to stay here just until the place stopped reeking of smoke, but had decided now that it would be better to go to a friend's house, last night being a bit awkward.

Well, perhaps my tone was a little brusque. I suppose the landlord might have thought I was quarrelling with him. While he
was staring at me, I could see all sorts of suspicions in his eyes;
more of what he has to say always leaks out from his eyes than
ever passes his lips. Later on, just a while ago in fact, I happened
across a Korean magazine in the bathroom. The landlord gets it
every month through international mail, a magazine put out by
some shamanist organisation. Well, as it happened, this magazine
was lying open on the page carrying a column by the landlord.
There was even a photo next to the byline, so there can't be any
mistake, no way it was written by a different person with the same
name. It was a kind of sketch-piece describing his lifestyle, the
lifestyle of a healer-cum-philosopher residing in Berlin. A certain
passage caught my eye, in which he claimed that while a minority
of wealthy exchange students, born and raised in Gangnam, lead
intemperate, disordered lives, cohabiting with foreign women as
much as ten years their senior—"in order to satisfy carnal desires",
that was the expression he used—the majority of 'genuine' students remain steadfastly devoted to their studies, even in such an
uninhibited Western environment. Wealthy and from Gangnam,
foreign women as much as ten years their senior; whichever way
you look at it, there's no mistaking that these words were aimed
at Yoko and I. Not, of course, that my background is anywhere
near as wealthy as he stubbornly persists in believing it to be. But,
going by the impression I got from living in his house for over
six months, he considered anyone whose circumstances were even
slightly better than his own, he who had been a scholarship student
at a provincial college and had his studies abroad fully funded by

the shamanist organisation, as wealthy. And you know, his describing me as 'wealthy' also held the implied criticism that such a state was the precise opposite of a sincere, spiritual life achieved through self-restraint and moderation. Of course, I didn't put myself out trying to correct these prejudices of his. There was no need for that. But here was this man almost ten years older than me, and studying philosophy, Dionysian Nietzsche no less, allowing such knee-jerk bias to form the basis of his worldview—that always struck me as incredibly bizarre. Perhaps the article he wrote was largely formulaic, not really something worth assigning very much weight to, and I can see that it might have been mainly intended to play up his sincerity and dedication in the eyes of the foundation who was supporting him. Nevertheless, it's still a fact that the opinions expressed there chime exactly with the impression I'd formed of him while I've been living here. That's undeniable. Still, it didn't occur to me to try and justify myself in some way. On the contrary, given that I was supposed to be leaving Berlin the following month, and that his loathing of me was already as rigid as his convenient worldview, he wouldn't have had the slightest interest in any excuses I might have cared to make."

Certain tribes hold the belief that the soul of the dead one becomes a bird and flies up into the sky. Certain other tribes say that you enter the underworld by passing through a door guarded by a monstrous dog; that the living cannot endure the gaze of that terrible hound and so are unable to pass through that door, while the dead find themselves translated beyond all terror. Various sea-going races who inhabit small islands load the dead into boats and push them out to sea, which to them is the eternal abyss of death. There are also tribes for whom bodily death is an encounter which takes place in the crown of a white birch. With their old, worn body balanced in the topmost branches, the dead one ultimately sinks into a dream in which they cross a slender bridge over the roiling waves to the world on the far shore. For some tribes, death is the kidnapping of the soul by the sea snake. Not wanting to pass to the next world all alone, the dead one entices the soul of another along with them, and there are also tribes whose legends tell of the souls of the dead passing to the western world. When they cross the distant western plain where human beings do not tread, they find a tree standing there, and a giant waiting in the branches who will take them up into the sky. The soul shifts form, appearing to humans variously as a tiger, a snake, an eagle, etc. In such a way, the souls of the Inuit are seals. An old woman of incredible age, a single-filament bridge spanning a river, sleep and dreams, the song of Orpheus, the jawbone of some fierce beast, fire, a pillar, a fantastical tree with white breasts, an enormous ancient cauldron giving off great billows of steam, three universes co-existing simultaneously, a coiled snake, a polar bear committing adultery with a human woman, the sacredness of a being who appears as a mountain of iron; there are also tribes who believe these things. For some tribes a hole opens up in the sky, for others their shamans use cigarette smoke, hallucinogenic mushrooms, or a particular cave through which to catch a glimpse of the heavens, slipping the bonds of consciousness to travel briefly back up to the moon. Here, rather than being an end point, death is simply a pathway, one of many human experiences.

On nights when the moon is bright, the shaman goes out onto the steppe wearing a cloak of white feathers, and beats a bronze drum while he prays. Without exception, fire plays an important role in all rituals where the deity of the underworld is entreated to send a soul back. The examples are countless, Kyung-hee thought.

I was reading a book when it came to me that the transmission of these nonessential gods and primitive beliefs, no matter the form they take, seems to influence only the members of tribal societies which have a particularly long and unbroken history of such traditions. Given this, I wonder about the collective soul of the widespread and artificially constructed new tribe known as the 'city dweller', who is no longer a part of any traditional society or race, and has never at any time held spiritual or religious beliefs which arise from any geographic specificity, or at least beliefs which are current only in a specific region, given that, even in regions where such beliefs had once held sway, the degree and duration of industrialisation meant not only that shamanism had lost its power but that access to collective memories of it had been completely cut off, with each individual inextricably bound up with things that would once have been foreign to them, psychological differences flattened, made to conform to an international standard now long accepted, a globally-current 'enlightened' standard that is considered the only one of value; the modern city dweller who has thus lost no few of their native, traditional, mythical elements, which defy explanation; the modern city dweller in whom the majority of us can now recognise ourselves. According to the book, at some point in the future, human beings are going to evolve into machines which exist within and are derived from nature; mightn't this 'present' time in which we are living already be a part of that future, mightn't the initial phase of a mechanical organism, which has neither an innate soil or a soul that would be in direct communion with such a soil, which has, perhaps, no longer a need for such things, be none other than the 'city dweller'? At that, Mr. Nobody laughed and answered: I'm a city dweller myself, but at the same time I'm also an ancient who retains old tribal memories. But that means I'm all on my own, that I've fallen away even from you! Kyung-hee cried out in surprise and despair. No, not that, you are my descendant, Mr. Nobody said to her. Mr. Nobody took Kyung-hee's hand and suggested that the two of them go to his land. Berlin was neither Kyung-hee's land nor his. But it's the land of city-dwellers, Kyung-hee said.

Kyung-hee said: he was walking towards me, from the opposite end of a gloomy alleyway; a small black car sped across his path and instantly transformed into a chicken, stretching its legs out as far as they would go. A big white rooster with a red crest, its sparkling wings half spread. "And so I ran up behind it and awkwardly shooed it away," said Kyung-hee, covering her hand with her mouth as she laughed. Mr. Nobody wondered aloud whether he had been the one driving the car. They were discussing Kyung-hee's dream. "No, you'd gone back home by then. The room whose window looked down onto a forest of black-leaved bamboo trees was yours, wasn't it. Nobody else would have dared to go into your room. The other room was full of people. They were a race of vegetarians, their bodies wasted into slenderness.

And I lay down among them. A mother and three daughters, all of them sleeping, they surrounded me on all sides. One to my left and one to my right, one at my head and one at my feet, they were each lying stretched out with their heads nearest me. With our bodies aligned in that way, we radiated out like the spokes of sleep. In this dreaming state, I ask, are we going the right way? Also still asleep, one of the daughters turns to look at me. The gorgeous silk quilt slips away to reveal her naked body, which resembles a hard piece of bleached driftwood. They introduce themselves as a fortune teller and her three daughters. The daughter baring her naked body holds out to me a scrap of paper with a single line written on it. 'Fate must comply with morality,' or some such phrase. I get the feeling that that sentence doesn't quite tally with the rules of grammar. Over this daughter's face, one of the other daughters' faces is overlaid. All of them sleeping all the while, they repeatedly overlay each other like that, one by one, at first only briefly before they break apart. But, as these palimpsests gradually last for longer each time, those daughters and mother flow into an inextricable entanglement, like four white torches fused into one. And so it takes a little time before I realise that they're now a muse sitting up on a huge revolving disc, hands clasped and dancing a soundless circle around me..."

While recounting the dream, Kyung-hee felt its vertiginous dizziness swoop back, every bit as intense as while she had been asleep. The two of them were lying on the bed when they heard the landlord-healer arrive home. The healer took off his shoes at the front door, went into the kitchen, put a frying pan on the gas ring, struck a match and kindled the flame.

The crackle and pop of the oil heating up, the creak of the hinge as the healer got a plate down from the cupboard, the clatter of a glass tumbler, could all be clearly heard. As could the healer's slippers on the tile floor. The healer thunked a plate of deep-fried meat down onto the table and washed his hands with a great deal of splashing. If you want to use the bathroom before you go to sleep, Kyung-hee whispered to Mr. Nobody, now would be the best time. "The landlord doesn't know you're here right now," she added. Just then, they heard someone going into the bathroom. It was Eun-hwan. "He's an engineering student, and you know, even though they live in the same house, he and the landlord never exchange so much as a single word. In fact, even if they come face to face in the hallway they just pretend that they haven't the faintest idea who the other is, and walk right on past." Mr. Nobody looked about to ask how on earth anybody could be so inflexible, so Kyung-hee hurriedly continued, "Come on, they're both still students after all, think about what it was like for you back then. You must have stayed in a dormitory, right? Someone puts a snow tire up on top of the wardrobe, then, while they're asleep, someone else drags it down and shoves it under the bed. You can't even conceive of such a thing as a private basement; there simply isn't the space. And so the stink of petrol ends up spreading through the whole house. Or what about those cramped dorms you used to have to share during high school, with so many kids to a room they were practically on top of each other? Finding a room like this for two hundred euros in Berlin is no mean feat. And the landlord might come in at any moment on the pretext of borrowing a mirror, so whatever you do don't poke your head out from under the quilt."

The room I lived in when I was at university was right by the elevated train, so naturally every time a train went by, which happened at one minute intervals until the early hours of the morning, the room would shake from side to side as though the whole building had been struck by lightning, accompanied by an absolutely thunderous din, Mr. Nobody said. Not just the building itself, when I was lying down I could even feel my bed juddering, he added with a laugh. And continued, every night spent in that house was like being in a train's sleeper compartment. Kyung-hee responded: "I see that. But this house is extremely quiet. It's a long way from the train station, so after dark it's pretty rare to even see another person, you know. And that means you're free to gaze out of the window for as long as you like, without the danger of some passer-by thinking you're staring at them. As a temporary place of residence it suits me. It's a great thing, and actually quite surprising, that I can feel so at ease sleeping in someone else's bed, using someone else's furniture, sitting at someone else's desk to write a letter."

Having finished his dinner, the healer let the plate clatter into the sink, picked up a damp cloth, and began to give the kitchen floor a vigorous scrubbing. He bustled about, wiping the table, washing up the dishes, stamping back and forth between the kitchen and his bedroom, his footsteps loud on the hallway floorboards. The sound of running water was audible from the bathroom. He filled a porcelain vase with water, carried it back to the kitchen and slammed it down on the windowsill. All in all, it was a clumsy, impatient, angry, repressed, clench-mouthed, highly-strung, cantankerous, ostentatious, excessive, tumultuous demonstration. Perhaps tonight the landlord will be unable to sleep again, Kyung-hee mumbled as she burrowed under the quilt, and will end up sitting at his desk writing a long article to send to Korea. Just then, something slid under Kyung-hee's door with a papery rustle. It was a slip of paper that the landlord had pushed in. It said, "Please keep the kitchen clean."

What did the room in your dream look like, Mr. Nobody asked.

"Yours had a large window, looking out onto an ashen scene sunk in dusk. You wanted to be alone so no one else was allowed to come in, but the door stood open. The house was not very wide, but had a series of rooms laid out in a long line, like the carriages of a train, connected by sliding doors. And there were many families there, not just the fortune-teller and her three daughters; each room was as jam-packed as a B&B during the midsummer holidays, with almost every available inch of floorspace taken up by thin Korean-style mattresses. All of the doors had been left standing open, probably because it was so hot, so I was able to look through them all the way down to the very end of the house, over all the bodies of the people lying down, to the scene outside your room's large window. The bamboo grove was in the foreground of a cityscape of disordered suburbs, the train station, wooden struts that had been erected over the brimming canal, an old orphanage, etc. There at the end of the house, all of this flowed by undisturbed. I'd forgotten about you as soon as I went into the room and lay down on the floor, and seemed to have been concentrating on gazing out of the window. After a while, though, the slender bodies of the fortune-teller and her three daughters started to disturb my concentration. It seems that—because of the scenery flowing by outside the window—I was thinking of your house as a boat drifting with the current, or else a train. Which is what made me ask the fortune-teller's daughter, are we going the right way?"'

The night wore on, and deep into the early hours they found themselves still unable to sleep. Toward daybreak, Mr. Nobody said again to Kyung-hee, "Come to my house. There are no solid walls or roof in that place, no tightly sealed rooms, so your soul will be able to wander as it chooses. Let's go to my house, to my hometown, together. What flowed from me is now in you. I am your land, your ancestor."

The following morning, the healer came face to face with Mr. Nobody in the bathroom. The healer had just had a shower, and was on the point of stepping out of the door when Mr. Nobody was about to walk in. When he first got out of bed in the mornings, especially on cool October days, Mr. Nobody felt that he ought to wander around the house without any clothes on, which was precisely what he was doing that morning. With a towel wrapped around his thick waist, and with one foot on the bathroom door sill, the healer looked up at Mr. Nobody, who was two heads taller than himself. Around the healer's expressionless face, drops of water were dripping from his hair to splash onto the floor tiles. Kyung-hee thought, all that water splashing over the tiles is extremely dangerous, he'll have to give it a quick wipe with a dry cloth. Only after a minute had gone by did the healer step aside so that Mr. Nobody could enter the bathroom. "Good morning," he greeted him. "As you're a guest, I'll make you some breakfast." Kyung-hee, who didn't shower in the mornings, heard all this while standing in the centre of her bedroom with the quilt wound around her, having flung the window open in order to air the place out.

Early and late mornings in the healer's house, the sunlight swept strongly into the kitchen and Kyung-hee's room. In the afternoons the sun's oblique rays slanted through into the hallway and a hon-ey-coloured stillness puddled onto the floorboards, and when the sun began to go down both the healer and Eun-hwan went out onto their respective balconies to soak up the back yard's silvered evening light, the scent of the night's beginning. In the healer's house was a second-hand vacuum cleaner that he'd fished out of the bins. However long you spent trying to get it going, it never actually sucked up any dust, just creaked and groaned and whirred, so Kyung-hee had opened it up once; a veritable mountain of dust was so densely packed inside that there didn't look to be space for a single mote more. But there was no paper bag, and so there was nothing for it but to leave it in its current state. Whoever was on cleaning duty had to get down on their hands and knees to mop the kitchen and bathroom floors. When it was Kyung-hee's turn she always filled a basin with soapy water to wipe down the bathroom mirror, bathtub, and toilet. Once a week, she wheeled a suitcase full of dirty laundry down to the laundry room. After buying soap powder from the vending machine and setting the washing machine going, she sat down on the bench and read a book while she waited for the cycle to finish. On weekdays, during work hours, few people ever came down there. The only people who did occasionally drop by were retirees living in studio flats which had no space for a washing machine, senior citizens,

⌐ho, for one reason or another, maintained a 'Berlin ⌐ung-hee glanced up from her book as someone shuf- ⌐wly in and transferred their laundry into the dryer; the ⌐comer looked to be in their nineties. Warmed by the autumn ⌐unlight coming in through the long window, and by the hot air produced by the machines, filled with the low, regular whir and swoosh of the washing drums, and the rattling of the dryer, the laundry room was, overall, peaceful. Kyung-hee looked down at the street scene, its sharply defined borders between light and shadow. Alleyways where, invisible to her, items of laundry fluttered in the breeze. The faces of people riding by on their bicycles like thousands of golden ears of barley, like ears of barley in the shape of arrowheads, passed into the scene, fusing into it as individual particles of its whole. For some obscure, incommunicable reason, my heart always seems about to burst... the whisper of a frightening dream, reassuring us that there is nothing to be frightened of.

As there was no living room, the three of them had to squeeze around the tiny kitchen table. The healer fetched a wooden stool from his room. Luckily there were hardboiled eggs in addition to the day-old bread rolls, plus butter and jam. Kyung-hee made the coffee. She even rummaged around in the drawer to find the Christmas napkins that had been stained by an old knife which a previous tenant, who'd been evicted, had wrapped in them after using. There was no dish or spoon for the eggs, so they settled on holding them in their hands to eat them. The healer let Kyung-hee have the sole plate, putting his own bread on a napkin, and gave Mr. Nobody the wooden chopping board. Kyung-hee brought

a bottle of honey from her room. As they each cut their bre̊
and spread it with jam and butter they were careful not to makℯ
any large or sudden movements, so they wouldn't end up jabbing
each other with their elbows. It wasn't yet eight o'clock. The only
person who used the kitchen to eat a proper breakfast at such an
early hour was the healer, who maintained regular hours at the
school and library. Kyung-hee solved the problem by eating the
morning meal in her room, and Eun-hwan always slept in late. Mr.
Nobody added a dash of milk to his coffee, and a good helping of
sugar. Kyung-hee gestured towards Mr. Nobody.

"This is my friend," she explained to the healer, somewhat
belatedly. "He arrived in Berlin last night." Hurriedly adding, "And
he's leaving Berlin tomorrow."

"I heard that you might be coming," the healer said, politely
encouraging Mr. Nobody to have some more coffee. "You probably won't be used to having breakfast so early in the morning.
City dwellers seem to get up later and later these days."

"I'm not a born-and-bred city dweller," Mr. Nobody responded,
"and I've always been an early riser. If I was in my hometown,
I would already have finished breakfast and be taking a walk
around the hill in front of my house. But for someone as young as
yourself to be getting up early every day, you must be an exception
to the rule."

"It's because I have to go to the library, of course, but even if
that wasn't the case the morning is still my favourite part of the
day. When the sun comes up and I feel its light on me, I notice a
marked increase in my energy." Narrowing his small eyes even further, the healer peered at the kitchen window, where the sunlight

was just beginning to come in. He turned abruptly back to Mr. Nobody and asked, stiffly, "But perhaps you are a Christian?"

Mr. Nobody replied that he wasn't. At that, the healer laughed out loud, loud enough for it to seem somewhat inane. "Then the three of us are non-Christian barbarians living in an empire of Christian culture, ha ha ha!"

Kyung-hee drained her coffee and cut off the healer's laughter by stating that she was not 'living' there.

Mr. Nobody, too, solemnly countered that he was only a traveller, putting up in Berlin for a couple of days.

"Well, if you look at it like that, then it's the same for me. I'm not a permanent resident either. On all official documents I'm simply listed as a foreign national studying here temporarily. All the same, I've been here for some years now. But the crux of what I was trying to say is that it's not an issue of whether you're a long-term resident... what I've felt since coming here is that the people in this place waste an inordinate amount of time debating whether or not a certain address counts as a hometown. Indeed, it's a characteristic shared by everyone who is conscious of their immigrant status. This naïve, inflated sense of having lost one's hometown. But really there's no such thing, huh, what is it about this 'hometown'!"

In that case, Kyung-hee asked, what was it that he had originally wanted to discuss. And the healer answered that he had wanted to talk about the sun. "In ancient Egyptian myths, the sun is described as male, the opposite gender of the German word, and the sky as female. Because, you see, the sun is what moves, moving into and back out of the body of the sky, which remains stationary.

The rosy morning sunlight symbolises a being which is born anew every day. The night herds us into the realm of dreams, burning out life's vitality. Throughout the night, the spirits of the dead seduce people in an array of constantly shifting forms, flitting from a small bird to a young girl, a peculiar dwarf to a butterfly with the head of a woman, making them claw the air in the flames of fleeting love. According to how the Egyptian myths have it, these are the shadow-apparitions of various dizzying objects arising out of the phenom-enal world, which the sun god 'Ra' sees while he travels in a cor-acle along the river of the underworld. In the evening, the female sky god 'Nut' swallows the sun. This swallowing is a receiving into the fleshly body. And so the sun spends the night travelling through Nut's body, just the same as he does during the hours of the day. Nut bends her long, elegant body over the earth in a soft curve. So that each of her four beautiful limbs touch the earth, you see, indi-cating the four cardinal directions. In ancient Egyptian murals, the female god Nut is depicted with her body bending over the ground like this. And in some paintings the blazing sun is drawn shooting towards the stooping Nut's abdomen like a burning arrow. When the next morning comes, the sun, having spent the right rowing a boat along the river of the underworld, leaves Nut's warm, moist stomach, which he had spent the night churning with his oar, and slips out through her genitals, which form the gap between the earth and sky. Heralded by the brilliant, flushed lustre of an incomparably lovely satisfaction. And in the evening he seeks out her genitals once again and burrows back in, like a cub that misses its mother's teat. Looking at it this way, don't you think that the sun's rising every day is a cosmic relationship rendered as a natural phenomenon?"

"And so it happens that Nut gobbles up her own offspring," Kyung-hee put in, doubting even as she spoke whether this was an appropriate response. "That is, she swallows something that's come out of her own body."

"Every time I encounter that myth it makes a deep impression on me, this unending vision of the universe as one in which the heavens and the underworld, birth and death, appear as separate things only in our eyes, whereas they are all ultimately flowing past as a single, interrelated whole, not as opposites but as each other's end and beginning." Mr. Nobody looked as though he had given this much deliberation.

"Those might not be the only things to form a whole, you know." As he had a mouth full of bread, the healer's words were somewhat unclear. "Given that the sun has intercourse with the body of the mother, what this amounts to is that the sun can be thought of as both its own father and its own offspring. A relationship in which it becomes, at one and the same time, ancestor and future. We can say that we are born from a gushing fountain over and over in an endless repetition, remaining all the while on the feedback loop of eternal life. The moment I apprehend the truth of this, my soul trembles as though struck by lightning. Because what it means is that though the individual is small and nameless, each of us is walking endlessly on, leaving footprints in the sand of eternity. I like the mornings. The spectacle of the sun edging its way over the border drawn by the horizon, blazing upwards through the clear sky, never fails to move me deeply. When morning comes, you see, and I stand alone in that light, all the various phenomena that have caused me pain and suffering the previous night crumble into nothingness. It is a time when the falsely beautiful bodies that had tormented us are extinguished. Bodies of seduction lose their mysterious pull and return to being nothing more than phantoms, nothing more than soulless shells. Extinction is their inevitable fate. Their fundamental essence is echoless death, no more than that." The healer's facial muscles quivered, his expression one of cold, wicked revenge. "Last night, amid the whirl of dizzying coquetry which those ashen demons always perform, I saw a marvellous sight: the towering tree of life, and the tree's bride. The bride was pressed up against the tree, with only a white veil to cover her naked body, while new leaves and branches were constantly sprouting from the trunk. Its fruits must have been incredibly heavy; the branches were so bent under the weight that they were almost touching the roots. But do you know what they looked like, these 'fruits'? Pitch-black mouths, caves yawning wide, lumps of red-black mud ploughed up like filthy wounds, deep pools black with mire..." As the healer carried on with his tale, his vaguely intoxicated expression suggested that he had become so carried away in recounting his memories that he had almost forgotten the existence of Kyung-hee and Mr. Nobody. "And then, as soon as I went up to the tree, right there in the middle of the trunk was the face of an old man, so old he looked to be two hundred years at least! Before I had time to recognise that face, in fact almost as soon as I caught sight of it, the bride who had been pressing herself up against the tree turned her head sharply in my direction; only then was I able to recognise that grotesquely contorted woman. Shockingly, the two of them were my parents, the flesh-and-blood bodies of my living mother and father.

They were open-mouthed and shrieking. Yes, and they were so intent on this that they seemed to have no interest whatsoever in their surroundings, I might as well not have been there. They were groaning amid their gruesome shrieks, the sweat was streaming off them, a disgusting sweet stink rolling off their armpits and groins, they were tangled together in one hideously drooping lump of laughing flesh, their fingers and tongues gouging each of the other's orifices, slurping greedily at the other's secretions, and on top of all that the white fabric which I had initially taken for a veil was in fact a wad of bandages stained with dirty blood, sticking out of my mother's crotch. Oh, I spent the whole night tortured by their screams, unable to tear my gaze from their animal writhing. There truly is no other hell! Now surely you can understand why I offer up such grateful praise to the fresh morning sun!"

Kyung-hee burst out laughing around a mouthful of bread. This is really too awkward a topic for the breakfast table, she might have rebuked him with a few words along those lines, but chose instead to let the healer carry on with everything he wanted to say, let him enjoy his revenge to the full. After all, where was she going to find a room like this in Berlin for two hundred euros? And, what was more, a room which didn't require an estate agent's fee or a deposit? By this point, Mr. Nobody seemed equally well aware of what the healer was trying to do, but didn't seem overly put out. Instead, and assuming a cheery voice, he said, "In that case, what you witnessed in your dream was the very moment when you yourself were materially formed! 'The moment you came into the world' in the true sense of the words, or 'the moment the world came to you'!" and roared with laughter.

The night before, Kyung-hee had crawled up a ladder. The ladder, formed from a withered tree, resembled Mr. Nobody's body. The white ladder was a pillar supporting the house and the world. With the wind blowing around her, Kyung-hee shouted several times, "You are my tree, my ancestor tree." A blanket which had escaped from the window of someone's house flew past right in front of them, undulating along its entire length. You are my house. My lovely person, my person made of earth. Unable to sleep, Eun-hwan had padded across the hallway floorboards and knocked on Kyung-hee's door, but neither she nor Mr. Nobody had paid this any mind. Riding on Kyung-hee's head, Mr. Nobody sang a song. Kyung-hee couldn't understand the song, as it was in Mr. Nobody's mother tongue. His song had a majestic, resonant melody, but contained more martial tragedy than pathos, and seemed to be ringing out especially in the cellar and the earth, disturbing the slumbering spirits of the dead. Mr. Nobody explained that it was a song about fireworks. Supporting the ceiling with both hands, Kyung-hee laughed. Eventually, she shouted out that she was touching the sky. "Look, your firework song has lifted me up to the sky! I see differently from before, hear differently from before, feel differently from before. Right here, this is space-time as it was before the Big Bang, that's how old we are. We are the world's parents."

By the end they were pounding the table and laughing uproariously. Breadcrumbs and eggshells bounced up off the plate, the knife clattered. Even the healer eventually burst out laughing, with a mouth full of egg. "Be careful of red cars," the healer said, giving Kyung-hee a gentle dig in the side, the expression on his face suggesting that he was being particularly generous with his advice. "I can't tell you anything concrete about your future, but what I can tell you is to be careful of red cars, and that if you carry on dressing entirely in black your spirit's vital energy will suffer." Kyung-hee replied, "I'm a traveller. Whatever belongings I take with me have to fit into a single bag, so all I have in the way of clothes are a black coat, a pair of black trousers, a black skirt, and a blouse. For me, this place is a point on a journey. I'm not able to be fastidious about the colour of my clothes. Also, my friend will be staying here tonight too. You don't mind, right?"

"A single night is no problem," the healer replied straightforwardly, as though there were no issue whatsoever, having eventually decided to give in. And he said to Mr. Nobody, "You're probably in pain after your long journey; I know how to give a quick back massage, so if you'd like I could give you one this evening." Mr. Nobody really did have a sore back. Not only because he'd spent many hours scrunched into the economy seat of an aeroplane, but because, as he explained, he'd had a chronic affliction for some years now, and neither doctors nor drugs could ease the pain; in fact, the only thing that helped was the dexterous hands of a Thai masseuse. "I'd be grateful for that," Mr. Nobody said courteously. "Only, I haven't washed myself with water for the past three years; I suppose you wouldn't mind that." The healer and Kyung-hee looked at each other in surprise. The healer, who showered twice a day, sniggered, and even Mr. Nobody laughed a little. "All the same, I take a kind of wind bath I've devised myself, using the air and a wet towel. Early in the mornings, at the rising of the sun who is both son and father."

I was intending to write my memoirs, Mr. Nobody said. I've had the manuscript nearly complete for many years now. But it turned out that it couldn't be published. Not yet, at least. There was no lengthy explanation for this; it was simply because he was afraid that what he'd written might unintentionally wound certain people, or that they might feel that he hadn't fully taken their feelings into account, which, again, was not what he intended. So he put the manuscript in his bag. He went travelling.

He and Kyung-hee were lying face down on the two beds in her room. Kyung-hee had no chronic pain and no particular desire for a back massage, but was there to keep Mr. Nobody, or else the healer, company. Having warmed up some kind of yellow oil, the healer now used circular motions of his hands to apply this to Mr. Nobody's back and the backs of his arms. According to the healer, the oil came from desert marmots. The healer's hands were white and plump. Since she had removed her outer clothing, baring her skin, Kyung-hee felt somewhat chilly. When the healer asked Mr. Nobody whether his back was starting to feel a little better, Mr. Nobody replied with a brief 'mm', his eyes and mouth remaining closed. The healer pummelled Mr. Nobody's back with the backs of his hands, so vigorously that Kyung-hee felt droplets of oil splash her face. The healer seemed in high spirits. His stocky frame was gathering speed, switching direction several times as he darted around the bed on which Mr. Nobody was lying. After squeezing the oil onto the palms of his hands and spreading it evenly over Mr. Nobody's back—the healer's arms were too short to manage this without switching mid-way to the other side of the bed—he swept his hands in soft strokes first upwards and then downwards, pressing down firmly on the spine, the armpits, and elbows, etc. Lacing his fingers together, he pressed down onto the individual vertebra one by one, hard. He performed acupressure on Mr. Nobody's shoulder muscles by manipulating them with one finger at a time. In all of this, the healer seemed to get a kick out of having control over another's body—the bodies of others being generally larger and stronger than his own, generally more beautiful—and out of governing another's pain. In spite of the chill, the healer was so engrossed in the massage that the sweat was thick on his forehead. And while he was doing this, he asked Mr. Nobody why he hadn't been able to publish the manuscript.

"As to that, various explanations exist, but the most overriding one is that my wife was opposed to it," Mr. Nobody answered. "You see, there were some things in the manuscript that she wasn't happy with."

"But do you mean that every time you, who call yourself a writer, publish something, it has to meet with your wife's approval first?"

"No, not that, but memoirs are very different from fiction. Individuals appear there under their real names, and all words and actions are given as statements of fact, even those which we wish we could forget had ever happened."

"But, and this is purely my own opinion, it's not as though there's no way around it. Couldn't you choose to state things in more of a roundabout way? Not actually lying, of course; just, for example, not directly mentioning whatever source of discomfort might happen to exist between the two of you. Aren't there times when that kind of evasion is life's correct response?"

RECITATION

"At first I thought like that too. I mean, it seems entirely self-evident. And I actually did give it a go. But the issue was that precisely that method of unspeaking silence, those vague explanations which, under the guise of considering my wife's feelings, I'd made deliberately blurry, ended up hurting her feelings irrevocably. As for explanations where I left something out, it later became clear that here there was the strong possibility of provoking a feeling of discontent, of making not only my wife but everyone who appeared in connection with the matter suspect that I had been somehow lax in my dealings with them, had treated my moral obligations towards them as something trivial. I mean, for the most part these were my friends or family, people who were important to me or with whom I was close. My wife was especially hurt, more deeply than anyone else. She still hasn't recovered even now. She felt that I'd made her look like an idiot, you see. Because I'd deliberately held back from mentioning things which might as well be public knowledge. But she would have been angry anyway, even if I'd done exactly the opposite. Granted, we hadn't been living together for all that long when this happened, but still, she was my wife, that much was clear. I received a letter from a lawyer. The upshot being that if I had the book published, I would be sued. But all that was years ago. Three years ago, now."

"It surprises me that there could be such complete inflexibility between a married couple." The healer craned his neck as he passed his ten stubby fingers over Mr. Nobody's back, searching for the places where the muscles were knotted together. "But what was the general subject of these 'memoirs' supposed to be?

You can't have been writing a book simply to lay bare all the trivial dealings which go on in a marriage?"

"For twelve years I was forced to make a living as a low-grade civil servant in the culture ministry, forbidden to write fiction."

"A civil servant in the culture ministry, that doesn't sound so bad."

"What's important is the word I mentioned just after that, 'forbidden.' Before then I used to teach foreign languages at university, but one day I lost my position there, entirely without warning. This was when China was in the middle of a war with Vietnam. And so I went to Vietnam as a war correspondent. After the war, in spite of my position having absolutely no connection with art history, I was posted to a museum. Whenever we had government officials visiting from Eastern Europe, especially Russia, I was tasked with giving them a guided tour of the basement rooms, showing them all the jewels and cultural assets. The reason they were travelling through our country being to search out any lust-worthy object. Eventually, when there wasn't a single thing left that they fiercely coveted, I ended up breaking loose from them, like a planet that has strayed out of orbit."

"No more cultural assets, but now you can write fiction again, so you're happy—is that what you mean?"

"That's correct. Fortunate in misfortune."

"You're not a patriot, then."

"That's right. Fortunate in misfortune."

"But now you've got the threat of your wife's lawsuit hanging over you! Your back pain probably started up around when all this did."

At that, Mr. Nobody opened his eyes. "That's right. Now I think about it, yes, you're right. It was around then, I think, that my heart started causing me problems. I was recently diagnosed with dangerously high blood pressure."

"I guessed from your complexion that you had a genetic heart problem. But your back is different. That's in my hands. How about now, doesn't it seem that the pain has eased up a little?" The healer fetched an old towel and wiped his hands on it with a satisfied expression. "My specialization as a healer isn't only the back. I can also cure tinnitus. If someone suffers from tinnitus, I bring my mouth to their ear and give them the warmest, most intense adhesion kiss in the world. Three times, usually. To first-time participants in my seminar it can look like merely a bit of fun, something done more for show than effect, but a kiss like that is the toughest, most energy-sapping thing for a professional healer like me. Because when the kiss is over, your mind is left as vague as if your soul had slipped away, and even your vision grows hazy. Not the one who receives the kiss, that is, but me, the healer. Ah, don't move, you've still got oil all over your back. Wait for me to wipe it off." The healer scrubbed Mr. Nobody's back with the towel he'd used to wipe his hands. As the oil slopped down over Mr. Nobody's sides, Kyung-hee worried about the quilt getting dirty. So she said to the healer, "Be careful, the oil's going every-where. If it gets on the quilt it'll stain the fabric, and we won't be able to get the smell out."

"The oil might have a deep colour, but it's not dirty. So you don't need to fret over stains. And if the smell makes it hard to get to sleep, there's some fabric deodorizer on the bathroom shelf, a good spray of that will sort it out. No problem at all. Actually, that stuff is so effective I almost never have to launder the quilt.

If an unexpected guest comes to stay"—the healer enunciated this part with a strange emphasis—"and they're wanting a new quilt, I just give them one I've sprayed with deodorizer. And no one's inconvenienced." The healer giggled behind his hand. He turned to Kyung-hee and patted her back, his hands still oily.

"How about it, would you like a massage?" Though Kyung-hee answered that she was even less fond of oil massages than of the regular kind, the healer had already started pressing his plump sausage fingers against her vertebrae and sacrum. "A twisted pelvis gives you a high chance of lumbar pain in later life, you know. And it's even more likely that your legs will become crooked, or that you'll end up with knee pain. It's not good for your internal organs, either; anyway, it seems like your pelvis is twisted." Kyung-hee, who had a habit of sitting crookedly and whose lower back was asymmetric, thought that this might well be true. Along with the advice about being careful of red cars and not wearing black.

"I had a gynaecological operation, a long time ago," Kyung-hee blurted out. "So that might have left me with a crooked pelvis, rather than back pain like Mr. Nobody."

"Ah, I see!" The healer fell briefly silent, and stole a glance at Mr. Nobody. "Of course, you do hear about women going abroad so they can have these operations in secret, but I never would have imagined that that sort of thing was going on in Berlin."

"I didn't come to Berlin to have an operation," Kyung-hee corrected him immediately. "That wouldn't make any sense. If anything, the opposite goes on; women from Berlin go to liberal neighbouring countries so they can have the operation without having to go through the formalities of pregnancy counselling or having to wait a long time to 'make up their mind.' Places like the Netherlands. And actually, all countries keep their patients' records private. At least that's what I've heard. Besides, my own operation was something I had done twenty years ago. It didn't happen in Europe. I was still a university student at the time. Back then, South Korea wasn't anywhere near as free as the Netherlands, yet, strangely enough, there was no need to go abroad to have an operation. The main reason must have been that there simply wasn't anyone who had that kind of money, I guess. So I remember them each, the bus stop in midsummer, the sycamore's every patch of shade, an elderly person clutching a fan and a man in army uniform, and the hospital. I stepped down from the bus and walked over to the hospital."

I'll give your ear an adhesion kiss, the healer offered Kyung-hee.

The single sun became a body. This body appeared in the form of a flash of light, surging in long waves up towards the heavens, from out of the empty air. It was a footless white torch. The body preserved the form of the fire. The body is bloodstained throughout its life and the body is mysterious. The body is a hotchpotch of things which the body has discarded. The sun blazes up, burning its own body. The body is of me. Or I am of the body. The body is open. Objects, thoughts, and perceptions pass through the body as they flow by. The body is embraced. As the body is warm, so it is cold. The body knows pain. The body knows how to tremble. Or else knows itching and softness. The body is hungry, the body cries. The hot fluid that flows out of the body is called blood or urine. The body suffers the touch of lips and hands. The body loves the body.

The body slips eagerly into sleep. The sleeping body is the soul's traveller. The body dreams. In dreams the body sees colours dance. A glittering which defies description constitutes the world. I call this the glittering of the blind. Bright dapplings which come up to the pupils and ripen there. But utterly resistant to description or memory. Lights without form, heading in some unknowable direction.

The image we end up seeing last in this life is said to be the moment of our birth, said Mr. Nobody. In that case, is it the future or the past? Kyung-hee asked. Almost at the same time as she spoke, a specific point on one of Mr. Nobody's mucous membranes passed over the keenly-alert spot on one of Kyung-hee's own, adhering closely. An invisible fire passed slowly over, burning vigorously. The tip of his tongue prised Kyung-hee's eyelids open, and took some time to lick the surface of her eyeballs clean. His tepid saliva soundlessly scalded Kyung-hee's eyes. Kyung-hee shuddered, now aware of the fact that she was not a person but some primitive organism made up only of duplicated sensations, a blind insect-cum-mutant butterfly with thousands of eyelids. With thousands of eyelids that open as one. It was an action suggesting that a certain prophetic affection—I will long for you—was going to haunt many more lives in the days to come, functioning effectively.

4. This particular street which leads from isolation

They first came to know of each other's existence through Mr. Nobody, or else through Maria. Mr. Nobody spoke of him as the cleverest of his sons, explaining that, from a young age, he had displayed outstanding artistic sensibility and linguistic skill, reminding him of a young Beethoven. But now the reality was that he, of all his sons, was having the most difficulty in making ends meet, and not only was it a struggle to provide for his family without relying on others for financial assistance, he had, in spite of his innate, superlative artistic talent, become one of those unfortunate human beings who fail to achieve anything, Maria said. He's a good guy, warm-hearted and mild-mannered. And yet, at the same time, a man with a strong sense of responsibility and justice. Unlike the majority of East Asians, he's found it difficult to adapt to the European way of life. He always had eyes for whatever was beyond his grasp; back in his hometown, while he was still a university student, I heard he even did some time in prison. After he got free of his father's influence, he married a girl who was pregnant with his child and became a father at a young age. Just like his own father did.

"How was your flight?" Banchi asked.

"That was just what I was going to tell you about; that I had a great flight, fantastic. Although the plane was delayed, and then the whole thing took around four hours, longer than usual..."

"And you still didn't find it tedious?"

"Well of course I did, it was as tedious as those things always are. But, surprisingly, the in-flight TV was showing *Out of Africa*."

"What? You went via Africa?"

"No, *Out of Africa*. The film."

"Ah, that. But what's so great about watching a film on a plane? And surely it can't have been the first time you saw that particular one?"

"Oh, you're quite right. I must have seen it at least five times already. But the *Out of Africa* I saw on this trip was the one I enjoyed the most."

"So the ones you'd been watching up until then were different *Out of Africa*s?"

"No, they were all completely the same *Out of Africa*."

"Well, it's been a long time since I saw it myself, so long that I can't recall anything of what happens. I guess it can't have made much of an impression on me. I always used to get it confused with *A Passage to India*, oddly enough. I mean, the titles aren't even that similar."

"Huh? What about India?"

"*A Passage to India*. The film, not the book."

"Ah, okay. I've seen it, now I think about it, but it was a really long time ago."

"I saw it in Vienna. Probably with Maria. I can't remember which cinema, though."

"I haven't seen Maria in ages."

"Same here. We only used to call each other for the briefest chats, but it's been years since we've managed even that..."

"It's the same for me, but I always think of her..."

"What? Just a minute, that wasn't what I was wanting to ask..."

"You already did ask me! About how my flight went."

"Ah, yes, that's right. So how was it?"

"I already told you it was good! Fantastic, in fact."

"A fantastic flight? I find that hard to believe... well, you're lucky, at any rate. I hate flying, you see. But is this all your luggage?"

"The bag's so heavy, I didn't want to rely on you carrying it for me."

"What are you talking about, it'd be my pleasure…"

"Banchi, where's the post office?"

"What?"

"The post office, one where I can send an international letter."

"Ah, you need Central Square for that. I'll drive you there tomorrow."

"Thanks, but there's no need. I can walk."

"Oh, it's no hassle. I'm taking my sons to the Children's Palace tomorrow so I'll have to take the car out anyway."

"I'll still walk, all the same. I like walking. I have to go every-where on foot, it seems."

"What? What are you talking about?"

"I'm going to send a postcard."

"Ah, a postcard."

Kyung-hee told the story of how she'd once gone to the post office of a central Asian city in order to send a postcard.

When you walk over grimy, irregular paving stones which are broken off at the edges, then go up the stairs whose edges have also crumbled, you find yourself in the post office's high-ceilinged hall; the skylight is very high up above the weak lighting and stacks of post boxes, so the interior is always gloomy, and the air is shockingly polluted, she said. As though there was an enormous invisible goods truck parked there inside the post office, constantly belching out exhaust fumes, Kyung-hee thought, feeling dizzy. There's clearly not enough oxygen in here, I can't breathe properly, I have to go outside. But Kyung-hee had to buy a picture post-card and send it abroad. And besides, the situation outside wasn't likely to be much better; the din of the vehicles as they passed through the square, the restless, nerve-grating blaring of car horns, the turbid air, would be just as bad outside as in. Kyung-hee had to buy a picture postcard and send it abroad. At the entrance to the post office was a notice reading 'Beware of Pickpockets'; as at most public facilities, this was written in English rather than the local alphabet. Kyung-hee went up to the counter and began to sort through a paper box of postcards. I have to go outside, on foot, always on foot.

Kyung-hee wrote a postcard to Maria. The gist of the message was that Kyung-hee had gone travelling, was still travelling, and that this travelling was likely to take her to Vienna, where she could visit Maria. On foot, Kyung-hee jotted down impulsively at the bottom of the postcard. It now read as though Kyung-hee was announcing that she was going to walk all the way from Korea to Vienna. Of course Maria would never believe this, would probably laugh at what seemed an amusing joke. As is always the case with other actual people, in practice Maria would have no idea. That Kyung-hee would really, actually walk that route. That she would really, actually walk that route all the way to the far end. But Maria would see. That Kyung-hee would be expelled from her own fantasy and end up wandering restlessly from one actual airport to another. Would pass by the terrorist security device, the automatic vending machine dispensing clear plastic bags for items containing liquids, the exclusive VIP counter which had been left completely unattended. Having been delayed due to a storm, the plane would fly so low as to seem to touch Kyung-hee's head, and the look on her face just then, entirely oblivious of the enormous plane circling above her head, might give the impression that she thinks that which is moving between one clouded item of vocabulary and another, creating past and future simultaneously, is not the plane but herself. Kyung-hee herself, real and actual. Solely through real and actual phenomena.

Kyung-hee was inside the Central Post Office building. Leaning against the table and coughing drily, Kyung-hee wrote one continuous letter so long it took up four postcards.

Maria, how are things? I went travelling. I'm still travelling right now. At some point during my travels I'll probably end up visiting you in Vienna. What I wanted to tell you is that a few years ago I left my home in Seoul, entirely out of the blue. But the thing is, even after walking all day and then some, I still couldn't escape from my native city. When I left the house I took the biggest suitcase I had, stuffed full with enough clothes and other items to last me several months. Underwear and socks, sweaters and t-shirts, a small blanket, a scarf and a knitted hat, a dozen pencils, a dictionary, books, vitamins and cold medicine, cough medicine, headache tablets, water-soluble painkillers, I even stuffed a sleeping bag into my spare shoes. After all that, you can imagine, the suitcase was practically the same size as me. Pulling that enormous suitcase along behind me as I walked, my way was blocked by bus stops and motorways, theatres and parks, metal fences and concrete walls, multi-story car parks and facilities for who knows what. And that's without saying anything of the heaps of rubbish that had been dumped by the side of the road, or the incredible mass of streetside hawkers. Before I knew it I was halfway up a hill, the sweat running off me. Only then did I become aware that the city was made up of countless red hills, like the surface of Mars. All objects that came into view as I went further up the hill did so by shooting up over the horizon, like the round moon rising through a thin layer of atmosphere. Houses and temples and skyscrapers and endless stairs, hills, cars, enormous doors leading into buildings and underground stations. It took all my strength to heave the suitcase up, grasping it with both hands, whenever I could spot the way forward up the hill, and this was made even more difficult by the fact that the footpath kept coming to a dead end unannounced and descending into a subway. Before I knew it, my straining forehead would be soaked in sweat yet again. The bumpy pavement slowed me up, and meant that the suitcase clattered incessantly. Worried about people getting in the way of me and my bag, I deliberately chose whichever routes looked least-frequented, which perhaps accounts for my ending up faced with a succession of steep, winding hill paths. After two hours of this wandering, well, you can imagine how exhausted I was. I sank to my knees in the middle of the path. It seemed that the city had seized hold of me and was refusing to let me go. As though it was gripping my umbilical cord in its clenched fist, I who had already disappeared some time ago, having become a goshawk's prey. Every time a human being thinks about their own origins, we have to make a concerted effort to drive from our minds the image of a hospital bedpan filled with a frothy mixture of blood, pus, and semen. In the seething spume of an open drain, which I almost stumbled into down some dead-end alley, I was able to recall those words. You said you keep a skeleton in your room, right? I keep thinking of it. There was a time when you said that you wanted to travel to Banchi's country, didn't you, to look at the rotting bulk of a dead horse lying exposed to the sun and wind, and you know, you suggested that the two of us go together. I keep thinking of it. I'll never forget how you said that you wanted to see the process by which an overripe flesh-and-blood body, a lump of muscle and fats, goes back to solid earth; to witness it with your own eyes, from beginning to end. You asked me to do you a favour, to stand at your side with an umbrella, so that if any birds of prey swooped down I could use the umbrella to chase them away...

Anyhow, there will never again be a time when I think of myself as no more than a lump of biology, as I did that day when I dragged my suitcase behind me, searching for a way to leave the city on foot. Do you want to keep my skeleton too? The day I became aware of the fact that there was no city gate. The river rises thick and fast from the neck of some rapids, then flows through the city in the shape of a horseshoe, curving back inwards rather than passing out of the built-up districts. The thing is, without being able to walk out of the city gate on my own two feet, I would never feel that I had, in actuality, left that city and gone out onto the vast steppe. Only through the dark unreality of the plane's radiation shadows would it be possible to experience the simultaneous switch, like turning the page of a book, of the world of my illusions, illusions such as day and night, moon and sun, black earth and clear water. I've met up with Banchi. I'm thinking of persuading him to go to Vienna with me, but I'm not sure how that'll turn out. What occurs to me just now: the person who told me about meeting a Japanese man at the opera who then threatened to kill them was none other than you, Maria. The Japanese man was short, with a pale face. He came and sat down next to you. He spoke to you, and at first you didn't understand, but then, after a little while, you did. I'm going to kill you, the Japanese man said, his face white. 'I'm going to kill you, your family, your friends, your insurance company, people who have promised to leave you money in their will because they like you, all of them.' You were shocked, and the shock was even more severe because you believed that you had fallen in love with that Japanese man, despite having known him for such a short time. Your head ached, and you felt nauseous. Only after the Japanese man had left the opera house, on foot, did you throw yourself flat in front of your seat, stifling your sobs as *Tannhauser* continued. Your migraines, your melancholy, your lethargy, your ageing, your swollen intestines, your anguished frowning, your foul stench, your clammy skin, your voice, your vague contortions, afflictions spanning your entire life, in an instant that Japanese man invaded your very centre, becoming the emperor of all your negative elements. A love like this! You sent me a letter filled with facts like these. Now, having lost none of their graphic intensity, they rise to the surface of my mind, with a vividness far exceeding what is necessary. As if I myself were the party concerned, the one who had held hands with the Japanese man in the opera house that day, listening to *Tannhauser*. If I'm remembering correctly now, I must have sent you a reply along these lines: 'There's nothing to worry about, Maria. He must just be in the habit of using violent language, he's not the type of person who would even dream of putting such threats into practice.

No doubt he goes around saying similar things to others as well. Besides, you have to bear in mind that he's trying to communicate his intentions through a foreign language, one he mustn't be too familiar with. In that kind of situation people are always reduced to using excessive expressions. With love, Kyung-hee.' By the way, it's heartbreaking, there's no space left on the postcard, so this letter will clearly have to finish here...

Banchi stepped into the post office building.

A light-brown cow, with ribs clearly visible and long, solid horns angled forwards, was wandering up and down the road. Rude, arrogant crows flew down low as though about to graze the cow's horns. The thick smell of animal blood and metal shavings came from the dust that the crows stirred up. Passers-by, paying no attention, dragged their feet through the thick dust on the way to some unknown destination. Huge, shaggy dogs followed behind them. Both the cars and the pedestrians seemed entirely oblivious to the changing of the traffic lights. The deeply flushed midsummer sunlight, the strong, clear alcohol filling a dirty glass, a goat tethered with a rope, the enormous sides of a glitteringly white modern building, the solemn melody of the national orchestra, the slender-necked actress who was performing on the stage, the arc of a rainbow which, after a sudden shower, fell to the earth like an arrow from between the clouds, a sheepdog pressed flat under the wheel of a car, a herd of stubborn goats bobbing their heads with profound indifference, blue cloth fluttering in the wind, designating something sacred, a swarthy woman looking down on the street below from a first-floor window, her exposed chest leaning out over the wooden frame, cat-sized rats threading their way around the legs of market stalls, unlit signs and display windows, a sombrely lit butcher's fridge, each dark red carcass still buttressed with the animal's skeleton, Banchi's printing shop, on the ground floor of a temple on the main street in the city centre, there Banchi makes picture postcards featuring his own translations of Indian sutras.

Banchi described his products as 'living pictures.' Through one simple action, he could instantly transform the picture on a post-card into an entirely different picture. Surprisingly, no digital tech-nology was involved in this. Instead, all you had to do was tug the bottom of the postcard and watch the vast steppe landscape morph into the image of the four-armed goddess Kali, or a glacier-cov-ered mountain, square-topped like a table, become the face of a young goatherd. Banchi explained that he had devised the trick himself, through the simple method of printing the pictures man-ually onto double-sided strawboard. As a birthday present or an expression of a particular feeling, doesn't this seem so much more sincere than an email or an ordinary postcard? Banchi suggested. "Banchi, do you have a patent for this technique?" Kyung-hee asked. Banchi stayed quiet for a while, perhaps because of the crudeness of the word 'patent', then responded apathetically that "such a thing is meaningless in this chaotic city."

Banchi's printing shop was located in the temple annex, next to the stairs leading up to the hall; the hall wasn't large, but as the place where the monks from each temple gathered to hold their meetings when there was a special event—for example, if the Dalai Lama happened to visit—it was ordinarily quiet and empty.

I could lay down my life for my family, Banchi said. "Perhaps many men in this country have similar thoughts. Not because there are any especially appropriate reasons. It's like with the sutras; we carry them imprinted in our blood."

They stepped out into the temple yard, where the tourists were nosing around in search of something worth seeing. The door to the central shrine was wide open, and the monks could be seen eating a meal, at the same table where they had been studying Buddhist scriptures. They ate with gusto, only pausing now and then to glare at the tourists, who were eying them unabashed. Not that they were the only ones for whom the act of eating was private; there were also a handful of European tourists who were at pains to avert their gaze. Dirty pigeons squabbled over feed in the middle of the disordered yard. The old women who sold the pigeon feed hung around at the edges. Young girls with braids fished coins out of purses to buy some feed. Every object in this city had broken corners. The temples and their bells, the monks, cars, stone steps, and buildings, the corners of the pigeons and of Banchi himself. Kyung-hee grasped Banchi's arm and said, "Banchi, what I meant was that I wanted to come here on foot." But Banchi didn't respond to those words, only saying "I could lay down my life for my family. But that doesn't mean doing everything that my family wants. In last year's elections, I voted against a bill to sell off the vast expanse of desolate land to foreign buyers. And this was even though casting a vote in favour would've left me five hundred dollars better off. Officially, no one lives on that land. What that means is that the land is not a place for registered citizens. In principle, it is only for wanderers.

And I am not a wanderer. Neither is my family. We're all of us long-time city-dwellers. Five hundred dollars is a lot of money in this city. My wife snapped at me: look, Banchi, you have two kids, why would you turn down such big money? You have to vote in favour of the sale and stop being so pessimistic about the future. When everyone else is taking the money, why should we be the only ones left sucking our fingers? The bad things you're imagining won't happen straight away, if we get political stability then all other calamities are nothing but fantasy. Please get rid of that dichotomy which says that all human desires are wicked while primitive nature is wholly good. Human beings have the right to make choices. Free yourself from this obsession that all outcomes, all new developments, are bad. And even if bad things do come about as the result of certain choices, perhaps they won't always be the very worst that could have happened, as you insist on believing... what I mean is, there are also lesser evils. Can't you accept that there might be reasons and explanations which depend on the choices of people other than yourself? More than anything else, the most important point is this: business is slow at the printing shop you founded, you have almost no income, and you have two children! On top of that, you shelled out such an inordinate amount for that Japanese copying machine that you still have to pay off the installments. The bank couldn't care less whether your desires are good or bad, how your choices might affect a single grain of soil or breath of wind in one corner of this planet's abandoned land. In other words, you have to cast a vote in favour and take the five hundred dollars. If you don't, that means only one thing, that you no longer love us, your children and me..."

"That's right, I'm a city-dweller," Kyung-hee broke in, as though talking to herself. "I didn't get a bank loan to buy a Japanese printer, but I did borrow money for other reasons. While the loan manager was transferring the money to my account, he said, 'Are you aware that the current world will be bankrupt by 2013? Or else 2012. There are various predictions to support it. So taking out a loan right now might well prove to be an extremely wise decision.' So I asked, in that case, what will be left after it goes bankrupt? The loan manager briefly bowed his head, as though consulting the loans guide on his desk. Then he looked up again and, while examining the faces of all the others who were waiting to borrow money, said, "It will probably be calm for a while. For a short while, at least, perhaps nothing much will happen. And then there will be a new Big Bang, and life will come again. The routine cycle of the universe, in which minerals die and flashes of light are born, will begin again. Don't you think?'"

They walked along the path in front of the temple, where young elms were dotted here and there. "I'm a city-dweller just the same, unlike my father I was born and raised in a city. I might repeat those words hundreds of times, I'm a city-dweller," said Banchi. "So, unlike my father, I do not know all the many dialect words to describe a horse. For certain tribes, words indicating horses are so innumerable they call to mind the stars of the Milky Way, or a rainbow's hazy remoteness. A one-year-old horse, a two-year-old horse, a three-year-old horse and a four-year-old horse are all described using different words, right. And not just that. There will usually be different names for each individual colour combination. A three-year-old horse with a brown mane and black-and-white dappled patterns, and a young white foal which was born on a stormy night, are described using different words in just the same way as city-dwellers use different terms to distinguish between a 'desk' and a 'well.' To horse tribes it's self-evident that those are entirely different species of horse, as different as a desk is from a well, and thus require entirely different species of words. And what all this means is that translating Sanskrit is no problem for me, but I could never write a book on horses." They crossed the road, taking care to avoid the speeding cars. Banchi said that here it was safer to cross the road in a group when the traffic lights were red than to attempt a solo crossing when they were green. "Because, you see, this city hasn't been civilised." Banchi used the expression 'this city' instead of saying 'our race' or 'the people of this city.' Having crossed to the opposite side, Banchi indicated the ground floor window of a bulky stone building.

"We lived here when I was young. In this very room. In this room, my parents gave birth to me and my three siblings, and this is where we spent our childhood. It's the dorm building of the university where my father used to teach German. The bathrooms and kitchens were communal. Because my father was a city hater, he was desperate to build a house in the suburbs for his sons. The first house he built was commandeered by the government, but somehow or other he managed to hold on to the second one. But it meant that he lost his position at the university, and ended up going to Vietnam as a war correspondent. This was when China invaded Vietnam, you see. Later, after he returned from Vietnam, my father got a job at a museum, and I attended a Russian language school. My favourite writer is Hemingway, but I can still look back on that time, when studying Dostoevsky and Pushkin first opened my eyes to literature, as a particularly beautiful period in my life. Ah, if only you knew how to speak Russian! Maria spoke it quite well. But I was studying German when I lived with her, so I insisted that we always speak in German. Perhaps you've come across something like my 'living pictures' in Korea?"

Kyung-hee shook her head. "Computer graphics technology means people aren't impressed even by really marvellous pictures. These days, even if a three-dimensional dinosaur backbone were to morph into a hologram of the Madonna, no one would bat an eyelid. They'd find it as ordinary as butterflies over flowerbeds. But Banchi, don't you want to see Maria again? If you'd like, we can go to Vienna together."

On foot, Kyung-hee did not add. And Banchi, a bashful amateur artist from the third world, who had once made it all the way to Austria only to fail to complete his course of study, merely replied that he could lay down his life for his family. As they walked, they passed a restaurant called 'Sisi.' Is that an Austrian restaurant? Kyung-hee asked. Of course not, Banchi answered. They have a portrait of the Imperial Princess Sisi hanging on the wall, but you can't really call it an Austrian restaurant. They have lamb stew, potato noodles and goulash on the menu, but no Weiner Schnitzel. "But this city has a European beer hall I could show you round, if you'd like. Genuine German cuisine. It's in the area near the German embassy, and inside you can look through a window at the beer-making facilities. The North Korean embassy building is next to the German embassy, but there's nothing to see there—only two days ago they cleared out the building and recalled the staff to North Korea. The building was torn down, and an enormous amount of dust poured down on the heads of passers-by. I thought of you when it happened. If you'd arrived in this city only a few days earlier we might have been able to get a front-row seat to watch the embassy being pulled down. I definitely wanted to show you it. The North Korean embassy was a special place for me, you see. When I was a child I used to pass it on my way home from school. I never failed to stop and marvel over the paintings covering its otherwise white walls; gaudy landscape paintings of the North Korean countryside, and paintings that record historical events, decorated with soft pink flowers. Paintings of tall, strapping men and charming young women, I had no concrete idea of what they were intended to show, but they gave the impression of being both solemn and sorrowful and, at the same time, touchingly beautiful and heroic. I would peep in through the iron gate at the embassy building, and oh, how incredibly dignified and majestic it was. It looked like a palace in some distant country. How I yearned for it, which seemed to embody those obscure, abstract names I first encountered as a child: moderation, elegance, honour, order, dignity, foreign country, alien. But now nothing is left of it. They left here without a trace."

"I don't know many cities," Kyung-hee said. "Back when there was only one city that I knew, my perspective was still closer to that of a visitor to this world than a fully-assimilated immigrant. Because, you see, I didn't know the language. When the foster parent was teaching me words syllable by syllable, there were still trams and bicycles in that city. My first memory of that city is of a young woman, probably blind, walking in the road.

Remembering what I saw back then, sitting in my buggy, it's odd; I wonder why she was walking in the road, rather than along the pavement like everyone else? Now that I think about it, that moment took place on the very first afternoon of my life. That day, a man was riding a bicycle. Some non-language afternoon on which the tram slid itself along, attached to an electric cable overhead. Clearly what it actually was was time passing by, or else the present-tense image of the eternal 'right this moment' of my illusion which, until now, has simultaneously and unchangingly progressed beneath my eyelids. The tram goes by over the woman's body. Without a sound. (I can't remember a sound.) The woman throws her arms up to cover her face and falls to the ground, and the man on the bike lifts her body up. That phrase, lift my body up, seems to have come to me not in my mother tongue but in some ancient language now long-forgotten. At the time I was still a visitor, not long since arrived in that city, and being pushed in a buggy, all the objects and scenes I saw, all the syllable-by-syllable language, not a single thing was familiar to me. And so I frequently thought in an ancient language, I was mixing up the ancient language and the new. I got the foster parent confused just like I did language. I confuse then with now just like I do with cities. I throw up my arms to cover my face and fall to the ground. The tram slides by over my body. And when I open my eyes, I discover myself in another city."

"You speak as though you were a wanderer of life! Or, one would have to say a wanderer of time."

"For a very long time I wasn't; such a long time, in fact, that almost all of my life had slipped by. I didn't want to know anything about wandering, I even had a job."

"A stage actor."

"A voice actor."

"That surprises me. Not that you had a profession, but that you were able to make a living through that particular one. In this city, even if such a profession existed, there's no way anyone could live off it. The very idea! If you look at my friends, they're all exceptional poets, writers, actors, magicians, painters, and healers, but at the same time they're actually taxi drivers, low-level legal clerks, sales employees in the airport's duty-free shop—at times they're Buddhist monks, functioning as a kind of tourist attraction, and also managers of small printing shops. The way I see it, my father is the only native of this city who supports himself solely as an artist."

"And he might be the wealthiest writer this city has produced. But Banchi, do you realise that we could set off for Vienna tomorrow, to see Maria?"

"No, I can't. I have to decide whether to cast an assenting or dissenting vote in this election."

"You have to make a decision right this moment? From what you told me, I understood that you had cast a dissenting vote in the last election, that the whole of your country had already completed the decision-making process."

"But sometimes, 'right this moment' can exist as something eternally delayed. That's what I've understood from listening to you."

They walked along the wall surrounding the North Korean embassy compound, the building itself having been completely demolished, leaving only an enormous dusty hollow.

Over the wall's railing, they could see a man strolling around in the dust. Aside from him, there was no one else in sight. Why does this thing we call 'the nation' have to exist forever? Kyung-hee asked herself, without expecting to come up with any convincing answer. Seemingly out of the blue, Kyung-hee recalled that the man who had been her first husband –officially, her only husband—had been a civil servant, and as a representative of the nation his job had been to investigate and negotiate with the market, though in fact it would have been more accurate to say 'agonise over the role of the nation in relation to the market', hampered by the fact that the banks and companies saw him as the ambassador of an entity that was steadily going extinct, a lonely diplomat des-patched by the nation. The movement of feet from one place to another, evoking the tactile sensations of lucid, vivid dreams, of the reality which is this abstract past. Opposite the embassy was the European-style beer hall Banchi had spoken of. Banchi guided Kyung-hee inside. The interior of the spacious hall was half in shadow, having no artificial lighting, and refreshingly cool; the vast majority of the customers who were occupying tables were European. Resting their chins in their hands, peering wordlessly into their glasses of beer with the sombre, even gloomy expressions characteristic of sandy-haired Europeans, they looked like refugees from some distant disaster. The light which slanted in through the entrance was suspended like a roof over their heads. One side of the hall was entirely glass, and on the far side were the facilities for fermenting beer. In the hall, ads reading 'Beer made using the German method' were dotted here and there. After a calm walk around the hall, Banchi and Kyung-hee went back outside.

Neither the staff nor the customers paid them any attention. Banchi led the way, his tall body bouncing lightly as he crossed the road. After the two of them had been walking for a little while, he abruptly ducked into a narrow shop, so small it didn't even have a sign. It was a printing-and-office supplies shop, with a handful of printers inside. My shop is similar to this one, Banchi told Kyung-hee, his casual gesture almost proprietorial. Kyung-hee nodded. And said, "Of course, it stands to reason that you frequent these shops, coming and going quite naturally, just as a nomad would. Just as a wild animal knows no borders." The people inside the shop merely regarded them with blank stares.

"At first I thought that this city and that city were completely different places, you know," Kyung-hee said. "Since, even leaving aside the geographical distance between them, all individuals necessarily encounter them one after the other, after a certain gap of time, and for that reason each city appears as a separate entity, showing their faces in a successive order. Just as a new life can begin only after another life has definitely ended, I thought that cities, too, existed like that. But if you try walking from one city to another, since there is an invisible vein of space-time running through all these cities, each of which has their own individual appearance, at a certain point it becomes a kind of airport of the mind; in this way, I think, cities actually exist simultaneously. And that in fact, rather than each city being absolutely separate and distinct, they interpenetrate, forming a palimpsest, though we may be unaware of this. And the same rule applies to one life and another. Before I had fully arrived in this current life, I saw the tram pass over my previous flesh-and-blood body.

So perhaps we don't need to focus our minds on a single place in order to give ourselves over to 'right this moment.' The more I focus on myself, the more this central self grows vague, and I become a derivative of myself, become divided into many simul-taneously-existing selves. I'm not a Buddhist like you, Banchi, or a practitioner of meditation. All I'm trying to say is that as my life progresses I become more and more diluted and spread out, permeating a part of the manifold universe. So eventually I myself will become the horizon of the whole world. Such a moment will come. But Banchi, right this moment you're great. Right this moment, even more than at other times, you're the best you can possibly be. I want to go and visit Maria with you."

"You always manage to settle every issue in the same fashion!" Banchi said, carefully but firmly extricating his hand from her grasp. "It surprises me that for you, two different cities can be identical, that it's so natural for you to get a city confused with things that aren't cities. And that, despite having received a per-fectly adequate education, you are entirely incapable of under-standing the difference between an assenting and dissenting vote. That you can be so careless of the difference between love and that which is not love, life and that which is not life. Or that to you, such differences are by no means conclusive. Yes, I'm surprised. You are surprising, you for whom a given issue and that which is not that issue are nothing but stars which glitter in sullen silence, drearily identical. Stars which produce no sound whatsoever. Stars which are formed solely of rock, without an atmosphere through which sound waves could travel. Where all that is visible is the horizon of light, drawn out like a long gold filament in the absolute darkness.

Only that horizon which is called 'the closed eyelid of the divine.'
Marvellous things can sometimes be true, you know. But though
I'm a failed visionary who sets out every night on an abstract
journey, searching for a single star, all the same, I could still die
for my family, the family of this life. I was born and raised in this
city where wolves still appear now and then, where the rich keep
pet crocodiles in their gardens while the homeless spend every
night wailing in despair. So there's no such thing as a zoo in this
city. I'm both surprised and frightened by how easily you can
think of this city overlapping with the one in which you were
born and raised. This word 'simultaneously', which you're so fond
of using, frightens me. It's not at all the simple, innocuous thing
you think it is. The power of repeated phrases goes beyond that
of language. You who, having appeared suddenly as a breath of
wind, will clearly disappear again after having poured out countless
individual words, as though this is nothing at all, are surprising.
Surprising and frightening. I marvel at you, you who skip so
easily from one city to the next. You're like someone reciting a
story which has neither beginning nor end, someone who lives
inside such a story. You're as dizzying as the indivisible universe.
You're like the old tale I heard when I was young, recited continuously over four days and nights. The words that come from
your mouth always sound like something being read aloud; you're
constantly saying what you are not; I think that sometimes you
yourself are that which is being spoken. You who have metamorphosed, become derivative of yourself, a metaphor of yourself,
endlessly diluted, to the point of transparency. You are strange
and surprising, but it's okay for you stay in our house even so.

For as long as you'd like to be there. We welcome you. You will see what an incredibly kind, friendly person my wife is. She won't be showing you kindness simply because my father telephoned to ask us for this favour. Whoever comes to visit, whether family, friends, or my guests, she always gives them her whole-hearted hospitality. She's a nurse at the hospital, she earns one hundred and fifty dollars a month. That's the woman for whose sake I have to decide whether to vote for or against. I have to decide whether to sell that vague land, that place which we city-dwellers have never been able to visit, and which we never will set eyes on in the future, either, whether to let the Japanese become its legal owners. Whether or not the Japanese buy the land, my body and that land are likely to remain utterly unrelated forever, mutually unknown entities, and I will never graze so much as a single sheep on it, and yet I'm involved in deciding the issue of its sale—it's incredibly perplexing. The 2000s were a truly difficult decade for me. And now all of a sudden I find myself involved in selling land. This will probably seem meaningless to you, but when I think of how I will end up seeing this land countless times in the dreams I am yet to have, this land which I have, of course, never actually seen, not even in a photograph, this present life already surprises me. In my dreams I will ride a horse across that land, a lonely old chieftain like my forebears.

That land from which my blood and bones were formed, upon which my ancestors lived, which will be forever unknown to me. But no, perhaps even right this moment I am really and actually holding a shabby bundle in my hand, leading my wife and children across that land, taking a lifetime to cross it on foot.

Land that it would take someone their whole lifetime to cross.
Given that to me this land exists in actuality as a second reality,
running parallel to this one, having to decide the issue of its legal
sale through a democratic ballot, here in this distant city, feels
like holding a ballot to decide whether I will see Maria again.
Your belief that two or more individual kinds of phenomena
can coexist in one world will never fail to surprise me. If chaos
is truly the fundamental nature of time, as you maintain, then I
will both see Maria again and not see her. Because those two outcomes will likely remain eternally undecided, or at least until the
day when all of our lives come to an end. In that case, what will
become of the land? What will become of that barren wilderness
which I've never seen, where no one has ever lived, and of the
ballot? Ah, what a load of nonsense this is! I've always hated such
senselessness! Let's put it aside. The government has said that it's a
wasteland, a barren steppe devoid of vegetation, littered with heaps
of stones and bleached animal bones, where blind field mice and
starving foxes burrow into the dried-up earth. Long-ago traders
who crossed mountain ranges and continents on foot did not use
that steep, rugged land as a route, and the only ones who ever
claimed to have set foot there were those who were murderers,
the banished, or those for whom a long period of wandering had
left their mind unsound. The modern age is the age of the map.
As it was no longer permissible for any corner of the world to
remain a blank, explorers went there and affixed their names to it,
making topographical maps of rivers and mountain ranges. And
so, for the first time, that place became 'territory.' I know that
I will never see that land. But I also know that I may well spend

my entire life encountering it in dreams, that it may become inextricably woven into a lifetime's worth of dreams. I am a city-dweller. I spent my childhood in a one-room university dorm apartment with a coal fire, and my children will grow up in a similarly cramped downtown apartment. A pauper's apartment which will crumble helplessly at the first earthquake. I have to sell the steppe wilderness littered with the bones of camels. I feel a sense of responsibility towards the issue. It is an uncontrollable vertigo. The vertigo of democracy, the vertigo of city life, the vertigo of density, the vertigo of rationality and actuality. How strange it is, that I myself came out of that land, land which I would one day end up selling off. My bones are formed from its soil. My father was born there. Until he reached the age of eighteen and went off to university in Leningrad, he lived in a tribal tent covered in wolf hides, and drank warm goat's milk. Between what the government is saying, what the explorers wrote down in their books, and my father's words, there's something that doesn't add up. I mean, were our ancestors banished criminals? Or might they perhaps, as my father maintains, have always lived on that land, might they even be living there still? Who are they? Are they perhaps none other than I myself? Either way, they are clearly people to whom nobody pays attention, people who are not seen. That's distressed me for a long time. But you cannot understand me, you cannot understand my being distressed by such things. The land is making even that distress, the last piece of my inheritance, into something both vague and 'simultaneous.'"

They walked without speaking for a while.

"I'm grateful to you and your father for letting me stay here,"

Kyung-hee said to Banchi. "Even though it's been more than a year since I last saw him." At that, Banchi peered down at Kyung-hee and smiled faintly. "It's been over five years since I saw him last. True, he always helps me out with money. But in my opinion, it doesn't look like he'll ever return to this country, not even if he were granted an entry permit."

The face of Mr. Nobody, whom they both missed, appeared briefly in their minds.

"Banchi, at heart you're probably perfectly aware of this, but there are certain things which are unchanging, no matter where you are or what you're doing. For example, someone being born when someone else dies. Or the moon being the sun's only bride, despite never once being able to meet. In my opinion, it's an absolute rule that when one door closes, somewhere else, another door which had previously been invisible appears. Don't worry about what's waiting outside that door. There's no need to be distressed because you want to change the world. There's no need to be distressed over what you want. You can hope for what you want in a way that is pure and without suffering. Irrespective of whether or not this wish is fulfilled. Even if you didn't actually make any effort to try and bring it about, you'd still be able to keep that wish intact for your whole life. I don't want to coerce you, I just want to tell you this as a suggestion, nothing more. You could go to Maria. It seems as though you could also return to that land of your father's right now, and live clad in wolf hides. But not only that: you could do both of these things simultaneously. What does it matter about long-dead explorers or the maps they made? Forget the gangs who call themselves politicians, who barely know twenty words to string together. Some of the government officials clearly have no desire to set foot on that land. They'll probably content themselves with giving it a once-over from the comfort of an aeroplane. I hope you'll stop driving yourself into deeper distress, wondering what they'll be thinking about inside that plane. If you go there you'll probably find that the hills join up as though stretching out their arms to each other, that during the brief rainy season the rivers flow naturally from one valley to another, that short-lived flowers are happy to go without names, blooming without regard for what they might be called. In that harsh wilderness, where the riverbeds dry up once the rainy season is over, the grasses will wither and die, but they will not call such a thing 'distress.' In that land onto which no borders have been drawn, where there are no soldiers, no flags, no permanent residents. Maria used to say that she wanted to go there, do you remember? Because she wanted to witness the entire process by which a dead horse's flesh-and-blood body rotted into the ground, to stand right next to it from beginning to end. Maria said, we ourselves are the only thing hampering us in making a decision. You yourself are the only thing preventing you from going to that land. And imagining that one concrete individual will make more mistakes than anyone else in this world, that you might be able to determine anything in reality—well, such things only hold true in your imagination, just like the belief that the decision will have any real influence on your existence. But I'm only saying this to you as a suggestion, purely that, so I'll shut up now."

Banchi's house was an old apartment in the city centre. It was a cramped house with only two rooms, but it was warm and, according to him, the best thing about it was that it was near his children's school. The best location it could be, as my children don't need to cross any dangerous roads, go down any dark alleyways, or past drinking joints of dubious repute. On top of that, there are even two scrawny poplars in the alley, next to the bins. Nature — isn't that a luxury in this city? When the children grow up, I'm planning to tell them how many green trees there are in Vienna and Leipzig. The largest room in Banchi's house functioned as a living room, guest bedroom, his study, and even a playroom for his youngest son, who wasn't yet a year old. On the shelves of this room were the sutras Banchi had translated; Hemingway's *The Old Man and the Sea*, his favourite book; several of his father's books, and the literary magazine he published in collaboration with some friends; he pointed this out to Kyung-hee. His wife made up a batch of warm soupy rice with lamb. She didn't know any German, so Banchi explained, "We went for a walk around the centre. We passed by the spot where the North Korean embassy used to be, and Sisi restaurant. There was a ton of dust in the road, same as always. On the way back I popped into the shop out front and bought two bottles of water for Kyung-hee, some vegetable juice for you, and Cola for the kids."

Banchi took a small notebook down from the shelves, opened it and showed it to Kyung-hee. The notebook was crammed with poetry, but all written in Cyrillic; only one poem had been written in English, the only one Kyung-hee was able to read.

Talking in bed ought to be easiest
Lying together there goes back so far
An emblem of two people being honest.

Yet more and more time passes silently.
Outside the wind's incomplete unrest
builds and disperses clouds about the sky.

And dark towns heap up on the horizon.
None of this cares for us. Nothing shows why
At this unique distance from isolation

It becomes still more difficult to find
Words at once true and kind
Or not untrue and not unkind.
　　　—Philip Larkin, [Talking in bed]

"In terms of how I myself read it, this poem is a record of the ulti-
mate sleeping place, i.e. a house," Banchi said. "I first came across it
back when I was living in Vienna, you see. Maria encouraged me
to read Larkin's poetry. I can guess how wildly exciting she must
have found it; not only his poetry, but his life, personally uninhibited and crammed with great achievements. I was a student newly
arrived in Europe, so I just found it all fairly baffling. Anyhow,
according to her, Maria once met Larkin in person, in London
some time in the early eighties. Though that was all I ever heard
about it. Not until I lived in Vienna did I come to realise that in
certain cases a house can be a place for those who wander while

staying put; that, unlike in my home city, many people lived alone, seeming to spend their entire lives wandering from one interior to another; that these houses took up residence inside their flesh, a vast number piled up in a single person's flesh; that to them, roaming was the fundamental essence of life, that the paths trod by their feet or swept by their gaze formed a delayed caravanserai of which they themselves were ignorant. And it seemed as though these feet-travelled paths were saying of the one who trod them, I am not a tree, which is why I leave this house for that. *And dark towns heap up on the horizon. None of this cares for us. Nothing shows why. At this unique distance from isolation.* From a certain point onwards, I began to understand all manner of sentences I encountered as records of houses and places of residence, cities and sleep, current and flow, visiting and leaving. The feeling that life is 'conceptualised space.' The feeling that the houses that had piled up like that would eventually reveal themselves as the final bed. The feeling that the substance of life is ultimately a conversation had in a bed which is a place that no one knows.

One day an unfamiliar young man with a small frame and a shaggy beard turned up at Maria's house. In t-shirt and jeans, dwarfed by an enormous backpack which looked to be at least twice his own size. Without even removing his dirty trainers, the kid went into our room, rolled his sleeping bag out on the floor, and lay down. And then promptly fell asleep. He was clearly dead on his feet. He spoke Spanish; he was Argentinean. The three of us lived together in that room for a while. Maria was entirely oblivious to his existence. When he ate, when he slept, even when he changed his underwear, she acted as though he wasn't even there.

After a few days of this I was bursting with curiosity, so in the end I asked, Maria, do you know that kid? And she replied that she'd never set eyes on him before, but she'd known that he would be visiting, which is why she'd cleared the space by the window, to leave enough room for a person to lie down. You know how chaotic Maria's room was. In keeping with her beliefs, she lived without any furniture, with all of her belongings—clothes, books, musical instruments, bottles of water, and plates of food—scattered over the floor. That was her way of life. How did this come about? I asked, and she answered, I'm Karakorum."

"She said she was what?" Kyung-hee asked. "Karakorum?"

"What's Karakorum? I asked, and she told me that it was an organisation which shared houses among its members, or else members among its houses. Shares houses among its members? I repeated, initially unable to grasp what she was saying. You mean, sharing houses with complete strangers? That's right, Maria said. "Karakorum provides houses for wanderers. Through each member agreeing to share their own house with any other member, that is. Anyone who has a house—here, the concept of 'house' applies equally to a single basement room, just a bare place to sleep, as to a mansion—can become a member. Once you're a member, it's your duty to provide a place to stay for Karakorum members from all over the world. No matter who they are. But there are no strict conditions such as your 'house' having to come up to a certain standard, like a hotel or B&B, or your having to provide meals and change the bedding. I mean, you can do all that if you want, but the basic principle is quite loose: a house, or a single room, or even just a space big enough for someone to roll out a sleeping bag and lie down, with a roof to keep them out of the rain, is fine. Even a room shared by several people—like we're doing now—is absolutely no problem. In other words, joining Karakorum means having simultaneous sleeping places all over the world. Whenever we travel to another city, the first thing we have to do is ask around the various Karakorum of that city to find a house that's currently accepting visitors. Jose (this was the first time I learned the Argentinean kid's name) lets wanderers stay in his house in Buenos Aires, and I do the same in Vienna. And there are Karakorum in so many other cities doing just the same. If, at some point, we end up travelling to India, we'd be able to stay in an Indian Karakorum's house. Were we to arrive at an airport anywhere in the world, we'd be able to go straight to a Karakorum. Now do you understand?' Maria said. I was as baffled as ever. 'We' would be able to stay? Even though I wasn't a member of Karakorum? When I voiced these doubts, Maria answered that since she'd put my name down alongside hers, I was a Karakorum too."

"In that case, your Karakorum was the room in Vienna where you lived with Maria, or is this house in this city also—to put it symbolically—the possession of a Karakorum?"

"Your guess is as good as mine. Back then, I rarely ever used the internet, so the online community known as the world of 'Karakorum' was a complete mystery to me. It's still a mystery now. But Maria can't have registered my address in this city. If she had, some wanderer of the world would have turned up at my house one day and strolled in without so much as a by-your-leave—just like we did with this city's European beer hall and office supplies shop, poking our noses around without even the decency to buy anything—and set up camp in this guest bedroom-cum-living room, squeezing in with my young son. And they would have insisted that they were a Karakorum, and, accordingly, had a room even in the forgotten city of Karakorum."

"And they would have been able to stay here freely, without even any rent..."

"Maria said that Karakorum is a world free from rent. Whether you stay in a palatial villa in Buenos Aires, a studio flat in Vienna, or even in the real ruined city of Karakorum. Even after Maria's lengthy explanation, there were so many thoughts running through my mind. What if Karakorum had truly existed? What if there had truly been a wide palace with sixty-four pillars, built of dark green bricks, and an ancient city of black walls and black mountains, in the heart of the steppe wilderness? A city like a divine eye, occupying the entire core of this world even while constantly shifting from place to place. What if there had truly been a city of wandering, which opened its doors to dust-covered wanderers who came there from every corner of the sky? That city of memory that is wandering even now, a city of the air made up of fluttering leather tents, ceilings with bells and drums suspended from them, and silk curtains, what if, rather than simply being a nostalgic memory which flashes into our minds one day, such a city truly existed in the same dimension as us? What I mean to say is, that wandering which you insist you possessed, that movement, those simultaneous footsteps which are time's true form, what if they were truly there, not merely as a linguistic component, no more than the expression of a shadow or paradox, unrelated to our individual existences, but there as an object, as flesh, as the smell of leather and skin..."

5. Is it surely night?

In that room, even in the moment of waking, Kyung-hee didn't slip fully out of that violent dream. The dream's conclusion had been a man in semi-transparent linen clothes. The man crossed a milky river of molten lime and receded into the distance, displaying a mysteriously broad, flat back. The clacking of some dead animal skeleton's ribs, suspended from the ceiling, grows distant. I grow distant from it. Some shore where the distance from the dream is growing gradually hazy. Kyung-hee woke there alone. The window was open; beyond it, the world was made up of ambiguous sounds and an aged, reddish light, so indistinct it could equally have been morning or evening. She recalled the scene of the dream's conclusion, a swarm of earth-coloured grasshoppers springing up from a vast expanse of dried ground, their bodies so transparent as to render them invisible. Every time her bare feet touched the earth, the winged creatures sprang up from between sharp blades of grass and narrow grains of soil, hundreds at a time; they vibrated their wings in the air, producing a slender fluting sound. The fact that she had woken up in a winter sleeping bag told Kyung-hee that she was, as ever, travelling.

There wasn't a single item in the room worthy of being called 'furniture.' But it was filled with so much clutter it was difficult to find any empty space: clothing strewn across the floor, moving boxes which still hadn't been unpacked, books arranged any old how, thick winter gloves, albums and posters, a china mug half-full of coffee, tall Wellington boots, a bag, etc. An enormous cello case stood next to the door, underwear had been spread out to dry over the heater, and a huge framed photograph leant against one wall. It was an ordinary-looking landscape photograph of a vast ranch, featuring a snow-covered mountain peak off in the distance, a faint green pampas grassland, and gently sloping hills. Cows were dotted here and there on the ranch, and among them was a man on horseback, apparently a ranch hand, his hands resting slack on the pommel. His wide-brimmed hat left the upper half of his face in shadow, his mouth and jaw revealed below the black. On the music stand, intended for practising the cello, was a newspaper clipping of a photograph of Domingo. He was on stage at the Bayreuth Wagner festival, during *Lohengrin*. Kyung-hee was dizzied by her inability to tell how long she'd been asleep, whether it was now morning or evening, or even, though the likelihood was slim, an unusually overcast afternoon, or a night of rare and especial brightness; whether she was hungry or merely thirsty, whether the air was cold and dry; her inability, even, to make out her own features. From the other sleeping bag there in the room, rolled out in the opposite corner to hers, unzipped, Kyung-hee could at least ascertain that she hadn't been the only person sleeping there. Two large moths with fluttering wings were quietly trembling over the floor, their lives exhausted. The sounds coming from outside the window were like the hoarse, thick cries of wild geese.

As soon as she stepped out into the narrow corridor, Kyung-hee discovered a small kitchen where, despite the lack of space, the door had been left open. She poured herself a glass of water, drained it, then took some bread from the fridge. She had no way of knowing whose bread it was but, overwhelmed by a sudden hunger, she decided to just eat it first and think about replacing it later. The tiny sink was full of dirty dishes, and the two-person table was cluttered with empty bowls and biscuit wrappers, dirty plates, a butter dish, and a bowl of prunes. After carefully pushing these aside to clear a bit of space, Kyung-hee made some coffee and sliced the bread. The sound of a door banging closed announced that someone had just gone into the bathroom. On the other side of the door a dog gave a low bark. Sitting on the stool and leaning back against the wall, Kyung-hee chewed the bread. And she thought about how long she'd been travelling for, and how much money she had left. The answer was probably 'almost none.' She recalled how, when she'd first had such thoughts, she would be struck by unease and a cold, slippery terror. Accompanied by a heavy terror which caused her heart to flutter, then sunk it in sadness. But that didn't happen anymore. 'Almost none,' but Kyung-hee knew a producer who had been wanting to record her voice for a few years now, and though they'd never yet managed to find a time that fitted in with both their schedules, she believed that he would help her out with some money. And even if this turned out not to be the case, the money issue was unlikely to cause any major problems for a while yet. Because Kyung-hee is Karakorum. Because she is a traveller who might be bound for Karakorum. And yet, an unrealistic stubbornness dwelled inside this optimism, a wild animal's fierce determination not to let life grind it down. If the day did eventually come when there was nothing else for it but to write a begging letter to her parents, it might be better for Kyung-hee to bare her teeth and gobble herself up.

Just then, someone stepped soundlessly into the kitchen. The young woman, who looked to have just stepped out of the shower, was so much taller and larger-framed than average that Kyung-hee was jolted out of her reverie, instantly imagined that she had come face-to-face with a beautiful young female giant, tall as a statue and with an expanse of white skin. With her wet hair twisted up on top of her head, and wearing a red bathrobe that looked hopelessly insufficient to conceal the hillocks of her breasts, the pale young woman strode over to the fridge, opened the door, and got some juice from a bottle, all without paying Kyung-hee the slightest bit of attention. And then, still without giving Kyung-hee so much as a single glance, she padded back to her room, her bare feet softly kissing the floor, and closed the door. As before, a dog's growling leaked in through the gap in that door, this time along with murmured words. A lilting radio, or else a boyfriend, Kyung-hee thought. The thought passed through her mind in an instant, that both of those things seemed the exclusive possession of plump youths of university age. Kyung-hee pulled on her jacket and shoes and left the house.

There was no sun in the sky, but nor was there a moon and stars, or even clouds. Neither could Kyung-hee spot the glinting body of an aeroplane or satellite. Is it night? If nothing else, at least it was clear that it wasn't night right now—because an old woman, people frowning severely, children with satchels slung over their shoulders, and a line of bicycles, were all passing through the streets. Most of those on bicycles were youngsters in jeans; an orderly procession following someone who had a flag sticking out of their backpack, marking them as the leader. It seemed to

Kyung-hee that she glimpsed the word 'Karakorum' written on the flag, but she couldn't be sure. She still couldn't shake the feeling that she had yet to wake up, that she was lingering at the veiled threshold of sleep. Arriving at your lodging after a long flight and then sleeping like the dead, it generally stands to reason that you feel like that for the entire next day, Kyung-hee thought. That you're itching to get out of the house and head off in whatever direction you choose, to walk on and on without any idea of a destination. Your steps guided only by the faintest light, like the shadow of a huge mushroom.

After a while walking like that, generally following the tram line but with no real idea in what direction, Kyung-hee came to an enormous, complicated main road. She was looking up at the opera house, with its elegant stone colonnade and a beautiful facade carved to look like draped fabric. The procession of bicycles which had flitted past her around half an hour earlier were now parked up there, the riders listening to the guide giving an explanation. They all had wireless earbuds, and the guide a wireless microphone, so he didn't need to bellow over the din of the traffic. For this reason, the handful of passers-by who wandered over, their curiosity piqued as Kyung-hee's had been, found it impossible to make out what the guide was saying.

Kyung-hee sat on a bench in front of the opera house. She examined the items in her handbag. A faux-leather wallet with some coins and paper money, gloves and scarf, a black ballpoint pen, terracotta-coloured lipstick, a brochure for the opera house, throat lozenges, a natural history encyclopedia, and an envelope containing a letter. This was on a company's letterhead paper.

RECITATION

"...and so, though this is extremely regrettable, our agency now finds itself in the unavoidable situation, due to a deficit having accumulated in the meantime, of being able to carry out only a minimum of the previously-arranged recording schedule, and, of that, the parts which it had been arranged that you would record..." Just then, it struck Kyung-hee that the shabby, grey-bearded homeless man sitting on the next bench was none other than the opera singer Domingo who, unfortunately, had vanished from public memory after singing "Nie sollst du mich befragen, noch Wissens Sorge tragen, woher ich kam der Fahrt, noch wie mein Nam' und Art". The man was wearing a long black cloak, had a grey scarf muffling his neck and jaw, and was sitting with his head so deeply bowed as to give the impression that he had fallen asleep. The wind scudded down to the earth from the height of the aeroplanes passing overhead, whipping the exposed skin of any who raised their faces to look up at the sky. Incited by the invisible sun, dust motes turned into radioactive particles of electricity before they even touched the ground, embedding themselves one by one in people's hearts. Sheets of darkly opaque fog were flowing over their heads like the shadows of huge black ships, heading out to the sky's open water. As though in submission to the fate that is nature, Kyung-hee bowed her head, returning her concentration to the faint, distant letter towards which she remained utterly indifferent. "...but were we to propose another project to you, might you be able to participate as a voice actor in a performance project, a project which would consist of a single radio artist performing onstage what was originally a two-person recitation..."

122

'Starbucks.' Looking up from the letter, Kyung-hee felt a strange sense of relief as soon as her gaze alighted on that sign; she stood up from the bench and hurried over as though having discovered a place of refuge.

Kyung-hee ordered two lattes. But only managed to get one. Several people—foreigners, tourists, opera-goers and people out for a casual stroll, Starbucks aficionados—were standing there clutching receipts, waiting for the coffee for which they had already paid. After Kyung-hee had taken her first latte, she waited for a while until a second latte appeared on the counter, conveyed there by the brusque hand of the salesgirl. Only this time, before Kyung-hee even had time to reach out, another customer whisked the coffee away. A disappeared latte. Unable to tell whether it had been the second part of her order, Kyung-hee continued to wait. A cappuccino dusted with cinnamon, an espresso, another espresso, and three lattes materialised in swift succession. But these latter were all small lattes, whereas Kyung-hee had ordered large, so she moved aside to let a noisy gaggle of schoolgirls scoop them up. The salesgirl washed her hands under the tap, then went calmly outside to smoke a cigarette. Kyung-hee waved to get the attention of another employee, a short, sullen-looking man who dragged himself over and asked what she'd ordered. Kyung-hee held out the receipt and pointed to the part which said '2 lattes.' Give me these, she said. You already got them, didn't you? the man snapped back. Only one, Kyung-hee retorted, speaking slowly so as to make herself clear, and that went cold ages ago. The man, who clearly couldn't care less, turned his back on Kyung-hee until he'd finished making not one but five lattes, which included those

ordered by other people who had just produced their receipts.
When he plonked the tray with the five lattes onto the counter,
the milk froth in each cup sloshed up, splattering drops of coffee
onto the tray. The door opened and closed again. While it had
been open, a pigeon had flown inside, causing a small but lively
commotion among those who had been drinking their coffee. As
it grew nearer to the time for the opera to start, there looked to
be a correspondingly greater number of people both entering and
leaving the Starbucks. Gazing out through the full-wall window,
Kyung-hee thought she saw Jelinek crossing the street. Looking
utterly ordinary, with a dappled scarf and a leather-and-wool coat,
alone, not attracting anybody's attention. And not paying attention
to anybody, either. Yet perhaps it was merely an illusory scene
which Kyung-hee's weak eyesight fabricated on her retinas. The
door was opened again and the pigeon flew back out, leaving
behind a faint henhouse smell, and Kyung-hee eventually got her
hands on the second latte. The man standing on Kyung-hee's right
turned to his petite, copper-skinned young wife, stroked her cheek,
and murmured, My lovely Cambodian woodpecker.

As Kyung-hee carried her coffee away from the counter, she
passed a table at which a middle-aged East Asian man was sitting
on his own, looking somewhat lonely. He caught her eye and
asked, where are you going? The man's hair was almost entirely
grey, but his face, voice, and gestures revealed a self-assurance
rarely seen among those who could truly be considered elderly.
His brisk, decisive attitude made him seem more like a young
man who had dyed his hair and eyebrows grey. He looked to
still have a little while left before he reached the age of ninety.

He was wearing a colourful striped shirt, neatly ironed, and brown cowboy boots that came up to his knees. He didn't look at all like an ordinary tourist, more like an artist or actor from some foreign country, here on a long-term stay. Kyung-hee answered as she always did whenever she was asked a question of this type; in other words, she blurted out the first thing that popped into her head, which in this case was that she was going to China. Because there were four young Chinese women, almost certainly university students, clattering out of the Starbucks right at that moment. Each of the students had their long, smooth black hair tied up in a ponytail, and none were wearing any makeup. Zipping their thick winter jackets right up to their throats, they headed bravely out into the flash of energy from the solar wind that had travelled there through the vast reaches of space. Perhaps, at precisely the moment they stepped outside, the girls would feel a silent sound wave pass through their bodies, a wave of melancholy that would feel, as it had once done for Kyung-hee, as though their hearts were breaking. For such a brief time that none of them even realised it had happened, the girls' bodies were soundboards resonating with the empty universe.

A stream of people poured out of the underground station, out of the buses which pulled up at the side of the street, all of them heading for the opera house. The East Asian addressed Kyung-hee again. Are you waiting for *Parsifal* to begin? Kyung-hee shook her head. She couldn't make up her mind whether to get the letter out of her bag and continue reading it, or whether to simply ignore it, which is what she would ordinarily have done, knowing that it was no different from any other form of long-winded international correspondence, i.e. reams of florid language with no meaningful content. Several people, probably tourists, got up from their seats around the same time and bustled towards the exit, chatting amongst themselves; the fragment of a sentence grazed past Kyung-hee's ears: "I stayed in a city that, in principle, I didn't know..." Which made Kyung-hee turn towards to the East Asian and inadvertently come out with the following.

"...the thought only came into my head just now, but this is a city that I don't know in principle. But, mightn't cities have some original form made up of sensations, like stories and feelings do? Sensations like, for example, the ominous gloom which all young people have in common, or the impression given by some bleak, melancholy suburb when an abduction is about to take place. Mysterious déjà vu. The phrase 'wandering aimlessly' must mean going somewhere entirely of your own accord, right? One day I'm walking along in the city where I live, when I bump into a European. As he brushes past me it occurs to me that we know each other. It seems as though that middle-aged man with the small frame and sandy-coloured hair is someone I met at the theatre at some point, who my German teacher introduced to me and with whom I shared a brief exchange, and it seems that the man also remembers this. But I can't comprehend what on earth he could be doing rambling around this Far Eastern city, alone, not attracting anybody's attention, and not paying anyone any attention either, truly wandering aimlessly. Perhaps with the same thought having occurred to us both, we each turn to the other in simultaneous recognition. We open our mouths at almost the same time, and produce almost exactly the same sentence.

Saying, I don't know where, but we met one time. At that moment, the thought struck me that the woman who used to work in that same theatre's cafeteria had also brushed past me somewhere. That woman probably would have asked me, would you like some tea, or, would you like some coffee?"

At some point while she was speaking, the thought briefly flashed up inside Kyung-hee that this meaningless speech was a kind of fluttering bridge helping their conversation not to grind to a halt.

They exchanged a few desultory remarks. They sat at adjacent tables and drank coffee. Kyung-hee said something about it being a good thing this is a Starbucks, because Starbucks is somewhere that people from China, Europe, or wherever, can feel equally at home—somewhere that literally feels as familiar as their hometown. It's the same with McDonalds, the East Asian supplied, nodding in agreement. "And that means wanderers must come to realise that their 'hometown' isn't a specific place in, say, China or Europe, but simply 'a big city.'"

"But if, after travelling many thousands of kilometres to a distant continent, wanderers were to arrive in an unfamiliar city only to encounter, of all things, an incredibly familiar cultural sign, appearing in an identical guise, and make a beeline for it, like a shipwrecked sailor swimming to an island, is that because they're sad or happy? I mean, what had they walked all that way to see?"

At that, the East Asian replied that it was simply discovery, not sadness or happiness, just as the beauty of a young woman whom you meet in one city or another is neither good nor bad, it is simply beauty; or, to put it another way, just as when we meet the same young woman in this city and then another, we feel as though she is two separate individuals, as though she can in actuality be separate individuals.

"But the young woman is a part of nature whereas the woman in the Starbucks logo is a man-made construct, a deliberately devised symbol, a contrivance of civilization like the Virgin Mary drawn on a shield! And not only is it artificial, it's actually a standardised sign like those used by the UN or international ships carrying radioactive waste material. You could even call it an international ideograph." This was Kyung-hee's reaction to the excessively placid look on the East Asian's face.

But the East Asian remained unruffled, saying "Starbucks is an attribute of the city, part of the city's nature, like the underground or the bus. If we fly to another city, many thousands of kilometres distant from this one, it would be easy to find a screening of the same film we saw here just before we departed, but that sort of thing doesn't make me feel any sense of loss."

"I've been to a big city that didn't have a Starbucks, but it did have an opera house, as beautiful as the one here," Kyung-hee said. The East Asian smiled, and said to her, "We could call such things the exceptional occurrences of this world. If I were you, I would try to simply enjoy those exceptions, not complicate them by over-thinking."

"Up until that winter, I lived a life entirely devoid of such 'exceptional occurrences.'" Kyung-hee continued to make conversation as she picked up her second latte. The coffee had gone cold, and the froth was giving off a faintly sour smell. "Because I was born and raised in a big city. Not that things are any different now, but I was an extremely ordinary woman back then, in many ways. As a child I took singing lessons twice a week after school. I wasn't dreaming of becoming some great artist. It was simply something I enjoyed. And people told me I had a beautiful voice. But the truth was that it didn't have much of a range, and my lung capacity was nowhere near sufficient to become a singer. Besides which, my pitch was unstable, a weakness which sealed my fate conclusively. Not even several years' harsh training was enough to fix it completely. And, as I got older, my tone gradually became covered with a film, similar in character to the 'blurriness' of a lightly-misted bronze mirror, or the ice of early spring. So from a certain point onwards, those who heard me sing would comment only on how 'very lyrical' my singing was. Nothing more. I was born with a voice that was doomed to fail. I was perfectly aware of that even as a child, and yet, oddly enough, it didn't feel like a major setback. Probably because my hope of becoming a marvellous singer and thus making those close to me happy—my family, for example—was unusually faint, especially for a child.

Ah, my parents were both professors, they employed a maid at home, and I also had one sister, who was around ten years older than me. No, maybe more than that. She might have been twenty years older, even. I can't remember exactly how it was; it's been such a long time since I saw her last. I have to admit, I can't even be sure of her name anymore. Perhaps this name is the origin of the doubt and unease that have clung tenaciously to me since my girlhood, the origin of the clammy fear, the obsession which pursues me, and that's what made me promise myself that my sister's name would never again come out of my mouth, that I wouldn't even allow the thought of it to enter my mind.

It's strange, but in my memory she was always an adult. As though she had been born with the fully-mature body of a grown-up. A body that was, in fact, larger than that of an average grown-up. Of course, that might all be down to the wild illusions about mature femininity which often affect young girls who have much older sisters. I know what you're thinking. You think I'm confusing her with my mother, don't you? But that can't be right, because to me my mother was never anything but an old woman. That's one thing I can be certain about, at least. Not only my mother, but my father too; I remember them as always having looked and acted like people who didn't have long to go before retirement. Late sixties, at the youngest. Small, round eyes behind thick glasses; short, stubby limbs like scraggy old branches; thin, lifeless lips, irritably pursed; pale, slack cheeks; mouths that looked so dark and damp as to be unhygienic, as though some kind of moisture was constantly collecting there; and on top of all that, they were unfailingly conservative and fastidious in their tastes. From my earliest memories, they existed not as adults in the prime of life but simply as the physical embodiment of old age. How I've described them, that's not just how I pictured them at the time—that's what they actually looked like, in the flesh. The kind of flesh nature would describe as 'waste material', that is. And, in keeping with their physical appearance, they were rule-bound sticklers, obstinate and intransigent. So it's not likely that I'm getting them confused with my sister. Anyhow, what comes to mind when I think of her now is that she was much older than me, and that throughout my childhood she seemed barely present, bizarrely so. She was always slow, or indolent and quiet, to be more precise, seemingly melancholy. There must have been occasions when I heard her speak, but I can't remember her voice, and whatever she said must have been nothing but a string of words which I couldn't understand. We didn't share a room, unlike a lot of sisters, so with that and the age gap I never even felt particularly close to her, like sisters generally do. It wasn't as though we were friends, you see. Though of course, I didn't feel especially unfriendly towards her, either. Unlike my mother, who was supposed to look after me, or my father upon whom our livelihood depended, she didn't have any particular role to play in my life. It was through skin-on-skin contact that I would have begun to be aware of her existence, as an adult with whom, though we lived in the same house, the precise nature of my relationship was unclear. So it was all somewhat perplexing, you see. Difficult to make sense of.

The way I remember her, she never actually did anything. Neither went to school nor had a job, that is. Thinking back on it now, it seems like she was one of those unemployed, unmarried women, incredibly common at the time, who, lacking the wherewithal to be financially independent, or at least lacking the courage and will, were unable to move out of the family home, and whose entire social identity could be summed up as being on standby for marriage, a kind of 'bridal reserve troops'! But we probably wouldn't have been all that pessimistic about her situation. Back then at least, the prevailing opinion was that young unmarried women—if indeed she was young at the time—were merely in a state of transition, temporarily pacing up and down the platform before finding their proper place, and so it wasn't strictly necessary to try and expedite the process. Because our mother also went out to work, we had a maid who came every day to do the cooking and cleaning, meaning my sister didn't even have any housework with which to occupy herself. As our parents were ruthless, frightening people, there was no way they would overlook even the smallest mistake. If I came back from school having lost a pencil or some money or if I came home late after going to play at a friend's house without permission, if I skipped my homework, if I told the kind of fib that little children are wont to tell, if I deliberately asked for more money than I needed to buy school supplies, then bought myself some secret treat with the surplus. They would threaten me, saying I would end up in a juvenile detention centre, then, once I was an adult, be transferred to prison straight from juvenile reform; that the punishment for children who were bad—ill-bred and ill-mannered—was being made to strip naked and stand in the school yard for an entire day. They even showed me some gruesome photos, saying that they were of convicts being harshly punished for their crimes. As well as my own sins of lying, frivolity, and carelessness, these crimes apparently even stretched to theft, meaning the perpetrators had to spend their entire adult lives in prison. The wretched, unsightly subjects of these hair-raising photographs were thin as rakes, staring at the camera with the blank, hollow gazes of corpses. My parents told me that part of their punishment was to be put on starvation rations. 'Just one more lie from you...' they would intone, boring into me with their gazes and striking horror into my young heart. 'We'll call the police and they'll come and take you away to a prison just like this one.

There, you'll also be whipped three times a day.' This is something I only found out later, but the photos they showed me were actually of inmates at Auschwitz. It strikes me now that they had a great many of these albums, full of prisoners in blue-striped uniforms. My parents also made threats about what would happen if I didn't do certain things; for example, that if I didn't walk around the house on tip-toe, as befitted a modest young lady, they would tie me to the radiator with a piece of rope, and I would have to eat out of a dog bowl. Much later, I chanced across an article in *National Geographic* which described steppe nomads doing something similar, securing their babies to the central pillar of their tent. Because the adults all have work to do, so they need to prevent their children from tumbling into a pot of boiling milk or crawling outside to get gobbled up by wolves. I was reading this article, and before I realised what was happening the tears were streaming from my eyes. Because it said they did it to stop their babies being gobbled up by wolves, which made them sound so incredibly kind and loving. Like someone saying they always make their baby wear a knitted cap so they don't get struck by lightning.

Don't misunderstand me; I don't hate my parents, or bear them any grudge. From their own perspective, they probably believed that they were doing the right thing. In their own way, they thought they were sparing no effort in raising their child. They probably knew no better than I what it was all in aid of, and that fact in itself qualifies every human being to be the object of pity. And yet, even though they were so strict, my sister was left entirely to her own devices. Even when I was being whipped in the kitchen she never paid any attention, just wandered around the house in her chemise, making herself some instant coffee or watching something on the black-and-white TV. What's more, she was a smoker, though only in the privacy of her own room. For the time, at least for a family who prided themselves on their respectability, this was eye-poppingly scandalous. And I'm certain that my parents knew this was going on, because every time she opened her door the smell of smoke wafted out. She kept a candle constantly burning in her room, but the popular belief that candle flames get rid of smells and smoke is mistaken. Unlike me, she slept in as late as she liked, wore whatever she chose, and came home late at night—not often, but certainly more than once. As a young child, I regarded her with a vague envy. Our lives were so different that I thought of her as an altogether different breed of human. It really wasn't easy to accept that she was someone who shared the same blood as me, whose status as my sister meant that society regarded it as perfectly plausible that the two of us might go out to see a film together, walking hand-in-hand."

That bespectacled monk passing by just now, sheltering under a small umbrella amid the hazy shade made by the wall of fog outside the window, isn't he the Dalai Lama? Kyung-hee was aware of this thought flitting unbidden through her mind. A young man sitting by the window, probably a university student, clearly had the same thought. From being hunched over his phone he jerked himself half out of his seat and touched his hand to his forehead, staring piercingly at the monk's retreating figure. His mouth and eyes were both wide with shock. He automatically blurted out, "That's the Dalai Lama! That's the Dalai Lama!" A clattering of coffee cups rippled through the café.

Otherwise, there was no reaction. Everyone remained absorbed in their own conversations, laughing and gossiping excitedly. But the young man's hasty outburst gave Kyung-hee the courage to say to the East Asian, "That student wasn't seeing things. I also thought I saw the Dalai Lama going by just now, a monk's robe seeming to flit past close to the window of this Starbucks. Only, a gust of wind blew his robe over his face, so I couldn't get a proper look at him." Without even bothering to turn towards the window, the East Asian said, "It's impossible that you saw what you think you did. Does it make sense that the Dalai Lama would appear out of nowhere, without any prior notice that he was visiting this city? You shouldn't imagine that every tonsured East Asian wearing monk's clothes is a Buddhist. Aside from street musicians, performance artists, and beggars looking for attention, there are also people who go around dressed like that purely for their own enjoyment."

"That winter, I saw her." Privately disappointed, Kyung-hee continued with her story. At some point the East Asian had moved to sit across from Kyung-hee, and was now leaning forwards, as though he was hanging on her every word. His black pupils radiated affability. But this kind of behaviour didn't sit well with Kyung-hee, who rejected the European belief that a person's eyes could tell you anything about what they were truly feeling. She found the East Asian's exaggerated attentiveness grating. It's just a simple story about my sister, so why is this person going so over-the-top in his role as a chance listener, is it nothing more than the superficial etiquette particular to the Far East, or has this story revealed something important about me, is it possible that he lived next door to me when I was a child, that he was one of the neighbours I've since forgotten, even as she carried on speaking these thoughts were running through Kyung-hee's mind, all in her mother tongue.

"That winter, I saw her. Really saw her, that is, in a way I never had before. One night that winter, I was in bed reading a manhwa comic. 'Manhwa' being on the list of items that were strictly forbidden in our house, alongside romance novels, which were considered indecent, swearing, sugary biscuits that rotted your teeth, and laughter, which was frivolous. And so, when I woke up in the middle of the night and discovered a dark shadow looming in my room, it stands to reason that what seized me, ahead of any ill-defined, instinctive fear of the dark, or of ghosts, was an all too concrete terror. I automatically assumed that the person standing there was one of my parents, that while I was asleep they'd taken the opportunity to go through my bag and desk drawer. That was the kind of thing they did from time to time. My heart contracted. What I felt at that moment was the wish to die right there and then, the genuine desire to be dead, to have it happen without a moment's hesitation and thus avoid both the heavy punishment which was surely imminent, and any contemptible, desperate fretting in the face of that punishment, one whose soul is as hideously crooked as their body, and whose mind has been cauterised. It really was a sincere wish, so much so that I didn't feel the slightest pang at the thought of relinquishing whatever life I would otherwise have gone on to live. In a movement which I hoped would look as though I were merely tossing in my sleep, I pulled the quilt over my head, but in doing so I knocked the manhwa, which had been next to my pillow, right off the bed.

The book thundered onto the floor, which shuddered as if in an earthquake—in what, to me, felt and sounded every bit as severe. Now there's no way out, I thought to myself. My possession of such an item was about to be brought to light, and they would ask me where I'd got the money to buy it. When that happened, there would be nothing for it but to confess all, yes, to confess that I'd swiped a note from my mother's purse the day before yesterday. I might even have to confess that this wasn't the first time. They would pick up the manhwa and beat me over the head with it. Or they would shunt me off to prison, their faces cold and unrelenting, just like they'd always said they would. At school I would be constantly harried, be made to feel the disgrace of what I'd done. My friends would all be informed that I was a thief and a liar. Trying to bury my head further down under the quilt, I was praying that if something had to happen then let it, whatever it was, for god's sake just get it over with. The black shadow stood by the desk, and though it must have seen the manhwa fall to the floor, it had remained entirely motionless. Far from snatching up the book and using it to beat me over the head, it was just standing there with its arms folded, apparently uninterested in my illicit reading material. As time passed I became increasingly aware of how strange this whole situation was, and though I was still terribly afraid, the need to know eventually won out, forcing me to push my head fully out from underneath the quilt. As soon as I did this I was confronted with a face which loomed so close it seemed practically to be touching mine. My reflexive response to the shock was to shield my face with my hands, even before I had time to realise who that other face belonged to; in that split second I'd taken it for my own, reflected in a black mirror.

After a few moments, though, I realised that it was my sister who had come into my room. And that there was something even more shocking than the mere fact of her presence: she was naked, without a shred of clothing on her. Two occurrences which surpassed the bounds of imagination! Granted, I'd seen her many times in a fairly slovenly state, wandering around the house in nothing but her chemise, and with her hair all dishevelled, but never entirely naked. Unlike the kind of accidental situation in which you get undressed before heading to take a shower and a family member catches sight of you naked, this was a revolutionary occurrence in which a person had deliberately chosen to be naked, and to flaunt that nakedness. Revolutionary, of course such a word wouldn't have popped into my head at that age, but I was still aware that I was witnessing an event of that character. Even now, I've no idea why she came into my room at that hour. It might well have been the first time she'd ever set foot in there. To me it was all terribly unfamiliar, troubling, even frightening. A burglar would probably have been far less of a shock.

I can't remember whether she acknowledged my presence in any way. Whether she asked me something, or even just spoke my name... this has only just occurred to me, but is it even certain that she would have known my name? Given the age difference, perhaps she would have thought of me as a small, mute frog being raised in her house. And had my lips ever pronounced her name? Had I ever even thought it? Over the course of our lives, we often meet people with the same name... names are like acquired behaviour, souls we learn to inhabit. I live within my name, not the other way around. It sounds strange, but how on earth would I have known her name? Anyway, I'll just say a little bit more, not about her name but about her naked body. Because it wasn't an ordinary body, you see, that just anyone might have. Her stomach, covered with gooseflesh and distended as though filled with the kind of gasses given off during decomposition, please forgive me, to a young girl it couldn't help but look like a nightmare."

Kyung-hee stopped speaking for a while and met the East Asian's gaze straight on; to find out if he believed she was speaking the truth, if he really was listening with the most sincere concentration, if he was absorbed in her story. Though the East Asian didn't avoid Kyung-hee's gaze, he nevertheless appeared somewhat aloof, as though he were gazing not at Kyung-hee herself but at a different, transparent body behind hers. Kyung-hee reflexively placed both hands on her stomach, one on top of the other. I wouldn't be able to do a two-person play, Kyung-hee thought. My voice simply doesn't have sufficient expressive power. And besides, I'm no stage actor. People would think I was imitating someone else's story. In other words, they would be constantly aware that I was performing. I'm sure of it. So I have to write a letter of refusal. The East Asian leaned back in his chair and exhaled loudly.

Kyung-hee had been too caught up in her story to notice that a faint light had crept into the scene outside the window. Under a sky thick and heavy as dirty cotton, countless shadows were passing back and forth, bundled up in coats, their backs to the light. Footsteps fluttered heavily. When a driver forgot to slow down to make a turn, their car would briefly resemble a lighthouse, the beam from its headlights scything through

forty-five degrees. Thanks to the discontinued light of the unlit
street lamps, suspended midway between the sky and the ground,
to the lidless windows darkly glittering, and the fragmented shadows darker still, and thanks to the ashen smog which was rising
up from underground and forming a thick blanket over the pavements, shrouding faces and muffling footsteps while at the same
time swelling every object with still more abundant contours,
the night's materiality—is this night?—as it unfurled in front of
the opera house was a tangible, material fact. Like faces of ash in
a volcanic cloud, like the real world seen only through a plastic
screen suspended over the stage, Kyung-hee thought in her mother
tongue.

"There was something very fishy about my sister's exposed
stomach. The old house in which we lived was a shabby, dull,
two-story affair, and was incredibly difficult to heat. Because of
money, that is. We could never just casually switch the heating
on. The only exception was if we had someone visiting. The
only heater in the whole house was a small electric thing that
lived in my parents' room. In winter we had to have a hot water
bottle every night. As a child I was constantly shivering with cold;
I seem to have grown used to it. I remember there were always
articles in the newspaper saying that the price of oil had risen.
Never any saying it had fallen. Isn't that strange...," Kyung-hee
murmured brightly, still staring into the East Asian's eyes.

The warmest place in the house was the small kitchen. As the room
had originally been used as a greenhouse it had glass walls on all sides,
allowing the light to flood in at all hours of the day. When Kyung-
hee stepped into the kitchen there was a young hawk on the floor.

The hawk's eyes were yellow as oiled paper and round as small Chinese coins.

The majority of its feathers were a bright, earthy brown, with a smattering of glossy blacks and whites sticking out here and there. The bright sun of the declining afternoon drew an arc of yellow light as it passed over them.

She thought of it using the name 'hawk' because she remembered having heard that word used somewhere. The actual form of the young hawk there in front of her was the very last thing she became aware of, after all other information related to hawks had passed through her mind. At first the hawk was still as a stuffed specimen, then it took a few crabbed steps, in fits and starts, springing up in the unrealistic manner characteristic to birds, but neither spread out its wings and flew up, nor went any great distance across the floor. The hawk shuffled slow as a venerable philosopher. A length of string was tied to one of its feet and on the other end of the string was an enormous dumbbell. The figure of the falconer in his triangular hat was nowhere to be seen. The hawk craned its neck this way and that at regular intervals, looking faintly mischievous. Kyung-hee laughed. At the hawk's being there.

Not knowing the difference between a goshawk and a black kite, the regular kind of hawk, Siberian peregrine falcons, mountain hawks and sparrow hawks, Kyung-hee was ignorant of the very concept which the word 'hawk' denoted, and yet here she was making free with that same word; dreamily, she surmised that this was all somehow necessary to complete her confession, a confession she had begun for no clear reason.

"…and she wrapped both hands around my throat and squeezed; before I had time to guess what she intended, I was choking. I was trying to say something, then I realised that my throat had closed up, that there was no sound coming out," Kyung-hee continued. "I was baffled, of course, but actually the first thing I felt was sadness. Yes, I felt sad, sad and uncomfortable; either because of the look on my sister's face, or because of the whole sequence of abnormal, exceptional occurrences which had brought this situation about. Even in the midst of this confusion, I was writhing in physical pain. The thought that passed through my mind just then was that I knew absolutely nothing about her, and so there was no way for me to judge whether there was some sound reason for her extraordinary actions, or whether she had simply lost her mind. I was seized by the conviction that I had to stop her, somehow or other I had to pit my own strength against that which I could feel in her grip. Strangely enough, in that very moment I recalled a scene that had taken place one gathering dusk, when someone had called her name. She was walking down the twilit alley. The alley sloped at a gentle gradient, lined by brick walls carpeted with soft, pale green moss, the scent of early roses coming from the gardens beyond. It was an evening in early summer, and I was on my way home from school. Our house was at the very end of the alley, right at the top of the slope. But, inexplicably, the person walking along the alley is not me but my sister. The retreating figure is that of my sister. The one returning from school is me, the one being spoken to by the objects which the sunlight touches is also me, the soft breath of the evening breeze and the scent of the roses are sensations I am experiencing, no one else; but the composite whole walking down that old alleyway with the rose branches trailing down over the red bricks, where the evening light has gathered, flushed the colour of rust, is not me but my sister. The strangeness of this strikes me. And then someone calls her name. I, no, she, turns and looks back. In that moment my sensations return to my body, I recover the whole that is I, and I carry on walking down the alley. Why of all things did I recall that preposterous memory, in that strange moment when my sister was strangling me? I grab her wrists and struggle to loosen her grip, squirming furiously to try and shake her off. Whether her face was telling me anything, that I don't remember. Perhaps she was suffering from some form of mental disorder which had been kept secret from me, or, though the possibility is so slim as to be practically non-existent, perhaps she detested me for some reason of which I was ignorant. As far as I remember, I never stole from her, never teased her or bothered her in any way. I'd barely ever looked at her, never mind disturbed her in any way. Or perhaps she'd simply started awake from a terrible nightmare and been caught up in a temporary madness. The fact was that I was somewhat ill at ease in her presence. Our parents treated me harshly, frequently beat me, but there wasn't that awkward sense of distance between us that there was with my sister and I. My parents had a direct influence on my life—more precisely, on my survival—and so my feelings towards them were an uncomplicated mix of fear and dislike. Even leaving aside the fact that my sister and I were not 'sisterly' in the sense of being close, I thought of her as terribly old, and since the two of us rarely came into contact I think that alone was sufficient reason for me to feel awkward in her presence.

Having a sister who is old is quite different to having old parents. Though at the time, perhaps I even thought she was as old as they were! Because, of course, it's not easy for a child to differentiate between adults of different ages, so to me anyone over thirty looked as though they belonged to a race whose members were all of an identical age. In light of that, I can't discount the possibility that my sister was actually much younger than I'm guessing. Perhaps it was only her oppressed, melancholy lifestyle, a day-to-day existence in which there was little hope of change, that made her look like an old woman. In any case, she was much taller than me, much stronger, and at least twice my size; barely an adolescent, I was truly incapable of contending with the pressure of her hands around my throat, a pressure which had all her body weight behind it. I struggled and writhed. But, at the thought that this was my first time seeing her face up close, even within the pain I still managed to notice how bizarre and improbable it was that, in spite of the fact that by that time my eyes had got used to the darkness inside the room, and the light from the street lamps in the comparatively bright alley were shining in through the gap in the curtains, I was completely unable to remember what her face looked like. An enormous hole, that's right, I only remember her face as an enormous hole or holes. The upshot of all this was that my breath was cut off, I could neither scream for help nor beg her to stop. I remember that, as I was struggling, my shoulder touched her stomach. That hideous stomach, which, as I've already explained, her clothes had always previously concealed, so enormously bloated as to appear quite bizarre. As hideous as a dead cow's. She said something, and only then did I become aware that she stuttered, so badly, in fact, that she was barely able to speak. No, it's more exact to say that this was the first time I recalled her stutter. The only thing I could do to prevent myself from laughing in her face was to affect a coughing fit, but she was squeezing my neck so hard that my throat was unable to produce the slightest rasping breath. Instead I tried to kick her in the stomach, with all the strength I had.

People tend to think that women always envy each other. Similarly, they believe that this envy also exists between sisters. But that kind of explanation would only be possible for sisters with much less of an age gap. To me, her hideous jar of a stomach rendered her conclusively unattractive, just a fat cow like other older women, while her stutter made her seem clumsy and wretched; such considerations seemed, if only momentarily, to free me from the pain my body was experiencing, but they didn't seem to have anything to do with envy, merely cold appraisal, as one might assess an inanimate object. And of course, it had never even occurred to me to compare her existence with my own. I'm certain that the instant my knee touched the perilously swollen flesh of her stomach, I fainted, laughing inwardly, or else slid back into a deep, unbroken sleep. The next morning I was woken by the alarm clock, the same as always. My throat's mucous membrane burned, feeling tighter than usual, and there were reddish-black bruises on both sides of my neck, but I just assumed that I'd strangled myself while in the grip of one of my recurrent nightmares. Which was something that had actually happened. I enjoyed thinking of myself as Desdemona of the tragic throat."

So what happened with your sister?, the East Asian asked

Kyung-hee, his voice composed as he ran a finger over the rim of his coffee cup. Did she apologise, or offer you some kind of explanation? But Kyung-hee said, I'm not waiting for the opera to start, I'm waiting for it to end. At that, the East Asian exclaimed, ah, so you're a fan of that famous singer too, I've heard that some of his fans think nothing of flying in from distant cities to see him perform, even from as far away as Japan. But Kyung-hee said, no, I'm not a fan of the singer. But it's true that I'm waiting for him. One day I decided that I needed to go travelling on foot in order to achieve a particular desire; somewhat embarrassingly, that journey didn't even last a single day, but the resolution did become the seed of the discontinuous, intermittent wandering I later embarked on. At one point I landed at a certain airport and went in search of accommodation, found something that looked suitable, noticed a theatre opposite and thus, entirely by chance, ended up in the audience for one of that singer's performances. He's not one of the really big names like Placido Domingo, but a decent number turned out all the same. Later on, I happened across him again in Berlin and then Shanghai. It seems to me that chance, in all its unfathomable mystery, had caused our paths to cross repeatedly during this particular period of our lives! I mean, haven't you ever read a story in which a person's hopes, their hours, their memories determine the path they take through life, but you have no idea how? That's how it is whenever one person encounters another in the course of their own fixed path; these coincidences, already fixed in advance, happen far more often than we think. So even if, after my wanderings have brought me to this city, during the few days I'm staying here there happens to be, of all things, yet another of his performances, that wouldn't surprise me in the least, she answered. Did you try having a frank conversation with your sister, to get to the bottom of what had happened? the East Asian changed the subject again.

"That might have worked," Kyung-hee said, "after enough time had passed, only it wasn't possible because, after that night, I never saw my sister again. She was nowhere to be seen when I got up the next morning, but that was no surprise, as she always slept in late. My mother had just finished getting ready to go to work, and was sitting at the kitchen table. I remember noticing how her eyelids drooped, their elasticity gone, and the foul odour coming from her skin, which she'd tried and failed to mask with perfume. She looked to have aged fifty, no, five hundred years in the space of a single night. I was all too aware that my mother was a dried-up schoolmarm whom her pupils found unlovable, as I myself attended the very same school at which she worked. No, rather than finding her 'unlovable' it would be more accurate to say that she was the object of hatred, especially among the older girls. The main reason for this being her age and her hideous appearance; her nervy, fierce personality was less of an issue. To most human beings, old age excites ridicule as well as abhorrence. And if an old person fails to conceal a strong desire for something, that is taken as a viable reason to inflict the most severe ridicule. Bearing in mind that desire is a sign of being alive—the dead are those who have moved beyond wanting—and that there is a tendency to consider old people as living on borrowed time, having been granted a temporary stay of execution. I was perfectly aware that the senior girls all wished my mother would hurry up and die.

That is, if there was absolutely no chance of her choosing to retire before they themselves graduated. Those girls were on the cusp of that ferocious, neurotic period in their lives, keen as a knife edge and marked by the tang of blood, and quite naturally had complex, confusing feelings about that sharp, stinging femininity that was in fact their own, which they had no idea how to respond to or how to demonstrate, and so their cruelty was in fact understandable. The rumour spread among them that my mother tormented certain girls because she envied their pretty faces. That she detested the femininity which was no longer hers. Girls who were older than me would stare hard at my face for a sickeningly long time when they brushed past me in the corridors. I knew exactly what that staring meant. It was fear of and contempt for the hysteria which was my future inheritance, collective sadism, animal curiosity, aggressive provocation, hostility, provoked by the menarche, whose object was unclear, and hatred of me, who was my mother, and in whom all these things were included and condensed.

That morning, though, staring at my mother's drooping skin, slack as a corpse's, which perhaps was what she genuinely was, I remember feeling for the first time in my life something akin to pity for her. Not only because her thick, yellow tears were spilling onto the table. She pushed the rice bowl and plate of fish towards me, hesitantly reached out to stroke my hair, though there was no special reason for her to have done this, said an absent-minded good morning to me as she sometimes did, bit her lip, sobbed soundlessly, then, unable to hold back any longer, burst into a grotesque stream of snivelling. I had an instinctive aversion to being touched by my mother and, wanting to avoid being infected by the elements which constituted her, I shifted away, though carefully, so it wouldn't seem that I was deliberately cringing back. If I only managed to keep away, I would never droop and spill and slacken like her. I remember watching as she blew her nose, seeing how twisted her wrist was, as though someone had stamped on it. Her own explanation was that she had rheumatoid arthritis from writing on that cursed blackboard for all those years. Her tears were yellow-tinged, dirty-looking. I stared, marvelling, at that unusually viscous liquid.

At the time, though I doubt my mother was aware of it, there was a game that was very popular among the schoolgirls, similar to the hallucination game. We arrive at school clutching our book bags and trudge into line. The playground in my memory is entirely, implausibly devoid of vegetation, constantly washed in an opaque, arid light. It is a scene of everlasting drought, the desolation of something from which all the healthy flesh has been gouged out, where the stones are frozen blue in winter. Not a single drop of water dripped from the rusted tap, and the tap itself, plastered with bricks and cement, was full of pallid moss; after it rained it would be swarming with earthworms. All day every day, songs inciting nationalism and patriotism boomed out from the playground speakers. As the school was used as a military drill yard on weekends, the yard would be crossed by trucks full of people in army uniforms. As though a part of the opaque dust stirred up by these trucks, some unidentified voice begins to whisper out among the children standing there. The first mouths to channel and pass it on belonged to the tall boys in the upper grades, then the long-haired girls who had abruptly materialised from behind the main building, pretty girls with charming, limpid eyes who were always top of the class and who were doted on both at home and at school, then the lovely little classroom prostitutes who, though there was nothing exceptional about their grades, were the objects of secret desire on the part of their perverted teachers; then the middle rank, whose mediocrity in other respects had led them to develop cunning and quick wits; and finally the rumour finds its way even to the indistinct majority, a bespectacled tribe so hemmed in by rules that it was difficult for any of their attributes, either their timidity or the exemplary way in which they fitted the mould, to be considered a characteristic. The fact is that none of us are our parents' children. Our true parents were gobbled up a long time ago by aliens—don't laugh!—and the old couple currently impersonating our parents are spies wearing the blood-stained shells of our parents that the aliens spat out. And there's nothing we can do about any of this. The naïve conclusion was that ultimately all we could do was guard our secrets, since if our 'parents' were to get wind of them they would include them in their nightly reports to the aliens, when they huddled under the covers and used a special device to transmit information about the earth in the form of radio waves.

You'll have guessed this already, of course, but not even a naïve young school kid would have taken a rumour like this at face value. Spreading rumours was just a bit of fun for them, a kind of game. And an incredibly popular one at that. For example, the rumour that a war was about to break out was always doing the rounds. Though it wasn't as though the rumours always passed from the stronger kids to the weak, from the privileged minority who were loved and had excellent grades to those who were run-of-the-mill, beneath notice. On the contrary, it was frequently the opposite... generally, the tribe that was strongest in the world of rumour were the flagrant exhibitionists, those with a particular aptitude for conjuring up fanciful scenarios, as they were the kind who enjoyed concealing themselves in secluded places, like spies on undercover operations. In the course of my childhood I participated in several collective rumour games of a similar sort. Now and then there were some extreme cases. When it happened that the first-year runts were the first to catch wind of a given rumour, then there would indeed be storms of tears, but the majority just took them as a bit of mischief, something to shiver at, increasing their enjoyment by pretending to believe them more than they actually did. Absurdly enough, as I stood there staring at my mother's yellow tears, I found myself recalling that rumour. No doubt it was extremely childish to imagine that those inhuman yellow tears might be a sign of alien genetics. It was probably due to that occasion that 'yellow tears' became added to the alien rumour as an identifying characteristic.

Just then, my mother told me that my sister had left home while I'd been sleeping. I was shocked, this all being very abrupt. After all, though it was theoretically possible that my old sister might leave home to get married or for some similar reason, it had never crossed my mind that this might actually happen, and besides, there was nothing normal about such a sudden disappearance. What's more, according to my mother's subsequent explanation, rather than my sister having left home to get married, she'd gone abroad to study singing. Apparently she'd spent the past few years preparing for such a move! That certainly came as a shock to me: that she was a fan of music, that she'd ever sung a single song, that she'd actually wanted or prepared for anything in her life. It was hard to believe, but then, even unbelievable things do come about from time to time. I don't recall precisely how I interpreted her departure, but I certainly found it less exciting than the rumour about metamorphosed aliens and fake mothers. I stared fixedly at the sight of my mother's yellow tears as they soaked into her blouse and dripped onto the table, stained the dish and spoon, and dirtied the corners of the knitted floor cushion. Conscious of my gaze, my mother spent a few seconds haphazardly fumbling with her face as though trying to wipe away her tears, then, abandoning that for whatever reason, clasped her hideous wrist with the opposite hand, then let both hands fall heavily onto her lap. My father shuffled into the room with his tie hanging loose over his shirt, wearing the knitted vest in which he usually drifted about the house. His socks so baggy around the ankles that they sagged right down onto his feet. On his way to the front door he stopped in his tracks and asked me why I hadn't written him a Father's Day letter. It was something we did every year at school, you see. I told him that I'd forgotten to take any letter paper with me that day, so as punishment they'd made me stand outside the classroom for the full hour. Mumbling to himself, he said that I could have borrowed some paper from one of my classmates. My mother, who'd been sitting there blankly making no attempt to wipe away her tears, her face a sallow, expressionless mask, curtly told my father not to start with that whining. For some reason or other a golden bee was buzzing to and fro between the table and the kitchen area, drawing a mysterious pattern in the air, though, as I recall, not a single fellow creature was there to interpret the sign.

Strangely enough, my father, who always set off to work earlier than my mother, was still hovering by the door, fingering the fountain pen in his chest pocket. Like someone trying to think through what they were hesitating over and why. The phone rang. Ours wasn't the kind of home where that was a regular occurrence, but when someone did call they invariably did so at an early hour. The maid answered the phone. It was for my mother, but she didn't want to take it. It was a call from the parents of a student in her class; their pet cat was due to be put down that morning, and since the whole family apparently needed to attend the deathbed, the child would have to skip the morning's classes. After the maid had hung up the phone, she relayed these words to my mother. My mother listened in silence, completely expressionless, but my father's face instantly turned the colour of earth. The reddish-black blood whirling beneath his skin, the decrepit tendons stretched to breaking point, were all clearly revealed, as though someone had grasped his tie and was using it to throttle him. I recall that his eyes briefly turned vivid red. Like a fish that had died a bad death. They were old eyes, engaged in a life-or-death struggle to keep the tears at bay. No one said a word. The atmosphere resembled that familiar tension when one person is about to strike another. Or when an event is imminent, superficially similar to a physical attack but actually quite different in character. Whatever it was, my father fled from it, hurrying to the front door apparently oblivious to the hindrance of his sagging socks.

A glugging sound bubbled up from his chest like when a drain runs backwards. He beat a hasty disappearance through the door, and still no one opened their mouth to comment. I recalled the recent 'oyster shell incident' at the girls' high school. My father taught mathematics at a school run by the same foundation as the one I attended; his position attracted every bit as much of the pupils' hatred as did my mother's. There'd been a rumour going around that, on top of being old and ugly, he wasn't even any good at his job, and only kept it through toadying up to senior management. Not only that, but he was never able to satisfactorily shake off the kind of scandalous rumours which often dog older male teachers. According to those rumours, my father had a thing for the plumpest of the older girls, the ones whose flesh rippled over their shoulders down to ripe, rounded breasts, and would deliberately follow them around, spotting his chance whenever they were climbing stairs to give their buttocks a quick, furtive pinch. Now, I'm not saying the oyster shell ballot itself was a rumour. It was something copied from the ancient Athenians, who used to hold an annual vote on the most hated person in the city, writing names on potsherds (the Greek word for which was almost identical to their word for oyster shells). Of course, the schoolgirls didn't have potsherds, so instead they used scraps of ordinary paper, which then went into an empty carton of instant noodles; a name was plucked out at random, and that person was the one chosen to be 'ostracised.' It was an open secret that one name was chosen more often than others. Of course, it was only a game, just a bit of fun. The high school girls were too old for the rumour that our parents were an alien race, so they must have needed a different game.

Had my father found out about this and been plunged into disgrace? Could that be why he had fled, with a similar countenance to that of the young hawk occasionally brought to our house by a relative, who hunted with birds, when that hawk had, quite out of the blue, splayed its legs and promptly died?

Some time later I happened across a hypothesis which sought to prove that there were no such things as extra-terrestrial organisms. It took as its premise the fact that intelligent organisms are only able to evolve in environments similar to that of the Earth. The sun was too big, the other planets either didn't have sufficient volume, were either too near to the sun or too far from it, too blazingly hot or too freezing cold… too much, that is, for the carbon compounds from which organic bodies derive to form strong, stable bonds. Anyhow, according to this hypothesis, of the billions of solar systems in the universe, fewer than you would think fulfil such criteria, in fact our earth might be the only place that does… it made me think back over the rumour game of my childhood; I felt as though the astronomer who had written this hypothesis had constructed an elaborately continuous and connected theoretical universe, linking it up and having it expand unchecked, for our sake, for the sake of our parents, for the sake of safeguarding all of our painful memories, of defending each of our points of view, and yet in spite of that I was unable to shake the suspicion that, were certain theses which the scientist had rejected outright (perhaps because the attitude known as the scientific, which we so readily place our trust in, is in fact extremely fallible) found to be true—for example, were some kind of as-yet-unknown consciousness with physical form able to exist even inside the sun's blazing flares or the tornado of an enormous planet made up of an icy core shrouded by thick dust, with no interest in responding to the language of radio waves which we have been periodically sending out for many years now (though we would never know the reason that terrestrial organisms didn't respond to our signal), were there to be certain unknown races living in a state whereby they no longer possessed either flesh, the conglomerate lump of an organic body, or even matter, were their existence to be entirely independent of phenomena, meaning that they had moved beyond being corporate bodies of oxygen, and that an 'environment' which could sustain living bodies was, therefore, largely irrelevant to them—in that case, using the conditions of Earth's environment as a basis for our scientific investigation into the possible existence of such organisms would be about as effective as studying a shrivelled caterpillar in a flowerpot that had died three years ago.

I don't know what became of my sister. According to my mother, she got married after finishing a long period of study, and is still living abroad. It's strange, but the foreign city my mother mentioned then was one which, coincidentally, has the same name as the one we're in now, so who knows, they might even be the same place. Even now, I remember her only as a silent face coincidentally derived from that which was decomposing, leaking out and slipping down; a suspiciously distended stomach, a female singer with a stutter; an old sister whose violent madness might have been the family's secret heredity. But there are also facts I don't remember. I can't remember the scene when my mother called her by my name. The old alleyway where, hearing her name being called, I (she) turned to look back; the fact that gradually, as I grew up, I outwardly came to resemble my old sister; the moment when, being struck by the intense feeling that my face in the mirror very strongly resembled someone else's, I had the astonishing presentiment that that someone might be none other than my sister; all of these disappeared from my memory. And after all, if you think about it, there's nothing remotely odd about sisters having similar faces. But I never did get a proper look at her face, so for me she is remembered only as a non-specific older woman; given that, I can't remember how I managed to become aware of our resemblance. For a time, things were peaceful without her. Not that they'd never been peaceful before, but, oddly enough, after she vanished I was no longer as frightened or nervous of my parents as I had been. Even when my father got colon cancer again, after already having had so much of his intestines cut away that there was barely anything left, though I probably forgot he existed due to the constant hyper-stimulation that is the life of an adolescent, I still didn't wish for him to hurry up and die. He's still living now, several decades later. At least as far as I know. Ah, and I grew up, and eventually left home. The dimensions of my body, which had been flat as a sheet of paper, swelled frantically after my sister disappeared, to the point where I was eventually even larger than my parents. Which was how I knew that I'd become an adult. On top of that, after my sister left there wasn't a single instance when I stuttered! I even managed to get a job reading aloud from books, though I'd already abandoned my singing lessons by that point. I tend to believe that, in their own way, my parents loved me very much. When it comes down to it, I don't think there's all that great a difference between someone saying, hey kid, try some of this fruit, and shouting, if your mouth twitches like that one more time I'll cut your lips into pieces with scissors, you little bitch! Since, to a certain extent, language is no more than a contrived, man-made symbol, like traffic lights or a flight attendant's uniform, like the sign for the bathroom or for Starbucks. In that way, I prefer the kind of love whose face defies interpretation. And I know how to smile when confronted with a love like that. Only that kind of love knows how to set me alight. But now and then I'm thrown into confusion, groping for words, or else memories, no, for thoughts; on-stage facing an inattentive audience, I wonder, am I the only one who doesn't notice this? Well, so, it looks like the opera's finished, people are coming out."

It was true. The doors to the opera house had opened, disgorging clumps of well-dressed people who streamed out into the street en masse. During this window of time the cityscape is strewn with clumped lights, which float swiftly or slowly. Orange candle flames on restaurant tables; the enormous ashen shadows that flicker brightly in front of them; bundles of fire blurrily reflected in invisible puddles, and on the surface of the canal; the streets are dotted with these flutterings of orange brilliancy.

"In the house where I was living a few years back, when I lay on the bed at night I could look through the open window and see aeroplanes cutting across Orion, their lights blinking on and off… like transformed sun gods, the planes travelled the entire length of the dark celestial sphere which made up the night," Kyung-hee said. It was difficult to judge the precise hour from the scene that was visible beyond the window, a tangle of dust, clouds, and thick fog, but, unlike when Kyung-hee had first entered the Starbucks—is this night?—there at least seemed no doubt that it was night. Small shards of light floating on the Earth's surface formed straight swift lines like swimmers cutting through water; only once they were very close could you tell that they were electric bicycles. Dark green coats and black coats, blue fabric tied to a pillar, a swatch of dark red velvet in the portrait of a Dutch painter, the long chocolate fur of a dog being taken for a walk in the fog, grubby flags, grains of soil in the flowerbeds, various shades of muddled brilliancy glimmering on the surface of a pearl, constituted the night of this city.

"Perhaps it wasn't a plane but a wandering star. Wandering stars do sometimes look as though they're passing in front of a constellation, you know. But, according to the theory that's held sway for a few years now, wandering stars are only apparent phenomena, not something that exists in actuality—merely specks of light which appear when the dust clouds on the far side of the sun momentarily exceed a particular density and the spurting explosive spectrum gets reflected; the night sky plays the role of a sleek black mirror or screen, making it look as though the 'star' is sliding along a fixed horizontal path. And since, coincidentally, the speed of that movement is similar to that of a passenger jet, the wandering star appears as a distant figure sliding across the sky, visible even for a short while after the explosion on the far side of the sun has subsided," the East Asian said, gazing out into the street. "And so, certain astronomers have in fact compared the phenomena of wandering stars to sun gods racing towards the morning, across the river of night. Though what's really surprising is the literature left behind by the ancient Chinese, who were the first to discover wandering stars. To them, the star was like a nymph engaged in a slow, eternal dance, unaware that she had died; thinking about it now, that description is scarily accurate."

Is this truly night? The sound of people collecting their thoughts and looking around grew to a ringing in the ears, cut through by a scream. Thief!, that ringing in the ears shouted. No, robber! Oh, this is Amok! Overcome with curiosity, someone who had been leaning against the counter waiting for their coffee ran outside into the street in front of the opera house. A black figure ran into the road, cutting across at a diagonal, and crashed into a man who walking over the pedestrian crossing. The unfortunate man doubled over and crumpled to the ground. A car sounded its horn and the black figure carried on running, thrusting people aside. The lights changed to bright red. Is this night? One man, seized by a sudden madness, was racing into the night's interior. The police immediately concluded that this marked the beginning of a radical demonstration, scheduled for that day, opposing the expansion of a nuclear power plant, but that demonstration was already underway in a different street nearby, and was in fact extremely orderly and well-behaved. The man who had fallen down on the crossing had been knifed in the side. The criminal had also stabbed a woman and two children, who had been walking in front of a department store two tram stops away, and, blindly wielding the knife when a number of witnesses pursued him, had seriously injured a further two people, both men. The criminal had jumped onto a tram and made his way to the front, hoping to attack the driver, only to be thwarted by the

driver's compartment being locked. Having to content himself
with spitting at the passengers and giving them the finger, he
then transferred to the underground, went one stop and got off at
a park, shouldered his way through the crowd that had gathered
to watch a band perform, who started screaming and scattering
as soon as they realised what was happening, though by this time
an uncountable number of backs and shoulders bore fresh knife
wounds; when, in spite of all this, the police had still not turned
out in any force, the man continued his blind dash, this time running along the river embankment, even finding time to send two
texts to his girlfriend, passed a bus stop and impulsively slashed
a poster which an animal protection organisation had put up
to indict Chinese bear hunters—the Chinese gather the bile of
living bears to treat toothache!—and went back up the main road,
then, without any particular will or intention, governed simply by
a rough inertia keeping him on the path he'd started down, on the
spur of the moment, stabbed at the buttocks of a person who just
then happened to be getting some money out of a cash machine
in a secluded corner; as a result of which, the person who had been
getting cash out shouted "Thief!", then, though it was clear that
no one was going to come running, shouted again, 'No, a robber!
Oh, this is Amok!' As this was happening, the man who had been
stabbed by the criminal's knife in front of the department store,
in the opening stage of this saga, had just come to his senses in
the ambulance and was informing the paramedic that he was HIV
positive, and though this whole business hadn't yet been reported
on an official news bulletin, many of the city's inhabitants had
come to hear about it through the radio waves of vague rumour,

and the anonymous perpetrator was said to be, variously, a hater of women, or else of children, or of the Chinese, and with all this chaos whirling around her, Kyung-hee leaned forwards in the Starbucks chair, looked down into her empty mug, and tried to focus on what the East Asian was saying.

"According to the literature of Orbis Tertius, the most important foundation of the Tlön school of philosophy can be said to be the negation of time."[2] The East Asian straightened up as he said this, sounding very sincere.

"What?" Kyung-hee frowned, baffled by the unfamiliar terminology.

"Or you might call it the negation of time's successiveness or continuity. If you take that as a premise, the future has real existence only as a form clothed in our current fears and hopes, while the past exists only as the imaginative form which we call memory. To make it a bit more a concrete, try imagining it like this: the world in which we are living, and all the lives contained within it, came into existence mere minutes ago; at precisely the same time, various fantasies about a continuous history stretching far back in time were implanted whole into the minds of the living, in the form which we call memory. The film *Total Recall* isn't a bad illustration of this, if you can remember it.

If you accept this, it follows logically that this world's expiration date has already elapsed, and that the sensations and happenings which we believe ourselves to experience, which we feel is life, are no more than the flickered reflection of faint, fictitious relics

2   Parts quoting Borges in W.G. Sebald's *The Rings of Saturn* re-edited and quoted at the writer's license

which the final stages of this by now vanished world have left to linger within the light. No more, in fact, than the death of stars constituting the vacuum which is the great mother, whose optical existence is made possible only due to a time lag.

Ah, these are not my ideas. Tlön, this is Borges' concept. And Sebald provides a very fine, lyrical gloss of this concept in his book *The Rings of Saturn*. All I'm doing is reconstructing his sentences. While I was listening to your story, cities made of time swam into my mind. The kind of cities which you must have seen with your own eyes, that is. You have alighted from the plane, gone through immigration and are standing in front of a bus stop information board, and there it is in front of your eyes, soaring up above the horizon like a white limestone moon, the earliest city, Ur. Ebla, which fills your field of vision with blazing terracotta. Uruk, city of Gilgamesh, king of the abyss, city of orange sand stairs, ruins decorated with basalt, and low hills, city where the hanged necks of condemned criminals form a mountain, city of the stained moon, city of tombs and of proto-pyramids. Or this city whose existence is simultaneous with these, which we are now physically walking through, just like travellers who discover 'Starbucks' shining like a distant lighthouse, illuminating the very heart of the night, their steps carrying them automatically in the direction of a woman of blurred green and grey water, feeling vertigo at the incredible breadth that lies between the very first and very last cities, I imagined cities that you had passed through like that and would pass through again in the future...If you're wondering why such thoughts came to me unbidden, it's probably because I had time to kill earlier today, so I spent the afternoon roaming this city; on top of the chill wind and overcast skies, this dull, dismal, depressing air meant that I could neither read a book nor go for a walk. So I got on the first bus I saw and rode it for about an hour, as far as it was possible to go in one direction, got off at some suburban bus stop near the edge of the city, where I'd never been before, stepped into a shabby movie theatre opposite the bus stop that had happened to catch my eye, and saw a film. It was probably some sci-fi B-movie, I'd never heard of either the director or the film itself, and the faces of the actors were also unfamiliar; in fact, now I think about it, it was the kind of film where it's even difficult to make an educated guess as to the year it was made. Whereas the lighting and direction, the dialogue and the actors' facial expressions, were, quite frankly, clumsy, the film's content was actually quite touching, even mysterious. So that the overall experience was preposterous, extravagant, and romantic, yet nevertheless curious, and, in the end, very lethargic, empty, and bloodcurdling.

The film opens with an unfamiliar man and woman meeting at some anonymous destination, just like we did. Surprisingly enough, that destination is the middle of a rocky desert. A place where withered cacti straggle up here and there from the ruined earth, and bald eagles circle through the sky, on the lookout for a carcass. The bus, which usually comes around once a week, spits the pair out and continues on its way. Believing that they have been alive for a very long time, they have come all the way here in search of the place where they will each meet their own death, a death that will be definite and conclusive. They desired only to make a final death entirely their own. Together, they enter ever further into the desert. At each step forwards, hallucinations unfurl in front of them one by one, wavering like mirages. The figure of a husband and wife eternally unaware that they had died or been separated long ago, memories of passion and of war, sundered people, people who part never to meet again, forgotten memories, memories of before the age of language, prenatal memories, memories, memories, facts and memories that are not facts, memories that are duplicated and amplified... the desert they had come to happened to be a specific place which stirs up memories. But their old memories have crumbled and split apart, and rekindle distorted like a virus within their agitated flesh. *It Must Hurt Before You Die*, that's right, now it's come back to me. That was the film's title. In certain senses, there's nothing at all unusual about it. In the modern sense, the couple are no different from patients who have escaped from the large-scale death factory we call a hospital. The price they have paid for this is that their own bodies bear all the burden of pain... gasping for breath, writhing in an agony of soul and flesh, they long for death to hurry up and free them from the countless memories whose revival is causing them such pain. Up to this point, it's an ordinary drama. But then a UFO from outer space comes flying out of nowhere, flat as a plate. A yellow beam of light screeches down from the alien craft, sucking the couple up. The audience members who weren't already nodding off burst out laughing at this part. Anyhow, the couple never actually 'meet' the aliens, as these latter are beings who have evolved beyond the need for physical form, able to exist as pure consciousness. The aliens take the couple to another planet, around ten billion light years away."

"What for?"

"Well. Who knows how aliens think? Even the director himself didn't seem particularly interested in their motivation. But my personal opinion is that they were curious about the 'agony' of those facing death. To beings who do not possess flesh and blood, that must have seemed a great mystery."

"So what was on the planet, then?"

"A desert, cacti and eagles, and memory."

"So you're saying it was identical to Earth?"

"No, not that, just that they seemed to have crossed ten billion light years' of space to somewhere resembling the desert of memory from which they'd been abducted, no, to have returned to that very same place. The audience is bewildered. The one difference is that in the new place the couple, like the aliens, also exist as consciousness without form. They think. No, they remember. To the audience, they now exist only as a voice-over. Might they actually have ceased to exist…? But if, in spite of that, their memories still continue on…?

Anyhow, they are not visible to the audience. The image shown on the screen is that of eagles circling through the air, gliding serenely down towards a recent carcass. There is a close-up of the eagles' glinting eyes, and the sound of their hard beaks crunching the beast's bones, raking at its flesh and sucking out the blood-clotted fat and intestines, can be heard for quite some time, in all its concrete detail. Takk takk takk. Slurp slurp slurp. But even in the moment of that invisible death, the couple's voice-over continues. Within the confines of the screen they converse, experience emotions, eventually seem to think, oh Time, stop, this instant, you are truly beautiful. They believe that they have died and come back to

life, that, unbelievably, they know passion once again, they enjoy
believing that they have fallen in love. They, their voices, their
memories, their hallucinations. The moment an eagle plucks an
eyeball from the carcass and swallows it, their consciousness speaks:
I believe in miracles, I believe in love, I believe that the future will
come to me. I believe in life. Oh, Light.

An odd story, then, but not actually all that unfamiliar. It's not
clear why, but listening to that episode about your sister made
me think of that film. Do our memories only ever live inside the
house of our bodies? And what is a body, really? A single body, for
example, might it be simply a single memory? And I don't mind
admitting that, listening to your story, the Inuit shamanist belief
in 'the soul's alter ego' was in my mind all the while. The gist is
that your soul, identical in form to you yourself, is your constant
companion, a walking stick-cum-ocean navigator which guides
your course, who gives a recitation of your life in advance of your
actually living it; on the day you genuinely become yourself that
soul-cum-alter ego dies, there on the far expanse of white snow
(please recall that the protagonist of the myth is an Inuit), leaving
only a shell behind. From that point onwards, not even a shaman
can tell you anything of the road that lies ahead of you. The visible form of your soul has disappeared, so you must set out alone,
in a direction of your own choosing. What your doings will then
be, no mouth has yet told.

I think it's possible that as a child, you lived through a very
peculiar time. For example, living under the same roof as your
own future, a future that felt like a stranger to whom you were,
nevertheless, strangely close. All parents can be seen as a past which

wears the future's clothes. We become parents, I think, because we hope to lie down alongside the ancestors of the past. This is something I'm always thinking about, but our being simultaneously past and prophecy, both our own future and something produced by our parents' bodies, is extremely significant when considered with the concept of time. It's certainly an important reason for denying time's continuity and successiveness. Since 'parents' are bodies in which hints of the future mingle with memories of the past.

A sister who is older, who stutters, who even has an unplanned pregnancy, might be interpreted as a separate individual who has the same name as you, your own image running in parallel. Since through her you lived out a portion of the future simultaneously, she is a premonition that the life which lies ahead of you might, as Sebald said of Tlön, somehow end up composed of the remaining fragments of a fantasy, relics of a transparent fiction. I thought that your name, your face, your future, had arrived in this world in advance and were waiting for you, like several layers of time disclosed concurrently, ensconcing themselves within your memories and watching all the while, still a part of you even now."

Kyung-hee went over to the theatre. After she'd been waiting around outside the performers' entrance for a little while, the singer who had played the lead that day appeared. His unusually massive frame and correspondingly large lung capacity were clearly apparent when he was on stage, but the figure who stepped out onto the road wearing a thick coat and with a shawl wrapped around his neck looked like an ordinary man, not especially striking, a bespectacled music teacher who was getting on in years. The street had darkened completely; lingering in the air alongside the thick, damp fog was the smell of iron in the blood. The police line had already been lifted, but the chalk outline of the person who had collapsed to the ground was still distinct. A gang of people crossing the street were twitching their facial muscles inexpressively and casually tossed their paper plate into the road after eating the final piece of sushi. One group, who were mainly women, detached themselves from the crowd and ran over to the singer, holding pens and programmes or autograph books out in front of them, and asked him to sign. With a friendly 'if you would.' Kyung-hee hung around at the back of the group, waiting until they'd all wandered off. After signing all the various things that were thrust under his nose, diligently shaking hands and maintaining an impression of general affability, by the end the singer looked almost done in. That this city boasts an unusually large number of opera programme collectors, determined to get a signature on every programme they own, is already well-known as far afield as Japan. The singer reached out and grabbed the opera programme that Kyung-hee was holding, scrawling a clumsy, mechanical signature in the blank space. "Your name?" the singer asked, pen in hand, aware that Kyung-hee was the last of the lot and therefore with the intention of displaying some extra friendliness. "Your name?" "Maria," Kyung-hee blurted out. The singer wrote the dedication swiftly and absent-mindedly, with a familiar carelessness. 'To darling Maria.' He then thrust the pamphlet at Kyung-hee and strode off in the direction of the car park. Someone was heard saying that the person who had been stabbed at the crossing had died. He was the only fatality from that day's Amok episode. Kyung-hee was shocked by the singer's non-reaction to the name Maria. "It's unbelievable," she exclaimed. "I expected him to at least ask me something about Maria." This was directed at the East Asian, who had left the Starbucks and come to stand next to Kyung-hee.

"It's because Maria is a common name," the East Asian comforted her. "He would never imagine that it was somebody he actually knew."

"But he lived with her for two years. A long time ago, but still." Kyung-hee sounded pained, as though vomiting out some stifling knot from inside herself.

"He must have guessed that it would be unwise to confuse you with that Maria."

"Ah, that's right, Maria was Karakorum, and an unusually liberal one at that, meaning she lived with lots of men. And lots of women too, of course. Now and then she even had couples paying her a visit, or no, to be more precise, paying her room a visit. Since Maria herself was only ever renting a room in a shared house. So in fact you could say that she lived with all of them. Each of them looked like travellers, and would turn up in front of Maria's door, entirely unannounced, with enormous backpacks. Maria never asked how long they intended to stay. Even after a month, two months went by and they still hadn't left, she never asked when they were planning to move on. She never even asked who they were, or whether they genuinely were the same Karakorum who'd contacted her in advance of their stay. So there were times when a Karakorum would turn up at Maria's door when there was already one staying in her room. But they were each perfectly satisfied with their own little corner, just enough space to lay out their sleeping bag.

Karakorums twice stayed with Maria in Japan, too. But were they really all Karakorum? A Karakorum husband and wife, a Karakorum couple, a singleton Karakorum, a gay Karakorum, a sixteen-year-old Karakorum and an eighty-year-old Karakorum, Maria's Karakorum lover, Karakorums who leave and Karakorums who arrive, a landlord Karakorum, a tax collector Karakorum, people who all had different body smells, an imperfect lover Karakorum and a three-fourths lover Karakorum, they lived together in Maria's room as though vaguely overlapping one another."

"And are you staying with this Maria now? Until you go back to China?"

"I'm not going to China," Kyung-hee said testily. "Why on earth would you say such a thing?"

"It's something I've always thought of doing myself," the East Asian responded coolly, and Kyung-hee remembered the lie she had carelessly tossed out. "Ah, what I mean is I'm not going there right away," she sighed. "One day the singer said to Maria, 'I've spent so much of my life roaming around, with one particular issue on which I never could make up my mind; only now do I feel able to come to a clear decision.'"

"You've told me so much about it, I think even I can guess what the issue was."

"That's right, he meant that he wanted to have a child, so he'd have time to watch them grow up before he died."

"And what did Maria say to that?"

"What options did she have? It meant that he wanted to leave her; he only phrased it like that so he could put a respectable front on it. At the time, Maria had already passed her sixtieth birthday, you see.

He said, Maria, my love. I will never forget your name."

They walked across the man's outlines chalked onto the zebra crossing. With all the other people. Once they'd crossed the road, the East Asian pointed left and said, "I have to go that way. It's nearly time for my appointment with some colleagues, and we've arranged to meet in an office on the opposite side of that road over there. By day it's an ordinary building where employees come to do their shifts, but at night it becomes our office. In other words, we only have that place for half of the day, in terms of hours, since our lease is only for the hours when the sun isn't up. And in my opinion, I sense that you will go in the opposite direction."

When Kyung-hee had left the house she'd had no plan beyond the vague intention of meeting the singer and letting him know—or else asking—how Maria was doing, but she didn't like the idea either of following the East Asian or of going in the opposite direction, so she said, "I still have to think a little bit more about what direction I might go in. So please go ahead to your office." Kyung-hee was left standing absent-mindedly in the middle of the pavement, and was still there a long time after the East Asian had disappeared from sight. Kyung-hee took a taxi. This happened because the taxi driver mistakenly believed that she was trying to hail his car—while standing on the kerb, she had stretched out her arm to sweep her hair up—and pulled up neatly in front of her. But Kyung-hee didn't feel the need to inform the driver of this misunderstanding.

They were passing through the city centre, past streets of silk, streets of smoke, streets of factories, streets of houses, and a riding school, to the natural history museum next to the Restored Catholic Church.

The taxi driver asked Kyung-hee if the cloth with which her handbag was embroidered was Chinese silk. And then, before Kyung-hee had managed to formulate an answer, informed her that his ex-wife had at one time worked as a salesperson in a Chinese silk store. And that that store, which dealt mainly with textile products from the northwest regions of China, was not that far from the Restored Catholic Church, or the Natural History Museum, which the two of them were on their way to. A Vietnamese acupuncturist had recently opened next to the silk store, and business was thriving at a tea house across the road, which sold Japanese mochi flavoured with matcha. And the driver turned swiftly to Kyung-hee and said, "Say to me what you look for in this city, in order to remind you of your homeland. I think I can show you that."

"Please don't go further than twenty euros' worth," Kyung-hee replied.

"Oh, that's far enough to show you somewhere new," the driver said cheerily.

The traffic wasn't good. No, rather than staying within the bounds of 'not good', it had crossed over into 'very bad.' Even bicycles were overtaking them. Kyung-hee got the natural history encyclopedia out of her handbag, flicked through a couple of pages, then gazed out of the window. The driver explained in a friendly manner that the traffic was so bad this evening because earlier in the day there'd been a demonstration against nuclear power plants. But the demonstration had in fact finished some time ago, and the demonstrators had either returned home or gone somewhere else, a rave, for example.

Kyung-hee concluded that the driver was still unaware of the Amok episode which had taken place in front of the opera theatre. A night where it looked as though making it past the crossroads that were right in front of them would never be possible, at least by taxi. Yet is this night? The fare was still less than twenty euros, but Kyung-hee was thinking that it might be better to get out and walk. She had seen a poster in the Starbucks on the opera square saying that today was 'museum night', an event which only happened once a year. On that night, every museum in the city centre stays open until at least midnight. But before Kyung-hee could tell the driver to let her out, two people walked in front of the taxi, appearing so suddenly they seemed to have materialised out of the strangely dark fog, and rapped on the rear passenger window next to Kyung-hee's seat. When the driver lowered his window and asked them what was going on, they pointed at Kyung-hee and asked to see her ID. Kyung-hee didn't have her passport with her. And so she did end up getting out of the taxi after all, albeit at someone else's bidding.

The two of them both looked young and alert; one blond with a gold earring, one in a black suit. The man with the earring got his own ID out of his pocket and held it out to Kyung-hee. They were police charged with tracking down those who were in the country illegally, though this wasn't something Kyung-hee could glean from their IDs; rather, she simply had to take the blond man's words on trust. After they had both shown Kyung-hee their IDs, the blond man lifted up his untucked shirt to give Kyung-hee a look at the leather holster attached to his waistband. But Kyung-hee was no more able to tell whether the blond man's pistol really was a pistol, or nothing more than a leather case he was wearing as part of his disguise, than whether their IDs were genuine or forged. They said to her, if you want you can call the National Police Agency directly and have them confirm our identity, but Kyung-hee shook her head. Instead, she asked them which direction the Natural History Museum was in. The blond pointed into the distance, indicating a vague direction that was neither right nor left. A car with its windows blacked out was parked by the kerb.

"We need to check your passport," the blond explained. Kyung-hee didn't ask why. She genuinely wasn't that curious, and besides, her passport didn't have anything much in it worth checking. "If you don't have your passport with you, would you please write your name here so that we can make enquiries?" said the man in the black suit, holding out a notebook. As she did this, Kyung-hee asked him if it was correct that the museums were open until midnight that day, and he replied that he didn't know. The man in the black suit got back into the car, holding the notebook in which Kyung-hee's name was written. The blond man had clearly been observing her in the meantime, standing close by her side though without much in the way of physical contact. This time, Kyung-hee asked him if it was museum night. Museum night was last week, he told her. This week, there's an exhibition of Burne-Jones' mythological paintings in the city hall gallery. The man in the black suit got out of the car, notebook in hand. And said to Kyung-hee, "I had a quick search done, and it turns out that we need to see your passport. There is no possible alternative. Our task is unavoidable: to check your passport with our own eyes..."

They demanded that Kyung-hee get in their car. And go with them to the house where she was lodging. Saying, just give us an address and we'll find it, anywhere in the city, no need to look it up. But Kyung-hee couldn't remember the address. "I mean, I only just arrived in this city this morning!" she said. "In that case, how did you get here from there? Did you take a taxi?" "No, I went to the opera square; I didn't see a performance, though, just had a coffee in Starbucks…" "How did you get to the opera square, then?" "On foot. I do remember, on the way there I followed the tram line for a while, and there was a pedestrian subway." When she'd walked through the subway there'd been a continuous clanging coming from somewhere above her head… and… ah, perhaps if she went to the area she'd be able to recognise the building by sight. "In that case, we'll take you back to the opera square and try retracing your steps from there, then you can let us know when you spot the road where you're staying!" The blond man presented this by way of a compromise, as soon as Kyung-hee had finished her long, clumsy explanation.

They opened the car door. Inside the car was a third man. He was a fat man with unkempt black hair, scrunched up awkwardly in front of an enormous telecommunications device. They had probably used that equipment to inquire about Kyung-hee's name. "But I… I'm on my way to the Natural History Museum. It's museum night, you see," Kyung-hee protested feebly. "It might already be past midnight by the time we get to my lodging, and then I'll miss my chance of visiting the museum." But the men showed no signs of backing down.

"That's a shame, but it's not our responsibility. If you were only carrying your passport on you as a traveller should, then there wouldn't have been any problem," the blond man said firmly.

"But you..." Kyung-hee let her retort trail off and glanced at the blond man's waistband.

"You've already seen my ID, after all. Or do you want to see it again?" He stuck his hand in his pocket.

"Perhaps my name told you something about me?" Kyung-hee asked faintly, but there was no answer. Unable to think of any further excuses, Kyung-hee complied with their demands and got into the car.

To avoid the traffic congestion, the car they were in chose to take a roundabout route through the back alleys. The fat man got out some gum and started chewing, while the other two remained silent. The car's black windows meant the interior wasn't visible from outside, but from inside the dark streets (now, curiously, darker still) could be seen, sunk in an opaque light. The lights were off in most of the back-alley shops. The car drove past a travel agency with a sign reading 'Syria Airlines.' The car's headlights shone through the glass wall of an office and illuminated the figures of two men doing something inside a store where the lights were off. Kyung-hee got the natural history encyclopedia out of her bag, opened it at random, and began to read. Probably bored and looking for distraction, the blond man asked Kyung-hee what she was reading. "It's an entry on anatomy," she told him.

"It describes how anatomy training was carried out in seventeenth-century medical colleges. Practising anatomy was very popular at the time, so it wasn't only medical students who attended; upper-class laypeople took part as well. They only used the corpses of men who had undergone capital punishment and for whom the church had given them permission to practise on, and during the practice they ate, drank alcohol, and performed music. And it says that they burned medical plants and incense to get rid of the foul stench." At that, the man asked Kyung-hee if she was a nurse. Kyung-hee replied in the negative. "Last time I was at the Natural History Museum, I saw a woman's uterus in a glass bottle," the fat man interjected with a snigger. "Beforehand I would just have guessed that it was round like a ball, but this thing was in tatters, like badly sliced meat, and weirdly puffed up. Like a decapitated chicken." "Well, it could hardly have been a man's uterus, could it," the blond sighed, clearly uninterested. "How would they have managed that?" "Perhaps it was a cancerous womb?" This time it was the man in the black suit who joined the conversation. "I don't know; I don't think so. The label didn't say anything like that." "Why a cancerous womb, of all things?" the blond put in. "It's in a museum, not a hospital's specimen room." Fatso spat his gum out into some paper, as though his mood had suddenly soured. "Perhaps it was a sheep's womb I saw, not a person's. It was really greasy," he said. Kyung-hee closed her book and looked out of the window. They had left the alleys and were passing slowly through some unfamiliar district which Kyung-hee didn't know.

"Look at those blockheads over there," Fatso said, pointing at a ground-floor office, the only place with its lights on in that secluded street. "So we're not the only fools still working at this hour!"

"They're not working," the blond corrected him. "It's an after-hours political meeting. Small political parties who don't have the money to rent permanent office space hold meetings at night.

As far as I can tell from the address, it's the office of this district's senior citizens's party."

Kyung-hee followed the men's gaze and peered inside the office. In the brightly lit interior, around a dozen people were sitting around a large round table, with one person standing up, presumably giving a speech—he was certainly gesticulating wildly enough. Were they really a senior citizens' party? They seemed old enough to form such an organisation, and also not. That is, if there were a fixed minimum age for such things. Though nothing of this could be heard from inside the car, the man who was giving a speech had his sleeves rolled up and was declaiming with great fervour. His hair was grey and his face was lined, but he didn't look to have yet reached ninety. If he were still no more than eighty-nine, people might hesitate to use the term 'elderly' to his face. The speaker rested both arms on the table, bowing deeply and breathing evenly. Then all of a sudden he turned in the direction of Kyung-hee's car; though of course, Kyung-hee herself wouldn't have been visible to him. All the same, he stared at her window for a good long time. Long enough for Kyung-hee to realise that he bore a surprising resemblance to the East Asian who'd sat with her for a while in Starbucks. Perhaps he really was the same man. Kyung-hee wanted to press her face right up against the black glass and get a better look at him, but the car hadn't stopped and was now at some distance from the meeting. Aside from that one office, the other residents of the street looked as though they had all agreed to be as frugal as possible with the electricity. The upper stories of the buildings were all residential use; aside from a couple of lit-up kitchen windows, the rest was dark, like the shops closed up for the night. "You're wrong," Fatso interjected. "That man was a foreigner; how could he belong to a senior citizens' party? And there were a few there who couldn't be called elderly just yet... if you ask me, they look like part of the Tibetan Independence Movement. And even if they're not, apparently there are plenty of radical Buddhist skinheads around these days." And the three of them turned and stared at Kyung-hee.

They drove through the opera square. Only from that point was Kyung-hee able to remember anything of her earlier route. "Now we'll follow the tram line," said the blond man. "At some point, we'll probably come across the subway you mentioned." In fact, the subway appeared at a much earlier point in time than any of them had expected. As soon as they had passed it, Kyung-hee was able to recall the street and house number of her lodging; when the blond man asked her, apparently without sarcasm, how she would have planned on getting back if her memory had continued to fail her, she wasn't able to come up with an suitable answer.

"Now listen, we'll all go up to your house together," the blond man said, ushering Kyung-hee out of the car. "To check your passport." The fat man got his gum out of his pocket and popped a piece in his mouth. The three men stood and watched as Kyung-hee fished the key out of her bag and opened the door. The flat was on the fourth floor, so they all panted their way up the stairs. Fatso was panting loudest of all, and seemed to be muttering something to himself, plainly put out. The carpet lining the stairs was extremely thin, so when the four of them happened to mount a step in time it sounded like a hammer clanging dully beneath them. Whenever Kyung-hee sped up the three men instinctively increased their speed to match her, following hot on her heels. Kyung-hee thought to herself that if she were to turn around then and there and say to the three of them, look, this flat isn't some secret hideout for refugees, there's no illegal immigrant Triad gangs with saw cutters for hacking off horses' heads, so there's really no need to trouble yourselves coming up here, it might well make for an incredibly funny joke. On one of the upper floors a door clicked open then slammed shut, unnecessarily loud, like a kind of warning.

They came across two elderly women, straight-backed and looking directly in front of them, making their slow, steady way down the stairs. It seemed an effort for their legs, stick-like in opaque tights, to drag their heavy, dull leather shoes down the steps. The quivering skin of their faces suggested the struggle to suppress a bronchial tube spasm. Skin covered with the thinnest possible faint, milky film, minutely, furtively decomposing. Rheum sliding out from four reddened eyes. Twin strawboard faces recalling a grey-haired Frida Kahlo. They passed by Kyung-hee in turn, weightless and scentless. The men stopped and pressed themselves up against the wall to let the women pass. Women who looked light as sinking dust, apparently through long resignation. If someone were to approach them, rest a hand on their friable shoulders and say, Maria, which one might actually turn to look back?

When she finally arrived at the door to the flat, Kyung-hee sank down onto the stairs. She'd pretty much run all the way up, without stopping for a rest, so now she was wheezing like a pair of bellows. A look of cruel anger glittered in the eyes of the three men watching her, anticipating that she was about to come out with yet another typical Chinese excuse. A look which told her plainly that if that were the case, they wouldn't forgive her for having dragged them all the way up there, they wouldn't give up their quarry. 'Dragged you up? No, I was thinking of going still further down into the deep earth, and it was you who stopped me, but I forgive you. Because right now I'm the only one of us who knows that you're getting paid to make a fuss about nothing.'

Kyung-hee was barely able to get any words out, as though she had become mute. Thinking that this was either due to her tongue having disappeared or to her having grown an extra one, she hauled herself up, inserted the key she was clutching into the lock and turned it. But as the lock snapped open, Kyung-hee suddenly doubted the wisdom of letting these men into the flat. 'I don't know for sure who they are, and since the flat isn't mine and there are other people living here, if a problem really did come up its scale and character probably wouldn't be the kind of thing I could cope with. And besides, one of these men looks to be carrying a gun, though admittedly I've only seen a case. I've never heard of European plainclothes policemen going around with guns to hunt out illegal immigrants. I've never even seen a gun with my own eyes. True, it's not as though I've heard everything there is to know about this world. That things I know nothing about nevertheless have a place in reality, I'll just have to make my peace with that. The gun I thought I saw is real. But does that have any bearing on whether or not I ought to let these men into the flat?' Before Kyung-hee had time to come to a decision, the men pushed the door open and swept inside, shoving past her without bothering to wait for her consent. They lined up in the hallway with their arms crossed, and said, we'll wait here while you fetch your passport from your room, in case you're nervous. Ah, so you really are policemen, then? Kyung-hee thought, but didn't ask.

After passing a closed door from behind which a radio could be heard and turning towards the bathroom, Kyung-hee tried the handle of what she thought was the room where she'd spent the previous night. But the door was locked. Perhaps it wasn't a room after all but a cupboard where the broom was kept or else some multipurpose space. So Kyung-hee went over to another room which adjoined the corridor. The room was exactly as Kyung-hee had left it. Except for the note which someone had left on her sleeping bag. As always, the window was open, and the room was even chillier than she remembered. All she could see out of the window was the cold cement wall of the building opposite, the two buildings so close together as to be permanently in shadow, or, if she craned her neck to look down, the rear yard where brown, withered stems of lily turf drew sharp shadows amid a straggling riot of grass. Stepping around the various objects strewn over the floor, Kyung-hee made it over to her suitcase and fished her passport out of the front pocket. She hesitated, then reached over to pick up the note that had been left on the sleeping bag. She unfolded it and read: "I woke up and went out to get some food, but when I got back you'd gone out. A call came from Berlin; they said that someone is looking for you. Someone who knows 'your Berlin address.' They asked me for the number of the Berlin healer's house. I'm planning to meet up with some friends from university and go to a pub in the centre. You probably went to the opera, right? We'll be at the 'Louisiana Blues Pub' on Prinz Eugene Strasse if you want to come along. Banchi."

When Kyung-hee came back to the front door with her passport, a university student who was staying in one of the other rooms was glaring at the three men, making sure they stayed out of her room. The girl had a packet of refrigerated ham in one hand, a plate of deep-fried meat in the other. The smell of food was making them all hungry. Kyung-hee held her passport out to the men. They went through it with a fine-tooth comb, a page at a time, checking the innumerable stamps that acted as entry permits or recorded the dates on which Kyung-hee had entered or left various countries. Though they hadn't asked for these, Kyung-hee also showed them her train ticket to Berlin and the plane ticket to Korea. Several minutes went by before the men eventually arrived at some form of conclusion, and handed the passport back to Kyung-hee. The student disappeared into her room.

"There's a reason for all this," the blond said, sounding reluctant to explain himself. "According to our records, you were registered as residing in this city more than twenty years ago, so finding you here now meant it looked as though you'd been staying here continuously, over a long period, without having obtained permission to extend your stay. In other words, you never got permission for an extension after the initial period of your stay had elapsed, yet there was absolutely no record of your having left the country. And so there was nothing for it but for us to obtain concrete proof that you did in fact leave. Now, having checked your passport, it turns out there's nothing wrong."

"How did this misunderstanding come about?" Kyung-hee asked.

"This is just our guess, but it seems to have been one of those cases where there are two people with the same name, or else one whose name was recorded incorrectly. It's rare, but it does happen now and then. Foreigners' names all sound pretty similar, you know, so it's difficult to tell one from the other. The operator makes a mistake with the spelling and it gets into the system like that. Your name is probably fairly common in your country, right?"

"That's right. Very." Kyung-hee nodded fervently, adding, "We differentiate between names that look the same in our phonetic script by writing the Chinese characters next to them. Ideograms, that is."

Uneasy, perhaps even hostile, in the face of this unfamiliar word, the three men stood in silence.

"In that case, do I have to go to the residents' government office and make an official statement about leaving the country?" Kyung-hee asked after a bit.

"No, there's no need for that now," the blond man answered with a shake of his head. "We'll sort all that out for you."

They'd only been doing their duty, so Kyung-hee didn't feel like the situation was all that regrettable, and after saying that she hoped they felt the same way, they left. After they'd disappeared, Kyung-hee couldn't stop thinking about the leather holster which the blond man had been wearing beneath his shirt. It's the first time I've actually seen one with my own eyes, she thought. It looked like a cattle prod that they use for jabbing cows in the head at the abattoir. Would the men really have jabbed Kyung-hee's head with a stick, or might they have been satisfied with boorish laughter? Had they gained a certain amount of enjoyment from the situation, or had they honestly thought I was a dangerous character? The student inched her door open and asked

Kyung-hee, "Have those men gone?" Kyung-hee nodded. "They were police, right?" Without waiting for Kyung-hee to answer, she said, "I had an encounter with a similar bunch myself. Last month I was driving back from a rave with my friends when these guys came out of nowhere and stopped the car. And told me to get in theirs, saying they needed to examine my passport. We'd had a bit to drink, you see. But we insisted on seeing their ID first, we wouldn't back down. We called the police and got confirmation that there really were policemen with those names. We didn't move an inch from the car until we'd got it all checked out, including what they looked like. Did you do the same?"

"No," Kyung-hee shook her head.

"And you still brought them all the way to the house?" The girl sounded completely flabbergasted. "What d'you think would have happened if they hadn't been policemen?"

"They are policemen. One of them even looked like he was carrying a gun."

"What? Don't you know how easy it is to get your hands on a gun? I wouldn't be surprised if you could get one off eBay. Does your boyfriend know about all this? Ah, that's right, he went out to the pub." The girl peered hard at Kyung-hee's face. "You could do with taking look in the mirror. Your eyes are exactly like a pair of flat wells, silted up with sand..."

The road was so narrow it was impossible for two people to walk down it side by side. So narrow you thought you could hear the sound of a chest heaving, breathing in and out, coming from the walls on both sides. This cramped road wound between buildings for quite a way. The walls slanted in over the alley as they went up, so that the sky appeared as a long strip of river, flowing between the eaves of houses. In this conical, three-dimensional space—road—made up of the darkness of the walls, the darkness of the shadows, and the darkness of the sky, which each have their own subtle difference in the gradation of light and dark, there was only shade and still deeper shade. Darkness like that of childhood sleep under the covers. The smell of mould came from the gaps in the damp stone walls. Like the bottom of a dried-up well in midsummer. It was a road for small foxes and snails. Phone cables, one of the symbols of modernity, trailed over the walls in a disordered mass, and formed clumps in mid-air like tangled hair. Before she started down this road, Kyung-hee had bought a bunch of yellow chrysanthemums from a street stall, and asked the seller the quickest way to Prinz Eugene Strasse. The seller had told her that she would get there sooner if she 'went round the houses' down this small road. The road was gradually narrowing, having already got to the point where Kyung-hee could have reached out and touched the walls on both sides. Had it been even slightly darker, she would have been reduced to taking one careful step at a time, groping her way along the walls. Kyung-hee was aware that if she were to start doing that now, walking along with both arms stretched out, the moment her fingertips brushed the walls her eyes would disappear, nothing would be visible, leaving the walls as her only object of sensory perception. Then what could it mean that Kyung-hee was now carrying a bunch of yellow chrysanthemums?

Kyung-hee noticed someone walking ahead of her, or so she thought; on closer inspection, it turned out to be not a man walking but the figure of a man standing still. Leaning back against the damp wall with his head slightly bowed and his hands thrust into his trouser pockets, he appeared to be standing sentinel, ready to scrutinise anyone who came through the alley. However long he'd been standing there, Kyung-hee was almost certainly his first passer-by. For a short while before she actually appeared, he would already have been able to hear the sound of her breathing, of her footsteps on the paving stones, of the newspaper in which the flowers were wrapped rustling softly in her hands. It didn't exactly seem the right place to have arranged to meet someone, or to be enjoying a leisurely stroll. The man was doing absolutely nothing, other than leaning against the wall. He was neither whistling nor smoking a cigarette. He was a young man; had he been a little taller, Kyung-hee might have mistaken him for Banchi, standing there waiting for her. She stopped next to him just to make sure. His face was expressionless. Perhaps you're one of Banchi's university friends? I came this way because I was told that this alley is a shortcut to Prinz Eugene Strasse; it's so dark, I'm worried that I'll get lost...The man made no reply, only peered closely at Kyung-hee's face from between locks of glossy black hair. His hands looked to be fidgeting uneasily inside his jeans pockets. Kyung-hee stood there in front of him for a while. The sound of his breathing filled the space between the walls and bounced back off them, magnified enormously. It rasped out of his nose in what was almost an animal snort, the sound of someone growing increasingly tense. As Kyung-hee stood there watching him, he jerked his head up. She'd seen a stage production once called *Puppet Show of Darkness*; this was like the time during that production when the white-bodied doll had swivelled its head to the side. The doll was inside a glass box, which was on a table. The box was filled with dust, which meant it could absorb any incidental sound or unpredictable movement, anything that wasn't a part of the production. A naked electric bulb hung behind the box, dimly illuminating its contents... As the man glared at the bunch of wild chrysanthemums in Kyung-hee's hand, a look of doubt and discomfort gradually filled his eyes. Prinz Eugene Strasse... Kyung-hee twitched her lips to form the words; even to her own ears, her whispering sounded loading with meaning. His limbs twitching in an abrupt, startled manner, as though his nerve-endings had exploded, the man jerked his body away from the wall. The smell of cold fibres and petrol wafted up from his clothes in a sharp smack, then quickly dissipated. He seemed to hesitate over which way to go, then hurried off down the alley in the direction Kyung-hee had just come. He disappeared into the darkness, walking so quickly he was almost running, with his upper body leaning forwards and his shoulders pumping up and down, like when a rebellious child finally leaves home.

Even after he had gone, Kyung-hee remained standing in the same place. She rummaged through her handbag and pulled out a map, but in that street, between walls that were black as blackness itself, it was impossible to make out a single letter. Rather than being simply black, the darkness of the street, a street which amounted to an unplanned gap between walls, the product of an architect's miscalculation, was closer to a very deeply-dyed, opaque blackish-red. Reminiscent of the pigment commonly known as Martian Red, or Florence Red, powdered iron produced when a meteorite burns, which cools into a blackish-red soil owing to a concentration of iron oxide. If you touch the tip of your tongue to that kind of soil, you don't only get the taste of ash, but also some salty, fishy notes. The darkness of mineral matter gave off a crunching sound like a black silkworm sitting on a mulberry leaf. While she'd been walking she'd somehow remained oblivious of the darkness, but now that she'd stopped Kyung-hee found herself so utterly overwhelmed by it that she was unable to take another step. Acting on instinct, she began to grope her way along the wall, her arms at chest height. She couldn't understand how the young man from a little while ago had disappeared with such swift, sure steps. Kyung-hee put the map, which she'd been pressing her nose against, back into her bag, then, sensing another shadow approaching from behind, whipped around and stared into the darkness, but there was nothing to be seen. A great mass of black silkworms were rustling on Kyung-hee's eyelids. They surged closer to her eyes only to pull back again, moving as one. They were the steady, repeated rhythm of the darkness itself. Forwards and backwards, forwards and backwards, then again forwards. Quietly inducing vertigo. They grew increasingly heavier, gradually weighing Kyung-hee down.

The black shadow stopped in front of Kyung-hee, looming over her. Kyung-hee knew that the shadow was standing still, observing her. It was a different person from the man who had disappeared a few moments ago. It didn't have the former's rough breathing; in fact, it didn't even look as though it possessed such a thing as body heat. After a little while, the shadow passed in front of Kyung-hee. Kyung-hee felt it. But it hadn't gone very far before it turned around and came back. And this time it opened its mouth and asked Kyung-hee: do you know where the Vietnamese kid is, the one who sells tax-free cigarettes here every night? Or are you his older sister? If so, then I should be able to buy cigarettes from you, right? Tax-free, naturally.

While the shadow was speaking his form gradually became more distinct, starting from the area around his mouth. He looked as though he was wearing a partial mask of reddish-black sand, revealing only the lower half of his face and drawing attention to his mouth. This mask, the only part of him that was visible, comprised sunken cheeks, a strong bone structure, hair that came down to his shoulders, and a jaw sparsely sprinkled with beard. Kyung-hee told him that she knew nothing about a Vietnamese boy who sold cigarettes, that she neither sold cigarettes nor even smoked them herself.

"Oh, I see," said the shadow's mouth. As a voice actor, Kyung-hee intuitively sensed that though the mouth was moving, it wasn't actually producing a sound, that the voice was coming out of some other part of the shadow. The impression of a metallic sound which, rather than being a void, had no physicality; the impression that, as with a radio broadcast, the main body of the voice was at some distance from the sound source.

"But you are Vietnamese, aren't you?" Something about the way the shadow asked this question suggested that, rather than being driven by even the mildest curiosity, he was continuing to speak simply because he'd already opened his mouth.

Kyung-hee didn't answer his question. Instead, she asked which direction she needed to go in if she wanted to get to Prinz Eugene Strasse.

The shadow gestured with his chin back the way he had come. "That way. When you go out onto the main road, that's Prinz Eugene Strasse right there." Then, before Kyung-hee had time to thank him and leave, he opened his unusually large mouth so wide it seemed it was about to tear at the corners, saying 'take a good look at me.' The corners of his mouth, which were like those of a fish, sprang back and up, revealing the narrow tip of his tongue poking out between white teeth. Kyung-hee had never seen a tongue so narrow or of such an intense, bright scarlet. Like a fish's gills... Alarm Red, the thought rose unbidden into her mind. The tip of his tongue, reminiscent of a pyramid, tapered into such a sharp point that it was surely not natural, as though the flat of the tongue had been deliberately cut into a triangle. Sticking his tongue out as far as it would go, the shadow started to wiggle it up and down, a frantic movement accompanied by a thrumming sound. It was trying to imitate a snake or devil; that much was clear. This shadow mustn't realise that I come from a cultural area where no one believes in angels or devils, Kyung-hee thought. The whole concept of 'evil' is alien to me. Wickedness is causing harm or willfully obstructing something, it's neither primal nor transcendental. An American Karakorum who stayed at Maria's house later travelled to Thailand, where his corpse was discovered in the food waste bin down a back alley in a foreigners' resort. Apparently all ten of his fingers were broken, and needles had been inserted into both eyes. Maria became aware of these facts when she saw his face in the paper. According to the article, his genitals had also been cut off, as punishment. Maria had informed Kyung-hee of this in a letter. Maria wrote, 'They must have tortured him simply to find out the PIN number of his credit card, but there dwells some primal, horrifying thing, frightening and depressing, in the form his 'punishment' took... if it was intended to punish the First World, that is... but in his punishment there is something else besides simple politico-economic discord. They seem to have wanted to go beyond mere pain or terror, beyond agony. To something like the awe and reverence you feel in the face of darkness and the abyss.' But I deny evil, Kyung-hee thought. Since, if there is no good, then there is no opposite concept either. If being depressed actually made me feel happy, that... the rustling of the silkworms of darkness snapped into silence. The smell of damp rot swirled up from the darkness, throbbing. The darkness increased in density and in front of Kyung-hee's eyes those things began to spill and slip down. Spurred on by the desire to elicit transcendent terror in Kyung-hee, like a primitive human absorbed, trance-like, in the friction needed to make fire, the tip of the shadow's tongue was continuing its quivering red vibrations, right in front of Kyung-hee's nose.

6. Absurdly, the sight reminded Kyung-hee of a particular day a long time ago, whose morning had been spent diligently studying the *Reader's Digest* she'd been given at the bus stop on the way to school, while in the evening she'd watched a film called *The Effect of Gamma Rays on Man-in-the-Moon Marigolds...*

Around half an hour later Kyung-hee came out of the supermarket. She walked over to the bench in front of the Volksbank where

193

Banchi was sitting. Banchi had Kyung-hee's already-withered bunch of yellow chrysanthemums resting on his knee and was absent-mindedly reading the text on the newspaper they were wrapped in, but wasn't touching either the flowers or the newspaper with his hands. The sun swiftly concealed itself behind the clouds. Banchi scattered the crumbs of his leftover bread for the pigeons. The newspaper rustled ceaselessly. As the wind was cold and heavy with moisture, altogether bleak, it was clear that right at this moment somewhere very far away, a grape-sized snowflake was about to fall heavily onto a Karakorum mountaintop. In Kyung-hee's hand was a bottle of blue-tinted nail polish remover. "I felt like I needed to buy something," Kyung-hee said as she sat down next to Banchi, as though by way of an excuse.

"Did you talk to her?" Banchi asked without looking up from the newspaper.

"Of course I did. But Banchi, Maria says..." Kyung-hee trailed off. Banchi only gazed at her wordlessly. "Now is an incredibly busy time for her, and also she said that you coming to call on her out of the blue like this has thrown her off balance a bit."

"I haven't 'come to call' on Maria. We were just passing by, and then the thought came to me while I was waiting here on this bench."

"Right, that's what I said too."

"I was aware that she would be busy. And that I ought not to disturb her while she's working."

"Right, that's what Maria thought too."

"And to be precise, I followed you. You were on your way to see Maria at the supermarket where she works as a cashier, and I was just strolling along after you."

"Right, I was the one who suggested you come with me."

"Is Maria doing okay?"

"Looks to be."

"Healthy?"

"Looks to be."

"That's great. And now's a busy time for her, but the fact is that she doesn't want to see me."

"It's not as though she actually said that, not in so many words, but..."

"I understand. In any case, if that's the way it is then there's no reason for me to sit here anymore!" Still, Banchi didn't get up right away. He only jogged his knees for a bit. Kyung-hee rescued the withered bunch of flowers that was slipping from Banchi's knees, and cleared her throat.

"So, Banchi, the friends you met last night were all from your hometown?"

"Most of them were."

"But there seemed to be people from other countries, countries a little further to the south. Or Tibet."

"That's right," Banchi nodded reluctantly. "There were a couple others, but they were from India, not Tibet. A long time ago, we were planning to set up a transnational organisation of young Buddhists, but nothing came of it; then the idea got revived at a certain point, and this time some of my friends living in Europe are being really active."

"And it's to do with Tibet, right?"

"I don't think so."

"What I mean is, yesterday while I was sitting in Starbucks I thought I saw the Dalai Lama walking down the street."

"What a load of nonsense," Banchi snickered. "There's no way a person like that goes around on their own in this city."

They sat there side by side for a while, each with their hands resting on their knees. Then Banchi asked, "Did you try calling Berlin?"

Kyung-hee shook her head. But said that what she'd in fact done was buy a ticket to Berlin. And that she would therefore end up going to Berlin. The supermarket's entrance was a glass door. There was a dog tied to the bicycle rack in front of the building, while through the glass shoppers could be seen transferring purchased items back into their shopping baskets. Beggars who had congregated underneath the roof which jutted out over the bicycle shelter were sitting waiting for loose change, leaning back against the tiled wall. I wonder why you never see any elderly beggars in this city, Kyung-hee said. Beggars and the homeless and hippies with piercings, where do they all go when they get old?

"I used to wonder that myself, a long time ago; Maria told me that they go to Australia," Banchi answered with a straight face. "But I didn't take her at her word."

The supermarket's glass door opened and a woman walked out with a basket in each hand. She set them down at the entrance and started flitting back and forth to the sale table in front of the building, which was practically overflowing with flowerpots and heaps of discounted fruit and biscuits. The cashiers were sitting in their starchy white uniforms. Every time they made a particular movement the till's metal drawer clanged open, then closed.

It seemed as though fireworks of static electricity were dancing from the cash in the drawer onto the backs of their hands. Most of the cashiers were women past middle-age, and they all looked much the same sitting there. "Just one euro, please, just a spare one-euro coin," one of the beggars muttered, as though placing an order. "Just a one-euro coin, to put towards travelling expenses to Australia."

"Mr. Nobody," Kyung-hee began, "once made a particularly harsh speech about poverty. About poor countries and poor people. Of course, his intention was to talk about countries that are poor because of greedy politicians, flimsy social infrastructure, and rampant corruption. As a concrete example, he talked about the plight of those without homes. People who are forced to live on the streets because they have nowhere else to go, forced to huddle underground during winters as cold as minus forty. He also gave a particularly gruesome description of an underground tunnel choked with sewage, teeming with rats the size of a human forearm. He said that he once looked after a woman who gave birth in such a place. And that, if you look at it in a certain way, the child's death, it having fallen into a drain as soon as it was born, was simply a matter of course, even lucky, in fact. And that, in spite of such poverty, politicians care only about buying houses in Europe and stashing bribes in offshore bank accounts. As soon as he'd finished his rant I told him that I'd been a part of an 'anti-society' group for a year during university. The homeless lifestyle was compulsory for all members. You had to snatch a night's sleep in various underground passages, and get your meals either through begging or at a soup kitchen. But it wasn't as though the group had

some political aim in associating themselves with the poor. They
were just kids who couldn't stand their parents or their parents'
homes. It was a form of social performance, designed to embody
a voluntary asociality. The boys viewed pickpocketing and sexual
harassment as a form of enjoyment; some of them even ended up
in prison. The girls chose to go against the social norm through
homosexual love, or, in a slightly more abstruse dimension, pros-
titution. It's true that they were constantly exposed to the danger
of experiencing even more serious things... but they didn't go to
prison purely on account of the homeless. They weren't all choosing to break the law just because they wanted to live the homeless
lifestyle. You've probably never tried it yourself, but I genuinely did
go begging on the streets. You, who see poverty only as something
to be eradicated and go around giving speeches to that effect,
won't be able to understand, but I've got a good idea of what
a poor person's ego can actually be... I can't understand what I was
thinking, now, coming out with such absurd stuff. I mean, I absolutely wasn't trying to ridicule him, the way he spoke with such
earnest solemnity, it was just a bunch of thoughts that happened
to come to me, turning into words and slipping out of my mouth.
But Mr. Nobody got angry with me. He said to me, 'You're all as
vile as the Americans.' And added, 'You imitate them, like monkeys.' So I told him, you saying that reminds me of the time when
I first came to Europe, when someone asked me where I was
from and then, when I answered South Korea, said, 'Ah, you mean
Americanised Korea.'

I didn't want to belittle Mr. Nobody's classical sense of responsibility. What right would I have had to do so? After all, I knew

that in a certain sense, as a typical third-world intellectual, he was aware of an unbounded, shapeless kind of responsibility that had been selected for him in the same way that he felt he had to dress a certain way. It's just unfortunate that, right then, my attitude appeared incredibly flippant to him. All it was was an intense, impulsive desire to tell him about the runaway life I'd previously forgotten, that period in my life when everything had been up in the air, to reveal something of myself to him, like wanting to bare my left breast in a restaurant—which, if it was to him, I could have done at any moment, with pleasure—but he completely misunderstood me."

"So you grew apart after that?" Banchi asked.

"I can't say that for certain. Mr. Nobody left Berlin the next day, you see, and went to some other country, but that was all planned in advance. He gave me the address where he would be staying. Plus the address for the third-world country that was next on his itinerary, and for another third-world country after that, a country I myself wasn't able to go to. He called me from that third country, and we talked for a long time. Then, after a few months, he returned to Germany, as he'd planned to. Not to Berlin, though, which was odd; instead, he stayed in some small city in central Germany that I'd never even heard of. During one of our telephone calls he gave a detailed description of the room where he was staying, what you could see out of the window, its precise location in the city—all far more detail than was necessary. According to him, the room wasn't far from that city's central station. The journey from Berlin, where I was living at the time, wouldn't even take two hours by train.

He told me that you could see a green hospital building from the window in his room. And that the window was covered with a tight-mesh grille. He said that if I were to alight at the central station, take a left as soon as I came out of the exit, and walk diagonally across the small plaza, I would be directly visible from his window. He also said that he went to the library every day to read and write, and that at seven in the evenings he always had dinner at Café Goat, in front of the library. He described his regular waiter at Café Goat, and the cute waitress. He said that, on the advice of his doctor, he chewed his meat slowly, didn't drink alcohol, and tried to avoid sauces that were enriched with sugar or dairy. He often chose that café as a meeting place, and his editor and her secretary came periodically to see him there. They got him work giving various readings and lectures, and organised his schedule in Europe. And, as he was entangled in an unresolved lawsuit with his second wife, a Russian, complicated by the fact that he himself was a political refugee, he also used the café as a place to meet with a lawyer. He would speak pityingly about you and your family, about the financial difficulties you were having. For a brief period he went every day to the studio of a painter who wanted to do his portrait. He spoke of all the loose ends he needed to tie up before he died. He said that as death came ever closer, his abstract wishes increased in number, and that the temptation to forgive himself, to forgive one who would soon turn to dust, grew stronger. He also spoke of his nephew's drowning. He told me that the boy had been only twenty years old when his rubber dinghy capsized during military service. He said that the other soldiers wanted to donate some physical training equipment in his name, so that his memory would be cherished for a long time. He spoke of relatives who had died and those who were still living, who had all become city-dwellers. He said that, before he put all of these notions to bed, left the café and went home, he waited for the sound of the last train pulling in to the central station. The last train from Berlin, which, after spending all of forty seconds in that city, headed off to the west. He said that he always kept my Berlin address in mind. My Berlin address, to which he would sometimes send long letters. The words poured out of him in a continuous stream, like a monologue, whenever we were on the phone. These soliloquies of his frequently lasted for almost an hour, with no pause for or expectation of any input from my end. It was his private autobiography. A private memoir, which didn't need to be run past anyone first. I was his sole audience. Listening with pleasure and rapt concentration.

With these descriptions of his life and thoughts being so very detailed, there were times when I genuinely couldn't believe that we were apart, when I was unable to shake the conviction that we had always been travelling together, ever since that day long ago when he invited me to his lost hometown. That this shared journey had already lasted for several years, and would continue for several lifetimes yet. Because he spoke to me in such minute detail about his room—saying, for example, right now I can hear the clock hand moving from three minutes past two to four minutes past—even now, in my dreams I sometimes see the two of us sitting side by side against the background of his pale blue wallpaper, sitting half a metre apart with our hands resting on our knees, listening wordlessly to the click of the clock hand as it shifts from three minutes past two to four minutes past; at such times, our attitude suggests that we are thinking about the body heat given off by each other's chest, about the temperature behind each other's eyelids. The temperature of the room, the quality of the light, the feel of the air, the sound of the water boiling in the electric kettle, the smell of the damp wallpaper, the black soil in the otherwise-empty ceramic flowerpots, the evening bustle of the station plaza leaking in through the open window, even the faint sound of the train's whistle, I remember them as though I had actually experienced them against my own skin. I feel them. And in my dreams I encounter them again, unchanged.

I remember one such day, him yelling straight into the receiver as though it were a demand rather than a statement, 'We will never meet again in this life!' An enormous lump inside my chest, what you might call a single, unbroken heart, collapsed with a thud, and I actually experienced vertigo. From that day onwards my body was the remnants of a fire that was sinking down, ever downwards. What I have now is burnt flesh. After that day I became my shell, oh, Banchi. I kept trying to track him down for a long time. One day I made a mad dash to the train station and bought a ticket going to the city where he was staying. This was on my last day in Berlin, the last day my Berlin address was still valid. The next day, you see, I had to return to Seoul. Standing on the platform and wondering why on earth I hadn't done this sooner, I watched the train pull in. The reality of those innumerable people each with their own feet, their own will, their own freedom and ability to move between cities, seemed scarcely credible. The train sped along without a hitch, and in less than two hours I arrived at the central station of the city where he was living. As I stepped out of the station, the hospital building appeared in front of me like a vision. The square in front of the station was tiny, and the windows of the ultramodern, green-roofed hospital building were each covered with a mesh grille, which seemed to be there to stop insects and bats from getting in. It was all exactly as I'd been told. Granted, it was my first time setting foot in the city, yet it felt as intimate as if those postboxes, flower shops, and bicycle lanes all somehow belonged to me. I walked beneath the awning of the tiny, al fresco Café Goat, where there were barely any customers braving the winter chill, arriving eventually at the house where he was staying, the room from which he'd said he would be able to watch me walking across the square to him. It was a day of bright sunlight despite it being winter, and as I stepped into the small, spartan room of an exile, I was wiping the sweat from my forehead. But he wasn't there. And not because he was out at the library, but because he'd returned to Russia. To White Russia, that is, which, to him as a university student, had 'inscribed distinctly into the flesh what it meant to wander the streets and train stations of the world with the face of an East Asian.' The country that had had a strong white fist, the country that had been like a cold steel net. Which was also the country where his second family was living. And only there did I come to understand why, of all places, he had chosen to stay in that city. Because of the hospital, which was famous for its cardiac surgery department. Had he been diagnosed with something? He must have known to expect me at some time or other, yet he hadn't left a letter behind, nor even a note. Only once a little time had passed did I realise what that meant.

The room where he had been living was empty, the bedding was neatly folded on the bed, and the minute hand of the old-fashioned Siemens clock made a snapping sound every time it went forwards. Snap, another snap, snap. I understood it as the sound of my life slipping down, trickling away one unit at a time. Snap, another snap, ever downwards, snap."

Kyung-hee stopped speaking and coughed.

"All the same," Banchi said, then paused. "All the same, you're going to Berlin, and perhaps this time he will be there waiting for you. He did get in touch with you, after all."

"Perhaps," Kyung-hee said thoughtfully. "Yes, I haven't tried calling the healer yet, but you're right, Mr. Nobody is the only person who knows 'my Berlin address.'" They turned in unison towards the supermarket door, because one of the white-uniformed cashiers had come out for a smoke. Cigarette clamped between her lips, the cashier tottered along the strangely blackened wall and disappeared around the corner. There, in an empty lot behind the supermarket, stood a lone Japanese rowan. An aged, late autumn tree which, although its gaudy crimson fruit had almost all been gobbled up by birds, remaining only as red bruises marking the sere and yellow leaves, was still as beautiful as ever. "What are your plans?" Kyung-hee asked Banchi.

"I'll stay here for a little longer, then go and spend some time with my friends from the Buddhist organisation," Banchi said. "In fact, some of the ones who came here used to work at a teak yard in south India. I'll inquire about a job at the hotel where I used to work, way back when I had to share a single rented room with several others. The hotel had a big room in the basement where all the dishwashing was done. When the plates and cutlery from the restaurant were loaded into the dumb waiter and arrived down in the basement, first we'd get rid of the scraps of food, then arrange the cutlery neatly in the dishwasher, set the machine going and then, when it had finished its cycle, take them out again, dry them, and send them up to the kitchen."

"And did you earn enough to cover all the installments for the Japanese copier?"

"If I'd kept on with that work then I probably could have managed it. But the thing is, I only purchased the newest model laser copier in the first place because I'd never imagined that the toner it needed would be so expensive, or that it would go through it at such a rate... I only found that out later, but by then it was too late, so all my calculations got thrown off."

"But what you really wanted can't have been to pay off the installments on the copier, right? Or, of course, a job in the dishwashing room of even a first-class hotel in a European city."

"What I truly want, though my family are opposed, is to stand in the square one more time with five thousand of my friends. And if I can't do that, perhaps paying off the money for the copier and starving to death here is the next best thing. Or going to the teak yard in India and becoming a lumberjack."

"Well, whatever it is, I'm all for it."

"Are you aware that there are fewer and fewer places these days where, as an alien, an outsider who believes in taking an objective point of view, you can squeeze your way in and be accepted? Let me tell you a story I heard during my university days, from a friend who'd worked as a woodcutter in that southern Indian teak yard by day, and been a supporter of the anti-government guerillas by night. While he was studying in Europe, he happened to read a pamphlet put out by an anti-government organisation whose essential position was that 'the scientific and technological advances and the spread of wealth in one half of the world correlates precisely with the responsibility of those who benefit from such things to redress the starvation occurring in the other half'; in other words, it was an eco-Maoist pamphlet about preventing forests and other natural resources in the third world from being swallowed up by the gaping maws of the multinational corporations. Well, he picked up a bag and set out for India. Thinking that the best way to establish contact with the left-wing environmental organisation who'd produced the pamphlet would be to get a job on the teak plantation. 'In the field', you might say. As a result, he wasted nine months there, on a wage that wasn't even equivalent to two euros per day. Everything he'd expected, everything he'd hoped to find, was there in that place. In other words, people who looked to have chosen a life of slavery, their hand forced by poverty and debt. There, it was perfectly natural for the entire life of both the son and the as-yet-unborn grandson to be mortgaged in order to pay off the father's debt. People are not aware that this form of debt is both horrifically inhuman, and, moreover, has no legal grounding, and neither do they seem especially concerned to find out about it. His first reaction upon arriving there and witnessing the situation would probably have been a smile of satisfaction. Since, according to his friend, that place was fertile soil for third-world Maoism.

But when he asked around, it transpired that no one knew

anything about any anarchist naturalist organisation, or the emergent Maoists of that region, and not only had no one heard of the pamphlet, the worst thing was that all his talk seemed to meet with blank incomprehension. Those whose trust he was trying to win were convinced that he was, variously, European, a Muslim, a Buddhist, a slanderer, an alien agitator, a vagrant, a tramp, a university student, or worst of all, a penniless American with puffed-up ideas. And this was a guy who'd never even set foot on American soil! Anyhow, one day the police made a raid on the village where he was staying, arresting the labourers whom he'd been working alongside, as well as the barber, the village's only teacher, even the old-timers who were considered local chiefs. This was something he only found out later, but apparently a police officer had been murdered in the neighbouring town, and the prime suspects were the Maoists whose activities centred around the teak plantation in the southern region. Only when he heard this did he realise that the villagers were living double lives, coolies by day and guerillas by night.

Naturally, he was arrested and investigated along with the other men, and though it became clear that he had no connection with any Maoist terrorists (for whom, ironically, he had spent over half a year in a fruitless search, unable to 'find' the very people who were in fact all around him) he still ended up spending six months in prison, because he didn't have an official labour permit. During his incarceration he came to a very slow, hazy realisation: that it had been a spectral pamphlet that had seduced him, and led him to fly all this way. The plantation workers were all Hindus from birth, teak-yard labourers and frightening Maoists, who were both transcendental meditators, terrorists, mystics, and the very smallest pawns in the profit system of multinational corporations and, at the same time, pawns of a revolutionary organisation. Like my friend, they were unable to understand the university-educated view of beliefs as something that one searches out or selects. They were people who had realised long ago that you cannot change your skin colour for the sake of an abstract belief. Since to them, beliefs were not the kind of thing that can be 'chosen', they felt no need to put a name to them or even think about them in any concrete fashion. And so when my friend asked them about the environmentalist guerilla organisation, they had no idea what such a thing might be. When it was actually themselves. The jungle itself, the teak plantation that was closely connected to London's financial systems, the workers' village, poverty itself as a kind of debt which you were born into, the colour of their skin, in other words natural existence. Once my friend found out that even the landlord of the hut he'd been renting was a cell of the guerilla organisation, he felt even more bewitched by the whole thing. Because this was a man who went around with a hunting gun and butchered wild animals, yet couldn't even understand the word 'Maoist.'

After listening to my friend's story, it struck me that while some people strive to reach the moon, the moon as a physical, actual object, other, very primal people are constantly directing their lives back towards their cave, their blood, their ancient language, as though answering the call of the spirits.

This is a vague and to some extent forgotten tribal concept, a little closer to the source than that of the broad 'race', which relies on the concept of cities and nations which have large-scale systems and organisations. They are searching for that stone cave out of which they once crawled as naked monkeys at the world's beginning. Only those who realise that the enormous whole is nothing but a fantasy, and search instead for their own direction, are the happy ones. Since they know their own cave. The happy ones are those who believe that their names are written on the wall of a cave somewhere in this world, written in wet ash, deer's blood, and red clay. Others give them names, neo-Maoists, conservationists, terrorists, Hindus, Buddhists, Muslims, Confucians, followers of the Gwangmu school, anything except Christians, but these labels have meaning only to outsiders.

I am afraid that the moment I cast off the garb of a poor, powerless, unidentified 'city-dweller', I will become a refugee, stripped of my citizenship, with no idea of the direction I should take. Aren't the tribes who have no cave of the soul thought of as the proletariat of technological society? It was only after my father left us that I became conscious of myself as belonging to the family of someone famous. Before that I was too young, although, because the Communist system exercised strict controls on all forms of what they called 'irrational historical consciousness', it took me even longer to discover that I was the descendent of an ancient tribe who spoke an ancient language. I then started to think of myself as a typical case of an individual who is severely estranged from the preceding generation. My father is still living, but I no longer know him. My father's existence is simultaneous with mine, his body is of the same nature, and yet I am unable to grasp even a tiny part of all the many things that he knows. Worse, I hadn't inherited a single word of his ancient language.

Since, under the Communist system, such things were classed as forbidden cultural property. He was one of the many people who left their hometown never to return. I was artificially pruned away. I possess nothing that can be explained without recourse to concepts. Granted, I work translating sutras, but my actual situation is one of being unable to move an inch without a pamphlet to guide my actions. This is clearly a symptom of the new concept of 'poverty.' This earth was originally the domain of primitive cave tribes; it occurs to me that city-dwellers have since been occupying it without permission. Perhaps, rather than being divided by a temporal gap of many millions of years, as scientists claim, cave tribes and city-dwellers are actually 'simultaneous.'"

"This just came back to me;" Kyung-hee said, "once, albeit for a very short time, probably only three or four months, Maria was married. Her husband was Japanese; apparently he'd been a pharmacy assistant in Japan, then upped sticks and came to Europe one day with no other thought than the longing to become an opera singer. He taught qigong and feng shui at an esoteric school which was only open on weekends. Apparently he knew all kinds of outlandish legends and prophecies from primitive tribes all over the world. His hobby was mysticism as a global phenomenon. Back in Japan he'd even written a book on the subject. On top of that, famous writers and scholars would stop by his pharmacy with some frequency and beg him to show them the rare medicines he had. Maria came to his school at the weekends. But one night, shaking Maria awake from a deep sleep, he accused her of having gossiped about his limp, so that now not only the teachers but even the students were aware of his disability, and asked in a heartrending tone why on earth she had done such a thing. Maria was lost for words, as not only had she never said anything of the kind, she hadn't even realised up until then that the man did in fact limp. It was only a very slight limp, the product of a long-ago car accident; so slight, Maria said, that it was difficult to make out even once you knew about it, and so the only people who were aware of this 'disability' was his family back in Japan. Even if you watched very closely all you would see was one of his feet dragging ever so slightly, the kind of thing you might dismiss as being caused by a too-tight shoe. In spite of that, the man adopted an extremely severe tone and said, do you know why I left Japan, wanting to be a singer was only an excuse, all I really wanted was to come to a strange land where no one knows about my physical defect."

"So that's why he harboured a grudge against Maria and followed her around like a shadow for several years, threatening to murder her!"

"Maria moved back into her own room after that. There was no way she could carry on living with the man. At the time she was working in the box office at a theatre, and apparently he even called up the other employees and threatened to murder them too if they were friendly with her. So she was forced to quit her job. Afterwards, she would feel regret and remorse when she looked back over those few months of marriage, the only time in her whole life that she'd spent away from her own room, as a non-Karakorum."

"So was this before or after her she worked as a receptionist at a yoga studio?"

"I don't know anything about that. I know she's worked as a

museum guard, behind the till at an Asian supermarket, and on the floor at a hippy clothing shop, modelling 'ethnic' clothes for a travel catalogue, as a cleaner at a youth hostel, as a street musician in Salzburg during the festival, as a picture postcard vendor, as a cloakroom attendant at the opera house. But this is the first I've heard of a yoga studio."

"It's a strange thing," Banchi muttered as though lost in thought, his gaze riveted to the supermarket entrance. "For decades, Maria provided countless wanderers from all over the world with a place to stay, but aside from frequently moving from one rented room to another, did she herself ever actually go travelling?"

"She often used to say that she wanted to go to the country where you live, Banchi, to see a dead horse…"

"Yes, but those were just words. In reality, she never went travelling. Considering that she was Karakorum, that's actually pretty ironic. She wasn't your average Karakorum, that's for sure. She must have put up more wanderers than any other Karakorum in the world."

"You said 'was' a Karakorum. Why the past tense?"

"Well, because I don't know for sure that she still is living as a Karakorum. It's probable, though."

"Thinking about it, she's the only Karakorum we know!"

"Did Karakorum really exist?"

"…"

"The ancient city of Karakorum, I mean."

"What are you talking about, Banchi? This is the twenty-first century," Kyung-hee said jokingly. "Something exists as long as it exists on the internet, never mind that nobody can see it.

I'm talking about the internet forum Karakorum, for wanderers who have their own houses."

"Ah, it strikes me that even if I hadn't had any firm intention to see Maria during my time in this city, I might have ended up bumping into her anyway. After all, I probably would have stopped by the supermarket once or twice. But now I know she doesn't want to see me, I'm not going to go up to her and start acting like I know her. All I want to know is that she's doing okay, that she's in good health. If I could just see that with my own eyes it would set my mind at ease, and I'd have no problem forgetting all about her. So if she gets in touch with you, please tell her there's no need to worry about me pestering her." "Tell her that you understand her fears," Banchi added, "but that I'm nothing like that Japanese guy."

"Well... I don't know how much longer Maria's going to work in this supermarket. Because she's doing cleaning work too, you know. She said she can earn ten euros an hour that way. No, twelve euros, it was. Anyway, she's working as an unregistered cleaner. Needless to say, that way you don't pay any tax, so it's even better. Apparently it's mainly foreigners' houses she cleans. And working two different jobs over a long period wears you down. So if she's going to quit one of them, it would probably be this supermarket job, because here she has to pay tax on her wages."

Kyung-hee finished speaking and coughed again.

"Shouldn't you buy yourself some medicine?" Banchi asked, sounding faintly worried.

"No, I can't take cough medicine. Drugs that dilute bronchial secretions can sometimes paralyse my larynx, and that makes me unable to pronounce certain consonants properly. For example, like 'ㅋ', the aspirated 'k' sound, or 'ㄲ', the tensed 'k.' It's a form of temporary dyslalia. For a voice actor like me, Banchi, that could be a serious issue. And besides, I have to call Berlin now."

"But you don't have any public performances coming up, so why can't you take some medicine? I'm no expert, but if it's a temporary thing, then even if you take some cough medicine, any symptoms will have worn off after a few days, right?"

"I'm afraid of contracting a permanent speech impediment."

"What are you talking about, that's not something you can just catch like a common cold."

"I'm being extra-careful because there's a family history of speech impediments." Kyung-hee stood up, clutching the bunch of flowers in one hand. "So it's best if I call Berlin straight away, before I lose my voice. Besides, I've just noticed that empty phone booth over there."

"If you go to Berlin, what will you order at the restaurant?" Banchi asked, also standing up.

"Fried rice at the cheapest Vietnamese restaurant. Prawns and tofu, with coriander."

"See, your pronunciation is perfectly clear!"

"Because I haven't taken any medicine yet, obviously! And I've already got a bottle of Noscapine syrup with me. The instructions say the recommended dose is one 5mm spoonful, no more than four times a day, but I've frequently taken ten times that and not had any problems. I'll take some if the coughing really gets to be too much, so you can stop worrying." Kyung-hee shouted all this back at Banchi as she ran over to the public phone booth. "My mother's had a gluten allergy for twenty years. Then last year she was finally diagnosed with non-Hodgkin's lymphoma. My father came through two bouts of stomach cancer hardy as a machine, but now he suffers from a pseudo allergy to all kinds of food additives and chemicals. Not only that, but certain acids and natural preservatives in fruit leave all his mucous membranes bloody. Blood leaking out of his eyes and rectum especially. So aside from the nurse's sweet saliva he can barely swallow anything but tasteless water!"

Kyung-hee splashed noisily through the puddles that had gathered by the roadside. Muddy water splattered all over her Wellington boots and the hem of her skirt, but she didn't pay any attention; if anything, she swung her arms even more vigorously, making her look like some huge speckled bird. Her flight was arrested when she careened into a fridge that had been dumped by the side of the road, and she almost fell over, but quickly regained her balance and carried on running, bursting into loud laughter.

"What's a pseudo allergy?" Banchi asked, trying to keep up with her.

"The symptoms are the same as for a regular allergy, but it's actually due to an intolerance for a particular medicine, nothing to do with the human immune system! Hysteric symptoms."

"Bwah!"

"So that's how I know I'm going to end up with some kind of pseudo dyslalia sooner or later!"

"And what are these so-called 'hysteric symptoms'?"

"Babies who were born in Chernobyl after 1986 suffered those kind of symptoms, did you know?"

"No, I never heard about that."

"Whatever it is, we can't stop it coming to us!"

"Whatever it is, for god's sake, calm down. Slow down."

"Some form of illness is inevitable before we die." Kyung-hee stopped in front of the public phone booth, her breath coming in loud gasps. She was still clutching the bunch of chrysanthemums, which had been reduced almost to bare stems. "I have to call Berlin, before I contract some kind of illness and my voice completely disappears!"

"It was a young woman who writes a magazine column," the healer yelled, so loud it made Kyung-hee's ears ring. "A young female journalist, can you hear what I'm saying?"

Kyung-hee replied that she could indeed hear him perfectly well, so there was no need to speak quite so loudly.

"Okay, it's just that there's always a lot of noise on this line, and the other person often struggles to make out what I'm saying, so I've gotten used to having to shout. Especially when I have to call Seoul, you can't imagine what a hassle that is. Though actually, the situation seems to have improved these past few days. Perhaps the issue wasn't having an old handset but the phone company's shoddy circuits. Anyway, I called Seoul yesterday, I only spoke a little bit louder than the other person, and heck, they probably could have heard me at that distance even without the aid of a telephone. But I'm no stage performer, you know; modulating the volume of one's voice at will is no piece of cake for an ordinary guy like me." The healer delivered this apology in as loud a voice as ever.

"You're saying a female magazine reporter came to Berlin to look for me?" Kyung-hee asked, somewhat perplexed.

"What on earth for? And how did she know I was here in the first place?"

"Well, I've no idea about any of that," the healer said brusquely. "It's not like we had an in-depth conversation. Maybe she wants to interview you? Given that she reports on public performances, arts and culture, that sort of thing."

"Why would she interview me?"

"Because you're an actor, of course," the healer said, as though this were blindingly obvious. "Supposing that she was coming to Berlin on business anyway, there'd be nothing strange about her wanting to take that opportunity to meet you, an actor, and interview you."

"I still don't get it. It's not like I'm even remotely famous; I've never had a single journalist want to interview me before. And why on earth come all the way to Berlin to interview me, now of all times, when I haven't had any work for ages." Kyung-hee's voice sank, trembling with despondency. "So which magazine was it?"

"Hmm, she did mention the name, but as it's not my field..." The healer dragged his words out diffidently. "Anyway, I was on the phone with your boyfriend and he told me that you're planning to come to Berlin anyway, that you've already bought the ticket."

"Banchi isn't my boyfriend."

"Well, whatever. Isn't it true that you've bought a train ticket to Berlin?"

"Yes, but just on the off chance that I might happen to feel like going there... so no one's come looking for me aside from this journalist?"

"No, no one."

"Any post?"

"Well, nothing that's come since you left."

"Ah, I see." Kyung-hee shivered and sighed. Involuntarily relaxing her grip, the bunch of chrysanthemums fell to the floor. All that remained in the hand that had been clutching the flowers was a bundle of newspaper. As the public phone booth was open, without sides, the exhausted Kyung-hee was forced to lean against the body of the telephone set. "Banchi and I might be going to another city. We're thinking it through now. Banchi's interested in forming a Buddhist organisation, not a political organisation, a 'poor people's Buddhist group' he's been mulling over with a friend. I'm not a Buddhist, but I think I'd like to help them if possible. So I might not be coming to Berlin, actually... if that woman gets in touch again, I'd be grateful if you could tell her that I'm not living there anymore."

"But..." the healer paused, as though deliberating over how much to say, "...in that case, what about the letter the journalist left for you? I promised her I'd send it on to you."

"No, why would she have left a letter at your house?" Feeling a lethargy-induced headache coming on, Kyung-hee, whose mood had soured along with her rising nausea, raised her voice without realising it. "And why should I read a letter from a woman I don't know?"

"I told you, she's a young female journalist..."

"Journalist or whatever, she's just some strange woman!" Kyung-hee's words came hard and fast. "I've no interest in meeting her!"

"Look, there must be some misunderstanding, this woman just..." the healer stammered, clearly flustered. "She just said she wanted to meet you one time... all said and done, she's a journalist, a female journalist, very young, and quiet as a sleeping cat. Surely it's okay for her to want to meet you? It doesn't seem such a terrible impertinence to me."

"I can't stand journalists. The way they talk, the way they write, their business cards, the whole lot of it!"

"Why are you getting angry at me? All I did was pass on a message. The young female journalist who wants to meet you..."

"I swear, if you say 'young female journalist' one more time..." A sharp retort was spinning around on the tip of Kyung-hee's tongue, and she only just managed to swallow it down.

"But you're the one who said you might come back here. Didn't you always say this was 'your Berlin address'? Weren't you the one who asked me several times before you left to let you keep this place as a fixed address, even though you wouldn't be living here anymore? To let you keep this address all the time you're travelling, so a part of you could stay behind, and anyone who wanted to find you could come and look for you here?"

"..."

"You told me you were going back to Korea. You acted as though you were going to look for a steady job in Korea and settle down there, permanently. And weren't you the one who begged me to write down all of the addresses you were using, of all the friends you were staying with, while you went gadding around central Asia, then to Europe, then to China, then back to Vienna, and to get in touch if someone came looking for you?"

"..."

"So all I did was pass what you told me on to her. To a young female journalist from Seoul. Saying that you were certain to visit Berlin again.

On top of that, I even shelled out on an expensive phone call all the way to Vienna. I don't suppose you have a problem with that? And now you're acting like I've done something wrong, I can't make head nor tail of it!"

"I'm sorry, and I'm grateful to you for letting me know. I should have said that earlier. Only, I don't have any coins left..." Realising that she'd made a mistake, Kyung-hee hastily tried to explain herself. But by this point the healer had flown into a rage, and there seemed no getting him out of it. The telephone receiver was bleeping every second, warning her that her money was about to run out, but the healer couldn't have cared less.

"You expect me to assess whether everyone who comes looking for you is someone you're genuinely expecting, and then pass that information on to you? What's that about?!"

"Of course not. I understand. I said I'm sorry. But my coins have run out, we probably won't be able to talk much longer..."

Bleep. Bleep. Bleep. Bleep.

"I've let you keep this house as 'your Berlin address' for several years by my reckoning, free of charge! I mean, you don't even pay rent!"

"And I'm grateful for that. But..."

"You had visitors over several times, and I never breathed a single word of complaint, isn't that right?"

The call cut off with a snap. Kyung-hee's two-euro coin had exhausted its effect.

Kyung-hee hung up the receiver, turned back to look at Banchi, who was idly scuffing his shoes against the kerb a few metres away, and shook her head. It's not him. It's not his letter.

Banchi's sullen expression told her that he wasn't particularly interested. Kyung-hee kicked the bunch of dried flowers that had fallen to the floor and walked out of the booth. And asked Banchi if he fancied going to Café Goat for some coffee. Banchi said he didn't want to. Oh, that's right, you don't want to do anything, Kyung-hee sniped, walking past Banchi and continuing along the pavement. Banchi didn't want to ask her outright about the location of this so-called Café Goat she'd dreamed up. Kyung-hee swung her arms as she walked, not looking where she was going, and a truck whisked by so close it almost sheared off the tip of her nose. She wobbled, coming within an inch of falling into the road, but just about managed to hold her nerve. The driver of the truck pulled up in the next alleyway, poked his head out of the window and stuck his middle finger up at Kyung-hee, fixing her with a furious glare.

"Do you know what just occurred to me?" Kyung-hee said to Banchi, who'd come up behind her. "When I first came to the city where you live, the roads were in such a wild, barbarous state that I was afraid I'd be knocked down and killed. But, as you will have seen just now, it was right here in the middle of Europe that it came this close to actually happening."

"It's your own fault, swanning across the road without looking where you were going."

"And the thought I had immediately afterwards was that if I did end up as roadkill here, and didn't have you by my side like I do now, you or anyone else, no one would ever be able to discover who I actually am, or no, to be more precise, who this body without a passport belongs to, where I came from."

"You do see articles like that in the paper, now and then."

"The body of an unregistered East Asian woman, who was not in possession of an ID card."

"They'd check the missing persons list first. You're ethnically Asian, yes, but you could still be a citizen of the US or some other foreign country, so they'll ask the various embassies here to verify your identity. And I guess they'll find out certain clues from your clothes and shoes."

"From the trademark 'made in China', you mean?"

"And they'll put up an ad about you in the police stations and the train station, and maybe wait for people who'd recently seen you or spoken with you to come forward and make a statement. From the look of the girl at the rented house where we're staying, you can safely count her out for coming forward of her own accord. Besides, she doesn't know what countries we come from, or even our names. If we didn't turn up she'd just pack up our things, stuff them in the basement, and forget about us. Just like every other inhabitant of this city, she never knew a single thing about us, and she never cared to. Thinking about it, the first to come forward would probably be those policemen you had the run-in with yesterday."

"I guess that's true. Perhaps they'd be my only eyewitnesses."

"And whatever they say about you would be your last official record."

"We didn't know who she was..."

"Well, that would be true, at least. And they'll say, it seems we got her confused with some other foreigner."

"We got her confused... Banchi, my chest hurts. That would

be the final sentence of my autobiography. But while I'm still living, I absolutely refuse to imagine what they might say about me after I'm dead. My final act of volition would be to refuse to know anything about that."

Kyung-hee stopped walking and started coughing, gasping for breath. With the practised movements of a genuine hobo, Banchi plonked himself down on the pavement, took off his trainers, turned them upside down and shook out the golden grains of soil that had found a way in while he was running after Kyung-hee. A line of reddish-black German-made tourist buses drove past. A line of decapitated horses, bearing equally headless policemen, clopped past over the pavement. Absurdly, the sight reminded Kyung-hee of a particular day a long time ago, whose morning had been spent diligently studying the *Reader's Digest* she'd been given at the bus stop on the way to school, while in the evening she'd watched a film called *The Effect of Gamma Rays on Man-in-the-Moon Marigolds*. Kyung-hee had identified with the young female protagonist of the film, who was preparing for a science competition. An identification which ushered in the absurd, unlooked-for hope of becoming an actress. As soon as the sun shrugged off the wisp of cloud that had been veiling it, Banchi's hair glittered like wet coal, such an intense, gleaming jet black that Kyung-hee found it almost unbearable. The colour had a hard, material quality about it, quite unlike something made of light, black as a chunk of obsidian just fished from the water, the rock which the ancients used in scalping. I will not permit such a blade to enter my body. I absolutely refuse to imagine it. Kyung-hee got the Noscapine syrup out of her pocket and immediately downed more than half the bottle.

Even supposing I end up bored and with no prospects, if I've aged so much that all the edges of my being are as worn as they can be, if I can no longer perceive colour, taste or smell, cannot endure life stretched out over such a deplorable length of time as a hundred years, and finally, worst of all, were to end up producing some kind of scribble that resembles a poem, my doing so would have absolutely no connection with my father, Banchi said.

I was walking along the bright, hot, dirty alley, where the sun's horizontal passage high above the embankment, a sun yellow as a ripe pear, cast a thin strip of deep shadow at the base of the left-hand side wall; at a certain point, I began to sense that someone was following me, Maria said. Maria sped up, and the one who was following also sped up; she slowed down, and so did her pursuer. The height of the afternoon. The houses which lined the alley all had their doors tight shut, each with a piece of white paper pasted onto them, bearing writing in a script that Maria couldn't understand; she thought that they probably meant something like 'everyone gone' or 'evacuated.' Maria didn't dare to turn and look back. Her Japanese ex-husband who, though many years had since flown by, was still sending her threatening letters at regular intervals twice a year, rose into her mind. Everyone close to Maria was aware of these persistent threats, and found it odd that she didn't call the police and demand their help. There was a reason for that. Maria bared her chest, exposing her operation scars to Kyung-hee. Next to her left breast, which was darkly tanned, cruelly wrinkled and withered, there was an unsightly hollow, as though the flesh had been gouged out with a trowel. The tumour had apparently been discovered in her mammary gland when she was still living with her Japanese husband. When she received the diagnosis, her husband was in Japan tracking down various medicinal plants, of all things. Maria informed him over the phone that she had to have an operation. Far from hurrying back, her husband returned even later than planned, after the date of the operation, but told her that the delay was due to his having hunted down a precious herb, and showed her several small, dried black roots. He told her the name of the herb too, but Maria said she couldn't remember it. He insisted that it was the only medicine she should take. It was a type of herb that granted eternal youth, one which the ancient kings of the East had wandered far in search of. Maria's husband looked utterly sincere when he told her that if she ate it, not only would she recover from her disease, but she would never die, not ever. But Maria said that she didn't want to live forever, just to grow old appropriately, as others do, in good health. I'd hate to linger on for two hundred years and be begging a doctor to put me out of my misery, Maria said, in a light, joking tone. But her husband shook his head. There is no 'appropriately'; either you eat this and live forever, or be reborn as a tumour in someone close to you. Maria peered at the roots, which looked like a lump of dirty coal wrapped up in a cloth. It looked like the mummy of a stillborn foetus, newly excavated from a Mexican pyramid. A lump of carbon from which whatever moisture it had once possessed had all dripped away over thousands of years, leaving the pulverised dregs of an organism made mineral. But in any case, what does it matter? Maria nodded in agreement. Not, of course, because she believed her husband, but because she didn't especially disbelieve him, either.

It's a divine discovery, one that a pharmacist can only hope to get their hands on once in a lifetime, he said. I'm giving this to you. And so you, Maria, will live included in my life. From now on, all that is my own will be eternally included within Maria's eternal life. At the time, he did not give any concrete explanation as to what exactly he meant by 'eternally included.'

When the bell rang and Kyung-hee opened the door, a middle-aged postwoman was standing there. She held out a letter. But she did not hand it over to Kyung-hee. Since there was no address written on the envelope, Kyung-hee doubted whether the letter was for her, and as the woman wasn't wearing a postal uniform, she also doubted whether she was really a postal employee. The postwoman declared that she was an employee of a private international postal company. The company delivers letters and parcels; as a rule, the expenses are cash on arrival. And so Kyung-hee could only take receipt of the letter after paying the special-delivery postage. If she didn't want to pay this fee, it was of course within her rights to refuse to take the letter. Only, in that case, Kyung-hee would, of course, be unable to obtain certain information about the sender of said letter. This is company policy.

Hello, said the female television presenter, speaking into the mic, and welcome to Wednesday's *Good Morning Show.* Let me introduce today's special guest. He's both a scholar with a degree on Nietzsche, a researcher in alternative medicine, and an East Asian healer. He's here today to give a brief talk for us. But before that, let's have a short demonstration. How about it, you said that when patients come to call on you, you first and foremost study how they look, the way they move, and concentrate not on what they say, but the way they say it. Could you explain what you mean by all that in a little more detail?

The healer said that, before thinking in terms of an illness, he first acquaints himself with the person holistically, examining everything about them that can be physically perceived—their voice, the words they use, the look in their eyes and direction of their gaze as they're speaking, the expression they make when he pours black vinegar into a glass, dilutes it with water and hands it to them, entreating them to drink this most sacred wine. In fact, he was usually able to discern from the very start the type of thing they either lacked or had an excess of, in their movements as they walked over to him, their gaze as they looked at him. Especially when he touched the patient's affected area—and the point that had to be made clear was that to him as a healer, every human subject in this world, himself included, was a patient—the degree of that discernment would be so intense as to make him tremble.

So what about me? the female presenter chipped in, so promptly it seemed she'd had the question prepared in advance. What can you discern about me when I look at you?

The healer replied, I could tell you now, but to be even more certain I would need to touch your chest, there's a sound coming from there.

Oh, that's the sound of my heart racing, said the female presenter, displaying a charming smile. The cameraman swung his camera around, panning slowly over an auditorium full of faces flushed with curiosity.

In that case, said, Kyung-hee, I choose not to take the letter.

The healer said, a letter for you from a young female journalist...

Closing her book, Kyung-hee turned to Banchi and said, the page I just read is about an Indian man who goes to India. The man's younger sister is trying to persuade him to go to India. He's spent so long travelling only in foreign countries, he needs to go and experience India, to be with the Maoist revolutionaries, even if it's just a one-off trip... the location of their conversation is, of all places, a city in western Europe, sitting outside a Berlin café. I seem to have encountered a similar scene in some other book. But why does it appear, incomprehensibly, to overlap with the conversation we're having right now, when the two are actually on quite different topics?

Goshawks flying through the air.

Were those goshawks flying through the air?

Despite the fact that I am not actually your sister, that I didn't tell you to go anywhere.

The healer got to his feet, stretched both arms out in front of him and gently pulled the female presenter's head towards himself. Displaying extreme agility—indeed, the whole thing was done in a way that seemed designed to create the most extreme spectacle— he slipped one hand beneath her collar and down to her breast. Though the female presenter's complexion didn't alter in the slightest, the complete lack of agitation visible on her face seemed, paradoxically, to reveal an extremely mechanical tension. The healer swayed on his feet, producing a babbling sound that could equally have been laughter or an order. Stay still just for now, I'm interpreting the shrieks from your heart, the healer said. As though these words were a command directed at them, the audience kept their gazes riveted on the stage, motionless even down to their fingertips and eyebrows. After several minutes of this, the healer exhaled heavily in a great whooshing sigh: you've been to Amsterdam, he said, the words seeming dredged up from deep inside. The tension, which had seemed at breaking point, slackened, and a ripple of light laughter passed through the audience. They started to rustle in their seats, shifting this way and that. That's right, the female presenter confirmed, giving herself a good shake, and I've also been to Tokyo and Beijing. But the healer only narrowed his already small eyes even further, saying, I will listen to what your second heart has to say. Second heart? queried the female presenter, louder this time. I once met a woman who had a second heart attached to her pelvis; she complained that it weighed her down on one side. She was bent at the waist as though she was lame. So did you heal her? the female presenter asked. With the healer's hand on her breast the whole time. No, she refused to let me give her a massage. She didn't believe in my healing skills, you see. She herself probably doesn't know this, but her pelvis will gradually have been tilting to one side all this time. That's the prediction I made. And the healer laughed out loud.

It just came back to me; apparently the name of that magazine is *Journal of Shamanism Abroad*.

The female presenter grabbed the edge of her blouse, gripped the mic, stared directly into the camera and said, we'll continue after a short break, so stay with this channel.

It's a quick quiz. Today's problem: what colour is a white horse? Or, how long did the Thirty Years' War last for?

When Kyung-hee asked, in that case what would the poem's

title be, Banchi answered 'The wife of the Saora tribe's shaman.'

I don't read poetry any more, said Kyung-hee. One day a theatre director came to me and said he was going to pay me per character for my on-stage readings.

After the first conversation finished, he asked his lover 'who are you?' and his lover answered 'I am a wandering soul.' (Andre Breton, *Nadja*, p. 56)

One of the audience members got up and walked towards the stage. The camera zoomed in on her face. It was a yellow face in which the eyes were unusually far apart, the sockets as flat and wide as a roof. The woman was as impassive as a dead horse. Her big square teeth added to that impression. The black hair that fell to her shoulders was already streaked with grey and hadn't been dyed in some time, so the white hairs straggled out of her centre parting. As though bleached time was sliding down her hair. Her lips and complexion were pale, almost grey. The woman shuffled her crooked body awkwardly forwards. A man who appeared to be her husband took her arm to help her up onto the stage. The woman, who was from East Asia, said she was a patient. The female presenter held the mic up to the woman's mouth, but it was her husband who spoke. Maria has a severe speech impediment, and has been barely able to speak for a very long time.

The healer clasped Maria's head with both hands. He breathed in deeply, then out. Maria just sat there on the chair, as still as a statue. The healer brought his lips to Maria's ear, gathered his strength and started to suck in the air, producing a thin whistle reminiscent of a siren. The whistling sound went on and on, showing absolutely no sign of stopping. The studio was packed with people, while crowded onto the cramped stage were Maria and the healer, Maria's husband, the female presenter, the other two panellists, one a folk psychologist and the other a folk doctor, and the cameraman with his bulky equipment, who was, of course, not visible on the screen. The collective tension had a material presence, expanding to fill the entire space, the pressure building to the point of explosion, all of which seemed almost visible. Everything was far too close, one thing stuck fast to another. The sound of breathing, the rough sound of breathing, the sound of the healer's stomach gradually filling with air and his eyeballs bulging out from the pressure, the sound of hearts racing, the sound of breathing through the nose, the sound of a suppressed cough, eyelids trembling, hearts contracting, the sound of saliva drying in the oesophagus and being swallowed, and the sound of the healer's lips ceaselessly sucking the air out of a human body. Her head slightly bowed, her posture utterly passive, Maria was letting her invisible contents slip out. As he struggled to inhale the air from inside her body, exerting all his strength, the healer's pupils darkened to a devilish black, his complexion transforming into that of a dead person. He was a fish flapping listlessly inside a basket, at the end of its strength. His hands as they clasped Maria's head were shaking from the effort. By now, the one with the illness looked to be the healer rather than Maria. The camera zoomed in for a close-up of Maria's face. Having been rigid as steel for some time, at a certain moment her expression contorted frighteningly. The muscles in her cheeks twitched furiously, seemingly a physical manifestation of the desire to speak. Someone burst into agonised sobs; this was neither Maria nor the healer but the female presenter, who had been standing there in a daze the whole time, the mic dangling from her limp grip. The whistling sound produced by the healer's respiratory action gradually niggled away at people's nerve cells, irritating in a similar way to white noise, and eventually seemed even to disturb the studio's broadcasting equipment. Noise gave birth to noise. A mechanical shriek could be heard now and again. Buzzing intermittent trembling or the scratch of skin being torn, the sharp crack of bones snapping, oscillations that whirred high and low. Symptoms of disquiet appearing as sounds of all kinds. Non-linguistic signs. The enormous rat trapped inside each person's head began to squeal and squirm.

The art of healing is one of the skills of the soul that are disappearing alongside ancient languages, said the folk psychologist to whom the mic had been passed. The ancient healers used to practice the sorcery of self-healing by chopping their own bodies into pieces and casting them into the air, then gathering the fallen fragments and birthing a new body from these. Once restored to life, they spoke of what they had experienced while they had been absent from their bodies. While their flesh lay dismantled they roamed the underworld, a journey upon which they encountered their spirit spouse. Men or women dressed in white. They married that spouse and had offspring. And when they were released from their spirit's spouse they were restored to life, returned to the phenomenal world, and recovered their former flesh-and-blood bodies. Back then, time seemed to flow differently in the two worlds. In the eyes of ordinary people, the healer cutting their body into pieces, then sticking it back together was collapsed into a single, brief moment, while the healers themselves claimed to have lived through many years, many decades in the meantime, in the world of the ground, the world of the departed, or the world of birds.

The young woman said that she'd found out something about who and where her mother was. Shockingly, the woman who was her mother turned out to be someone she already knew well, at least in name. Because the young woman had long been one of the few people to have an interest in a certain extremely minor field of art. By this time the young woman was already an adult, so it wasn't as though she still needed parents for protection or nurturing, yet she still felt the desire, a manifestation of pure yearning, for some kind of personal knowledge of her own mother. And so she made up her mind to set out in search of her... and a kind of female Odyssey began.

Eventually, the healer had to be forcibly detached from Maria. Though by this point he was unable to breathe and his eyelids had turned inside out from lack of oxygen, he didn't know how to remove himself from her. He looked to be in urgent need of artificial respiration, but luckily returned to normal after a short while. The camera showed the disordered stage and the shocked, baffled audience. The female presenter resumed her sobbing. The folk psychologist was sitting stock still, save for his quivering legs.

Maria ate the black roots.

You will never die, Maria's husband said.

Kyung-hee's German teacher wrote her a letter which said, in the period when death was impending, I would stare fixedly out of the ward window at the triangular roof of the train station immersed in the final dusky light of the declining sun, and, when the final train to Berlin for that day was just pulling into the station, would succumb to the illusion of having spotted a rare Amur falcon flying through the air, its red feet and slender body outlined against the sky, and give myself over to the fantasy of, in two days' time, illegally marrying the woman who had just then opened the door and come into the ward...

Defining, citing analogous terms, enumerating samples, explaining, rephrasing, communicating, imitating, speaking in poetry, composing haiku, speaking without the use of certain indispensable words, speaking using only certain other, entirely unrelated words. This was the method of instruction which the German teacher had used with Kyung-hee. One day Kyung-hee claimed that she had forgotten everything she'd learnt and refused to have any further lessons.

Even though I changed city and language, it was no use. This giddy vertigo, the feeling of something ceaselessly sucking away at me.

...the fantasy of having her be my final hometown earth.

One day a young woman came to see me, the healer said once he had recovered. A young woman whom I'd never met before. And yet, she knew me—because she was a journalist at a magazine which had once carried one of my articles. In my opinion, the article I'd written was embarrassing, nothing more than the childish product of an excessively conceited student. But she said that my writing had made a very deep impression on her, and because she praised its purity, calling it writing which evinced a firm, sincere will—though such words must be ten-a-penny in conventional introductions—well, even granting that her looks were no more than mediocre, I warmed to her from the very beginning. So I decided to hear her out, and do her the favour of forwarding the letter she was planning to leave behind to the mother who had long since left her. Even while I agreed to this, though, I could be quite certain that she was mistaken as to one particular fact. Namely, that the woman she called her mother was no such thing! But if anything, the fact that I of all people knew what she did not made me still more kindly disposed towards her. As if, though this is something of an exaggeration, she were my never-before-seen fiancée. Her eyes were far apart, and in spite of her youth hers was a face which had something vague, something unclear about it. Rather than the usual curve, her eyelids drew a flat line across her eyes, giving her a sleepy look. Her eyes drooped under long eyelashes. It was an unusually wide, tranquil face, whose expression when at rest was one of impassivity, which could, according to the circumstances, be interpreted as unfeeling. There was no blush to her skin, which was sallow as a pear. When she smiled, the smile didn't reach her eyes, and neither did she have a bird's lively skittishness. What with describing it now, her face, her form is coming back to me in still greater detail; I lack the confidence to judge whether my recollection of her corresponds to the reality, or whether it is an impression created by my breaking the original impression she made down into atomic fragments and combining these anew in my language, entirely as I pleased—an impression, in other words, of rearranged pixels. She was sitting at the kitchen table writing a short letter, and I was watching her do so. As the French windows which opened onto the kitchen veranda had no curtains, mornings would generally see the kitchen flooded with unbearably strong sunlight. And all of its surfaces would glitter as brilliantly as though the kitchen were a kingdom of brass. The sunlight fell upon on her right cheek as she bent over her writing. Like a rocket's concentrated beam. Though I was standing in the shade, watching her made my own skin throb as though it was itself struck by a fierce ray. But the actual temperature of the solar energy was quite low, low enough for her not to notice its impact, or be aware of the risk of getting burned. Curiously, she was barefoot. Summer had been over for a little while already. The kitchen floor was very cold. And so she was resting her right foot on her left, toes curled, as though embracing the one with the other. I had a strong desire to examine one by one the wrinkles which clasped the sole of her foot. And to try and visualise the simmering and bubbling occurring on her burned right cheek and the sole of her right foot. Just then, the phone in my room rang. I wanted to stay and watch her for a little longer, but I had to take the call. Leave the letter there when you're done, I shouted to her as I went to my room. I'll put it in an envelope and make sure it gets to your mother! I said this even though I knew that the woman she thought was her mother was not. I even called her by her name, as though we were intimate. As that name would strike your ears as terribly strange and foreign, for the sake of convenience I'll call her simply Maria. Maria made no response. As I stepped into my room she turned her head, perhaps about to say something, but at that point the receiver was already midway to my ear, and the kitchen door blocked my view of her. Whether she hadn't quite caught what I said, or whether she'd said something in reply and I was the one who hadn't heard, I'm not sure. If, when the call ended and I returned to the kitchen, she, Maria, had still been sitting there at the table, mightn't I have been able to explain to her, quite calmly, this feeling of mine regarding her mother who was not her mother, my sense that her pseudo mother had sat just like that in just that spot, that queer and contradictory facts about Maria had come out of her pseudo mother's mouth; yes, there are times when I think I could have explained it, though it's difficult to describe, that experience of what seemed a form of tangible contact between human beings separated by time, the physical closeness and distance between us that this produces...

7. I become the low hills' lupins

Kyung-hee wasn't exactly famous, true, but we still thought of her as an actor with a certain amount of renown among stage professionals or lovers of recitals. And so when we got in touch with various theatre companies and audio book publishers to try and find out her contact details, and came up against the fact that no one had any information about her, this left us at something of a loss. To put it simply, none of the people we got in touch with had heard of Kyung-hee. The stock response that kept coming back to us was that there was no recital actor of that name. What's more, one person even informed us that the breed of artist who could be called an 'actor specialising in recitation' no longer existed in South Korea, that the renowned stage actor-cum-singer who had passed away many years ago would probably have been the very last performer to specialise in recitation and solo voice acting, that these days one was more likely to encounter stage recitation, if indeed one encountered it at all, as something which radio actors dabbled with as a sideline. Of course, that person later clarified their remarks, saying that they'd meant the kind of actor who enjoyed such a level of fame among the general public that they could appear on television broadcasts. Now and then, people showed signs of confusing stage actors specialising in recitation with writers of fairytales or radio actors or puppet theatre voice artists, ventriloquists or even magicians who used their voices as part of their act. There was a reason that we had to meet Kyung-hee. But everyone we telephoned said in chorus, there is no recitation actor named Kyung-hee, if it's not a pseudonym then it's probably a false name, or else a lie. It can't be, we said. If we said that we'd invited Kyung-hee to our house and hosted an at-home recitation, the listener would express their superficial admiration by saying in wondering tones, 'Oh, you must be so wealthy! Only the upper classes could hold a private recitation in their own home!' Though at the same time, they didn't forget to add that, though the situation might well be different elsewhere, there are some things that South Korea simply does not have, and that one of these was a recitation actor by the name of Kyung-hee. But none of them could give us a convincing explanation as to why they were so sure on this count. It sounded as though, rather than indicating that there really was no Kyung-hee, perhaps it was simply that the phenomenon of a woman by the name of Kyung-hee was insufficiently noticeable, and the voice of a woman of that name was fated to go unrecognised. Just an empty exclamation. "An at-home recitation, well I never! What uncommon class!"

Having been drawn to Korea by an utterly inexplicable,

irresistable impulse, we cannot forget the sight we saw at a small countryside school. When, after a fairly lengthy bus journey, we eventually alighted at a stop quite far from the built-up areas, around evening, we were immediately confronted by a cacophonous war cry drilling into our ears, with an accompaniment of screams and roars. It was coming from the small playground in front of the bus stop. In the centre of the playground there was a long pole, tall as a flagpole, with scores of children thronged around it, shouting a single name over and over again in a rough chorus. We were rooted to the spot; that name was 'Kyung-hee.' Since the constant refrain 'there is no Kyung-hee' had been coming at us from the mouths of so many people, theatre professionals and those who were connected with the world of the stage, that chance encounter went beyond surprising—it was miraculous. The children were raggedly chanting the name of a girl who, dangling perilously from the upper section of the pole, could neither move further up nor come back down. We couldn't tell whether the intensity which laced their voices indicated wild encouragement, hate-filled curses, severe collective scolding, or a simple madness that had nothing to do with any of these. Despite being clearly terrified, and lacking the means of crawling further up the sports pole, the girl didn't look to be thinking about retreating back down it either. She was trying to hide herself, frantically burying her face in her arms as though fleeing from something, but the position she found herself in offered little hope of this. Not only did the children not tire, their screams of Kyung-hee, Kyung-hee! were growing gradually more aggressive. Compared with the confident, strapping children screaming up at her, this girl called Kyung-hee cut a fragile figure. We stood there for a while. We listened to the yells bursting from the mouths of the enraged children. That was the first, and perhaps the only Kyung-hee we encountered in Korea.

Having found a kind of refuge, though a perilous one, there at the top of the pole, Kyung-hee had almost no physical form against the dark-washed sky. So there was actually nothing odd in everyone having told us that there was no Kyung-hee. There in that playground, already strewn with twilight and tinged red like rusted soil, the evening was rapidly spreading as though slipping down from the surrounding hillocks towards the flat land. It was the moment in the day when the contours of objects, where a given form begins or ends, grow rapidly vague and become confused with one another. The white pole became a sharp metal pillar, boring into both sky and earth. As a form of appendage suspended from the wretched human whom they were calling Kyung-hee, who clung to it like a little monkey, the pole seemed to be testifying with its whole body to the confidence of matter, the integrity of matter, the immortality of matter. Morning glory flowers bowed their heads and shrank into themselves. Propaganda banners fluttered and subsided of their own accord, and we froze in a pious shudder.

Later, a teacher emerged slowly from the school building and, looking somewhat shifty, explained to us that the child called Kyung-hee had been stealing her friends' money, and that when the student body, unwilling to take any more of this, had gathered in a simultaneous display of anger, the frightened little girl had displayed a superhuman strength in crawling to the top of the pole, which had been set up ahead of the district athletics competition the following week.

We did visit several recital stages, but if these had names then nobody knew them. Theatres exclusively for recitals were usually found a little way out from the city centre, in residential suburban areas or in shabby single-story buildings near train stations. On days where there were no performances these places were locked up and, as they would have neither a business sign nor a notice board, could easily be mistaken for basement offices; only when the evening performance was soon to start would the door be opened and a makeshift ticket office set up, usually nothing more than a shabby fold-out table. At some point, we'd become convinced that as a recital actor, Kyung-hee must be known by a stage name. And that this explained why we'd been unable to track her down so far. So we decided to do the rounds of as many recital stages as possible, without bothering to find out the name of the performer. Strolling the city from one recital to another. And with the expectation that, sooner or later, we would stumble across one of Kyung-hee's performances. But we never did get to see her standing on-stage. Not only that, but we learned that not even the scant handful of regulars attending the recitals, who all knew each other by sight and had naturally become quite friendly, knew anything about anyone who might have been Kyung-hee. As time passed, what we already knew about Kyung-hee, what we'd thought of as concrete facts, became vague. As the concrete Kyung-hee grew more and more vague, the symbolic Kyung-hees standing on-stage drew ever closer, little by little, through voice and gesture, and we would experience a simultaneous receding and approaching. As with the countless screaming voices, all directed towards the tiny figure outlined against the dark sky, dangling perilously from the very top of a pole, those disembodied voices which formed a symbolic pointing finger, crying Kyung-hee! Kyung-hee! as though they had seen through to her unrevealed essence. For example, each time, late at night at our lodging, we listened, deep in thought, we would hear a crisp, continuous whispering coming from the other side of the wall. We fell into imagining that an impromptu recital was being held in the next room, that a female recitation actor was reading a long text in an uninflected voice. But the more we strained to catch the details of what was being said, the more the whispering persuaded us of Kyung-hee's absence. Kyung-hee had been discontinued. Kyung-hee was finished. Kyung-hee had boiled down. Kyung-hee had been annulled. Kyung-hee had been dismantled. Kyung-hee was the burnt-out past. Kyung-hee had become no one. Kyung-hee was nothing. That woman lacked the fact of being Kyung-hee. Kyung-hee had been extinguished. Kyung-hee was within the sleep of sleep. In other words, doubly asleep. Kyung-hee was with a woman who no one knew, with no way to tell the two of them apart. Kyung-hee was three-fourths Kyung-hee. Notification of the fusion of Kyung-hee's components. Kyung-hee had slipped down in the form of low hills... The whispering continued night after night, lingering into the hours of broad daylight, clinging to our ears as we rode the bus or the subway or wandered the streets of Seoul, and we didn't know how to shake it off.

Oddly enough, this unaccountable whispering reminded us of when we'd attended a recital and seen a tall woman in her sixties recite several poems, standing stock still and with her greying head bowed at almost a ninety-degree angle. Such whispering paradoxically notified us of Kyung-hee's non-existence through the image of Kyung-hee that appeared, changing name and place here and there within imagination and memory. The recitation actor's voice sounded like Kyung-hee's, her silhouette was not especially different from that of the Kyung-hee we knew, and so, fully expecting that she was indeed none other than Kyung-hee, we were unable to tear our gazes from her throughout the recitation. But once she'd finished the final poem and raised her head fully, so that the lighting streamed down onto her face, not only was it the face of a completely different person, but the voice instantly transformed as well. This seemed scarcely credible, but perhaps it was due to a particular acoustic effect caused by the stage's peculiar construction, which consisted of various circular levels like a snail's shell, or perhaps the actor having had her neck so sharply bowed, like someone who had just been hanged, and having maintained that singular posture throughout the performance, had exerted an abnormal pressure on her vocal chords. We couldn't tell the precise cause. The name of that performance was *Primitive*, and the title of each poem she read was also *Primitive*.

Primitive 2[3]

Wild beasts are born, go by, die.
Since they go to the land of endless cold,
To the cruelty of endless night, the heart of darkness.

Birds come, then fly away, and die.
Since they go to the land of endless cold,
To the cruelty of endless night, the heart of darkness.

Fish come, then disappear, and die.
Since they go to the land of endless cold,
To the cruelty of endless night, the heart of darkness.

People are born, eat, sleep.
Since they go to the land of endless cold,
To the cruelty of endless night, the heart of darkness.

The heavens burn, eyes cave in.
The evening stars shine.
On the earth, a harsh chill, in the sky, light.

People went to that place: those once prisoned in life were released,
The shadows were gathered in.

---

3   *A pygmy burial song quoted by Octavio Paz in his essay collection. The title of the essay in which the song is contained is 'Primitive'; 'Primitive 2' is the title assigned by Bae Suah to the song as re-quoted here.*

Had we not, one such day, had our attention captured by the faint sound of the radio coming from behind a shop's partition; had we not pricked up our ears and realised that the sound was identical to the ghost whispering with which we were by then familiar, we would have taken what those voices had been saying—phrases related to the non-existence of Kyung-hee—as read, would have dismissed our chance encounter with Kyung-hee at the station, our intense absorption in the story she had told us then, as simply a scene from an unusually solid, tangible dream that had lasted for several days. A dream as a long as an ancient epic poem, a dream which we had dreamed collectively, a dream made up of long-winded, riotous imaginings like those of Apuleius' *Golden Ass*, a dream of waking from a dream, part of a dream of entering a dream, and the dream is the sickness that people who have lived for too long a time on nothing but books, painkillers, the radio, and audiobooks, end up contracting at the end of their life, a sweet form of compensation.

Everything began as a kind of muttering. It was a language of muttering which recalled rough, hard, broken rocks and earth and bleached bones and grainy sand, the sound of a two-year-old horse's tendons trembling, the sleekness of a smoothly-eroded limestone floor, a cave bat's breathing, a flute made of swan's bone, a planetary ring of colliding rock and ice kernels, whispering made up of hard ironware with irregular edges, the sound of bones burning in a fire and soot gusting up like a storm cloud, a bearskin drum. The shop we stepped into was a general store on the outskirts of the city, which sold soap and cigarettes, sugar and soy sauce, etc. We couldn't understand how we'd ended up there, so far from the subway station. The area was still technically a part of Seoul, but it was more like the ruins of an abandoned construction site than a city; dirty puddles were hidden here and there between mounds of soil, and black mosquitos swarmed around the straggling clumps of grass. The place was littered with various items which had been dumped there illegally, such as fragments of galvanised iron; an old-fashioned, busted TV; a rusted iron stove and an armchair with its stuffing hanging out; a doll missing its eyeballs; a wrecked birdcage. And, on the hillocks which were scattered around, sporadic clumps of lupins, of a breathtakingly intense purple. The sticky spiders' webs strung between the lupins gave off a sweet scent as they strained and bellied in the wind. Who was it, we wondered, the one who thought to sow lupin seeds in the ruins of this decaying city, a place which wasn't even their hometown. Nearby was a paddy field, left fallow now for many months, and the low hills continued beyond that, and on one of those hills was an old two-story house, long abandoned. An obsolete building, whose demolition had been postponed for some reason. Walls that had once been painted white were now black with soot, crumbling in places, and the iron plating on the steps leading to the front door was rusted right through. A construction consisting of large windows, a flat roof, and a first-floor veranda over the ground-floor living room. A building obliquely recalling the standardised lodgings of security guards, the jerry-built fashion of the 1970s. The same thought flitted through our heads simultaneously; had a teacher lived in that house with his family? The shop faced onto the road directly opposite the house.

As soon as we went into the shop we noticed two enormous

bees stuck to the tacky lid of a box of sweets. The place was deserted, but the door leading to the space at the rear was open. Though the shop seemed very poorly stocked, the glass bottles lining the shelves were particularly eye-catching. Each bottle was filled with sweets of a different shape and colour. Yellow and gold as the eyes of a sick child, bloodshot red, frog green, glassy eyeballs on which time could get no purchase, things armed with an intense monotonous sweetness. The reason for their presence soon became clear. The rear of the shop looked to be a factory for making sweets. A makeshift partition formed of a wooden board covered with a grubby quilt had been erected in one corner of the shop. The voice gradually became more distinct, though it was still mixed with radio static. From the first, we'd guessed that the sound was coming from some kind of machine, like a radio, television, or tape recorder. This was not the voice of an ordinary radio DJ speaking into a microphone. Ringing out with sufficient volume to fill the space known as the stage, while maintaining a crisp clarity; pouring forth accompanied by a certain degree of pain at having to push itself beyond what was innate to it; that was the kind of voice it was. As the voice came, it brought a physical body with it. And when it left, that physical body left too. That thing, attempting through the use of an archaic physical body to outdo the future of the technology known as radio waves, was a sound that gave the impression of being truly human, almost primitive. We were rapt before we knew it. The sound of the sweet factory's machine ceaselessly rotating over there inside the shop; the sound of the sweet, sticky sugar grains dispersing inside the machine like drops of water spraying from a fountain;

the sound of a wide roller shifting slowly, as in a mill; the sound of sugar lumps being stretched out as you do for taffy; the sound of cooled sugar being chewed; an unidentified crunching; the sound of a faint late summer afternoon collecting on the factory floor; the sound of sugar fragments stuck to the soles of shoes; the sound of a rat-piss-stained, flower-patterned countryside quilt sagging down; the private amplification reigning over the darkness of the shop, unalleviated by artificial lighting; the sound of low sunlight slanting onto the moisture-clagged dirt floor; and the sound of the recitation coming from the radio. The sound of the vocal chords, made up of muscle and mucous membrane, which command the space of the stage, carrying to its outer reaches, the singing voice of the Saora shaman's wife, singing an incantatory tune.

At the sound of someone singing above the shaman raised his head.

At that moment his soul left his body.

His wife was standing by the brazier in the middle of the tent.

The water in the pot came to the boil, and

She put a branch of young spring elm into the pot, intended as medicine for her husband. A pale green bud had sprouted from the branch. It was the first bud of the year

Which she had searched the frozen ground to find.

When she removed the lid the steam rushed up,

Filling the tent. In that white rush, she saw her husband mount a white bird and fly off.

Though she reached out her hand to seize the tail of the bird, she failed.

The bird ascended vertically to the mountain of cloud which reared up into the distance,

Leaving behind a single white feather.

She went over to her husband's sleeping place. Her husband's flesh-and-blood body was lying there intact.

Though his mouth was parted and his eyes open, his breathing could no longer be felt.

His white hair was scattered in all directions,

His eyes glowed red with burst capillaries.

A thick, pliable vein coiled around his whole body like a dull green iron chain.

There is a place I love, he had said the night before.

Above a tall tree,

In the bosom of the wind,

A lonely place rearing up from within the clouds,

The edge of an inaccessible cliff.

The white bird's feather bobbed on the boiling water.

People on horseback, black hoods pulled down over their faces, raced past outside the tent.

They were holding crescent moon knives in their hands. Each time one of them brandished their knife the moonlight scattered into fragments in front of her eyes.

The liquor bottle and mirror broke.

The wolves howled.

The wind raged. A ram gushed black blood and black milk flowed from a woman's chest.

The brazier's fire went out.

The shaman's wife was eighteen years old, the abundant black mass of her hair reaching down to her chest, and her white fore-head round as the moon.

She stood in a daze in the tent, into which the cold air had suddenly flooded.

Father of the tree of life, let me follow him, send the white bird, the shaman's wife cried out.

At that, the feather in the water transformed into a winged bird. And a voice from somewhere said,

You mustn't think for long, the ground will split but the gap in the rocks will soon heal up, thick moss will conceal the cleft of the entrance.

Only if you mount the bird this instant will you be able to follow the one who has already died and left for the underworld.

You mustn't think for long, the sky will split but a light that no one knows will stitch up that crack in an instant.

You mustn't think for long, the dead go at a speed that the living cannot match.

You mustn't think for long, don't turn to look back, go dancing lightly forwards.

His memory goes with him,

His self grows distant with him,

He goes only forwards, his footsteps stop for nothing,

He will soon have forgotten everything...

Just then, someone emerged from the sweet factory at the rear of the shop, went behind the partition and switched off the radio. The voice abruptly disappeared. The man flicked the wall switch and a dim light began to glow in the small bare bulb suspended from the ceiling, but this made no difference to the overall level of brightness in the shop. A continuous drone came from the bulb, like the buzzing of bees. The roller was still lurching effortfully around in the room at the shop's rear. We asked the man if he happened to know the name of the artist whose recitation had just been broadcast over the radio. We weren't expecting much, given the shop's almost depressing level of shabbiness, the extreme wildness of the surrounding environment, the poor village setting in which everything was tumbling down, the rough, boorish ambience of the buildings, and, more than anything else, the fact that the man looked so old and infirm we were unable to guess his age. He raised his head to answer, revealing clouded pupils from which the power of vision had clearly been lost, and explained that, rather than a live broadcast of a voice actor reciting a piece in the studio, this was a pre-recorded recital that had been made into an audiobook. The difference, that is, between listening to the same piece of music on a record and as a live broadcast in a recording studio with an orchestral accompaniment. *Saora Shaman's Wife* had been repeatedly recorded, he'd already listened to it in three different versions. He added that, however, rather than the recitation having been recorded in the audiobook publisher's studio, it was a live recording, done directly from an on-stage recitation in Seoul. And that he preferred on-stage recitations, which inevitably include incidental noise such as the strange echoes produced by a larger space, the actor's footsteps and the creaking of the stage floorboards, the audience's coughing, and thus feels more alive than a neat, clean studio recording. Pleased, we asked again whether he knew the name of the recitation actor, saying that the voice sounded exactly like that of an actor we knew called Kyung-hee, whom, admittedly, we had never seen on stage. The old cataract sufferer, a devotee of radio recitations as well as a sweet factory worker and store clerk, nodded. I know the voice of that recitation very well. I've heard recitations by that voice several times. Even among a group of voice actors, I'm confident that I could pick out that actor's voice. But as to the voice's owner, which is something different than the voice itself, I've never been especially concerned to know. And so it stands to reason that I'm ignorant of the actor's name. True, the recitation actor's name is mentioned at the very end of the recording, but it isn't as easy to pick up on as the title of the recitation or the name of the writer. Moreover, a reciting voice can sound different on the radio from live on-stage, or from the actual voice, and since it's also possible for it to sound similar to the voice of someone else whom we already know, lay-people, people who aren't recitation fanatics like me, might get the actor confused with someone else, he explained. In that case, we asked, trying to maintain a shred of hope as we paid for a paper bag of prunes, could you tell us whether you've ever heard anything about a recitation actor by the name of Kyung-hee, whether a recitation actor by that name exists, whether such a thing is possible? The man deftly ran his fingers over the notes we handed to him, checking the amount and denomination, and gave us the exact change. He answered, even though I'm a recitation devotee, and could probably recognise many recitation actors' voices, I don't know the name of a single actor. Why on earth should I know a recitation actor's name, surely that's as unnecessary as knowing their face. And so we tried again, saying in that case we'll put the

question a little differently, given that the voice which had just
been reciting *Saora Shaman's Wife* is familiar to you, might you be
able to tell us where that voice is now? Whether there's anything
you can tell us about that voice? Oh, he said, I've heard that voice
give recitations many times. What's more, I know that the voice's
owner recently gave several performances at a particular theatre.
They kept giving out the details on the radio, you see. Like a type
of advert. If you'd like, I could tell you the name of the theatre.
I'm not sure of the precise location, but a theatre specialising in
recitation, the name...

A few days later we were walking through one of Seoul's residential districts. It was close to miraculous that, just then, inexplicable
chance operated in such a way that our attention was drawn to
a poster on the door of a shabby building. The poster was only a
crude black-and-white thing upon which dark, sombre hues and
indistinct forms flickered. Besides which, the print was so small
and blurry it was impossible to read without going and peering
at it close up. As we were walking along the road and our gaze
lighted upon the three-quarters silhouette of the stage actor on
the poster, in that instant we saw Kyung-hee's image. So we went
up the poster and read what was written on it, and learned that it
was advertising a recital of *Saora Shaman's Wife*, to be performed
that very evening, in the basement warehouse of that building.

We were incredibly excited at eventually finding the theatre,
having had only a vague name to go on. So we wanted to go
down to the basement right away, and find out about the actor
who would be performing this recital. Of course, we would have

to sit through the performance first. We went down two flights of stairs, and found a small door without any form of signage. We knocked on the door and an usher promptly emerged. We had to purchase a ticket before we could go in. Though our spirits sank when we saw the actor's name, printed in clear type on the ticket—a name whose three syllables bore no resemblance to 'Kyung-hee'—the photo, which was a little less blurry than the one on the poster, was further confirmation that we'd been right to get our hopes up. Our surprise was such that we inadvertently voiced our thoughts out loud, so she really is a recitation actor. The usher turned to look back at us, frowning, and said, obviously, she's the Saora Shaman's wife. Despite the lack of any artificial amplification, his unusually low voice dispersed rapidly through the space, like a wave with a long wavelength. When he opened the door the galvanised iron plate became partially detached and dragged along the cement floor, producing a sound which grated on the nerves in an extremely unpleasant manner.

We would never have guessed that the cramped, recessed space was in fact a performance stage. Around thirty cushions had been arranged on the floor of the dark hall by way of audience seating. The lights above the tiny stage were off. The explanation being that there was still a little time before the performance began. So that day we were the first of Kyung-hee's audience to enter the theatre. Several more people arrived over the course of the following hour or so, up until the start of the performance. Our seats were at the very front. The other audience members were a teenage couple, whose love of small theatres was probably due to such places being dark and sparsely attended, three middle-aged women who seemed to be a group of friends, and several men who were there on their own, ranging in age from twenty-something to sixty-something. Finally, after a young woman who looked like a university student had come in and found a seat, the usher closed the small door and brought up the lighting over the stage. It was a typical recitation stage, not aiming for any experimental or dramatic effects. The only props were a screen suspended at the front, with an entirely ordinary chair to the left of it, so that the performance depended solely on the voice.

And that was how we encountered Kyung-hee again, or thought we encountered her. Dependent on the white lighting which illuminated nothing of her face, as it was set up to focus only on the script she was holding and the movement of her feet over the stage, and moreover was not especially bright. Dependent on the utterance known as 'voice' being produced by the vocal chords of a tall body cloaked in a black ankle-length costume. Dependent on the material fact that the human body is a musical instrument which generates sound waves, producing emotions and feelings which vary in accordance with minute differences in the shape of the internal tubes which pierce this instrument, producing sounds which make up an atmosphere particular to each individual. At some point we'd taken a look at the minutely detailed anatomical drawing of the human vocal chords in the natural history encyclopedia which Kyung-hee always carried around with her; it bore a surprisingly strong resemblance to the reproductive organs of a woman with her legs parted.

We had a copy of the letter that had been sent to Kyung-hee. The letter might have already arrived at Kyung-hee's address;

it still isn't clear whether she actually read it. Presumably the letter had gone via several addresses before eventually reaching us. The very first and last of those addresses being what Kyunghee had dubbed 'my Berlin address.' The letter was initially sent to this Berlin address, then, presumably having been transported to Korea in some traveller's luggage, for whatever reason that traveller then posted the letter back to the Berlin address from a post office in central Seoul, then, after many months in Berlin, the letter passed along some unidentified route to Shanghai and then on to a central Asian capital, was sent from that city's central post office to an address in Seoul, and finding no one willing to receive it there, was sent back to the Berlin address with the stamp 'addressee unknown.' This time, the person entrusted with getting the letter to Kyung-hee made several copies and sent these out to various addresses in Kyung-hee's notebook, which she'd probably left in Berlin with the rest of her luggage; the letter we received was one of these copies. It was over two years since the letter had originally been written, and the writer was no longer living. The more hands the letter passed through, the more distant it grew from its initial character, from the myth of its genesis. The person responsible for passing it on would add a brief note to the envelope before handing it over to another party; judging by these memos, it seemed that of those who had received the copy, we were probably the only ones to have actually met Kyung-hee, and so we resolved to give her the letter in person. This, we felt, was our final task.

That day, no more than two metres lay, in reality, between ourselves and Kyung-hee as she stood on the stage. But when we reached out to pass her the letter, her long sleeve concealed the hand that clasped it, and though, perhaps because the air was so damp, our ears could detect no rustling of paper, though the letter vanished into that voice, which seemed another of the stage's illusory devices, we were seized by the feeling of having seen it reach the opposite riverbank, far in the distance.

I don't know much about my father. Not only because he is an old man of ninety. Given that all fathers will reach the age of ninety at some point, unless they die first, it's difficult to assert as a logical extension of this that no one knows much about their father. For a long time now, I've been unable to shake the suspicion that my father is already deceased; that those who speak as though he were still among the living do so purely because they do not wish him to die. And so they say to me quite coolly, 'A call came from your father', or 'Your father sent me a letter.' In that way, he remains alive. And perhaps for precisely that reason I, his son, am also able to live. I want to know how the various records he prepared for my life, while he was working as a trainee journalist at a magazine, will be spread out before me. He wrote a will, an autobiography, various newspaper articles in addition to his regular column, and many letters; he even wrote some poems in his younger days, though I must admit I've never read any of them. The magazine editor hired me because I claimed to be attending night university, majoring in humanities. But that was a lie.

Unlike with my father, the word 'mother' always called up a feeling of closeness for me, intimate and affectionate. I always carried her photo in my wallet, a stylish profile shot from her younger days, part of her actor's portfolio. I had the vague sense that I resembled my mother in terms of physical appearance, and that that meant my voice and delivery must also be similar to hers. If anyone who had loved my mother was still alive, no doubt they would also love me. I've lived in the same city as my mother my whole life. I even bumped into her once, quite by chance, in the city centre. I didn't recognise her straight away. She was at least twenty-something years older than the mother in the photograph (which had been taken before I was born, of course). But my mother was none other than the woman in that photograph; age hadn't changed her into someone else. It was in a subway station where our paths crossed; a few seconds later, my feet were carrying me in the direction of her retreating figure. In other words, it wasn't me who chose to follow her, but my feet. She was wearing a black coat with a wide collar and carrying a large lilac-and-pearl bag. She must have a script in her bag, I thought to myself, the script for a recitation that she'll perform this evening. Each time she changed direction, the hem of her coat swept around as though she were dancing lightly. At that point, I'd never seen her on stage. I'd never seen her in person at all. All I'd done was listen to several radio broadcasts of her recitations. Now that I think about it, I can't understand why I never went to see her perform at a recitation theatre. Strange, isn't it? It would be closest to the truth to say that it simply never occurred to me. Probably because I'm not particularly a fan of recitations. I assumed she was on her way to the theatre. She got onto a train, and I followed. I'd originally been on my way to meet someone, but at a certain point I forgot all about that. I was busy gazing at her silhouette, reflected in the carriage window. It was around the time when most office workers commute home, so the train was fairly packed. She got off after two stops. She'd been standing there quietly, without giving any indication that her stop was coming up, so I was unprepared when the doors opened and she abruptly slipped out. I had to make a mad dash to get off before the doors closed, and by the time I'd shoved my way off the train and onto the platform, she was already on her way up the stairs. My feet sped up, but she was no slouch herself. Only once I'd panted my way up to the ticket barrier was I able to dodge in front of her. I wanted to get a look at her face, you see. But as luck would have it, she was rummaging around in her bag for her purse and had her head deeply bowed.

After a few seconds of me walking in front like this, I looked back over my shoulder to check which direction she was heading in. But I hadn't expected her to be quite so close—practically treading on my heels--and as she was walking very rapidly we only narrowly avoided a head-on collision. We were both startled, and I took a reflexive step back. She'd been charging forwards, but I'd turned around quite hesitantly, and now, flinching back, was unable to keep my balance. I stumbled, and ended up thunking down on the floor. She was the first to apologise, apparently considering our collision to be her fault as she'd been walking along lost in thought. I'm very sorry, she said, helping me to my feet. I was still a little shaken, but hearing her voice made me too happy to care. But she darted off before I had time to say anything in response, swept away by the surging rush hour tide. It all happened very quickly, but I had time to notice that her walking speed, the speed at which she disappeared, was much greater than that of those around her.

I went around telling people how, in the twenty years since I was born, my one encounter with my mother was when I was out one day and bumped into her by chance, literally bumped into her, as in I actually ended up on the ground. But no one believed me. I would have been happy to inform my father, if he had still been in a position to understand human speech; regrettably, this was not the case. Only then did it occur to me that if I wanted to meet this mother of mine, an actor who gave frequent performances, all I needed to do was attend one of her recitations. As I've already mentioned, though, I'm hardly an aficionado when it comes to such things, and besides, I was worried about choosing a particularly unpopular recitation and ending up conspicuously alone in the audience, and so I never did go and see her on stage. I did, however, sit in a café opposite the theatre where she was giving a recitation, stationed by the window so I would be able to see her emerge after the performance. When she did exit the theatre, she was accompanied by a bespectacled man, which threw me somewhat. I'd assumed she would be alone, so I couldn't make up my mind whether to follow her as planned or just stay where I was, avoiding her altogether. It wasn't as though I had any particular intention beyond just following her for a while, like last time—in other words, until I could no longer keep up—then going back home once I'd lost sight of her. But while I was hesitating over the best course of action, the two of them walked right over to the café, came in, and took a seat at the next table. There wasn't anything especially odd about that, as it was the only empty table in the tiny café. I pretended to be engrossed in a magazine, but the writing was just shapes on a page. They ordered one regular coffee and one espresso.

They talked, mainly about the performance she'd just given, and about the one coming up the following month. Though the man had an affable look about him, as though permanently amused by something, his desire to dominate the conversation was still obvious. Judging by the way he spoke—loudly and at length, frequently repeating himself—he was almost certainly the producer of the upcoming performances. She, on the other hand, spoke relatively little, favouring brief responses over introducing any topic of her own. Yes, no, really, I assure you there was, that's right, that doesn't make sense, I don't think that would be possible. She gave the impression of wanting to make her voice as unobtrusive as possible. The way unusually tall or large women often hunch up, trying to make themselves seem smaller. Her hands were in constant, seemingly nervous motion, either rotating at the wrists, pulling at her hair, or folding the napkin into complicated shapes only to smooth it out and start again. At one point, she even straightened each finger in turn and examined her palm. Like the kind of gesture an actor might make while performing a 'vaguely conscious character' in a one-person play. Though their conversation was on general topics, as I listened I began to suspect that they were either a married couple, lovers, or having an affair. I've no idea what gave me that impression. Not only did they neither touch each other nor discuss anything especially private, they actually used honorifics when addressing each other. I kept my gaze firmly on the magazine, staring at the same page for an awfully long time. When I eventually flipped it closed, the man turned absent-mindedly in my direction and muttered, "*Journal of Shamanism Abroad*? All these magazines have such weird names."

The magazine's name seemed to catch my mother's attention. Having just finished re-straightening each of her curled fingers, she turned and glanced keenly at me, no, at the magazine cover. Conscious of an implicit question in their gaze, I told them that it was a magazine for shamans living abroad. It's not distributed in Korea, so it's no wonder you don't know it. And added, but I'm not a shaman, I'm a journalist, I write articles for this magazine. Really, the man said, a journalist at your age!

"Well, I'm only a trainee," I answered, "I'm still at university."

"Is the magazine available in Berlin?" This time she was the one who addressed me.

"Yes, it is. The company that publishes it provides financial support for some foreign students to study there. There's also a Korean shamanism research foundation who give out scholarships. And several of those students write pieces for the magazine."

"Coming across something I never even would have guessed existed—admittedly, not something directly related to my field of interest, but still—it really puts a spring in your step. Invigorating, you know," the man said, sounding as though he genuinely was staggered by his chance encounter with the phenomenon of Korean shamans abroad. This exaggerated response turned out not to be entirely groundless, as what the man then went on to speak of was clearly intended to show off his membership of that intellectual minority who are interested in ancient culture and cave art, prehistoric and primitive things. The many cave paintings overlooked by UNESCO, forgotten ancient artworks, figures of the female body used by the earliest members of the human race in shamanic and divinatory practices, etc.

It was clearly a field in which my mother had no interest. Or at least, not in the way that the man did. He rambled on, displaying a fragmentary knowledge mainly gleaned from things he'd heard secondhand or read about in magazines, and showered me with questions to which my answers consisted partly of my own fantastic notions and partly of lies concocted then and there (though he seemed entirely oblivious to my shamming). The longer the conversation dragged on, the more evident my mother's boredom became. She yawned. I noticed that while she was yawning, under the table her hand darted to the man's thigh. It looked like a signal for him to quit this stifling talk so they could get out of there. He plainly wanted to stay and brag some more, but he couldn't ignore such a clear sign. He was sorry. From the impression I got that day, he seemed the regretful type. He even shook my hand as he stood up, which seemed bizarrely formal given the circumstances of our meeting. He gave me his business card, saying that my mother would be giving a performance the following week, and that if I had time I should come along. It's something that a woman like yourself, very young but with a wise head on your shoulders, and engaged in specialised journalism, would be sure to find interesting, he said before he left. My mother stood mute by his side, like a tall umbrella.

Did the letter from Berlin ever reach my mother? I stayed in the café for a while after they'd left, lost in thought.

The bird bore the shaman's wife to a barren tract of reddish ground, by the side of a large river; it landed in front of the small hut that stood there. The hut had walls of flat stones, a roof of rags and tree branches that had been washed there by the river, and was so low you had to stoop to enter.

The river's fierce clamour shook all the world, like thousands of stones tumbling down from a high mountaintop.

The river was a bright grey. Each time the swift current crashed against the rocky riverbed a burst of angry spume was thrown up, as though threatening to engulf the shaman's wife.

There was neither boat nor boatman on the river.

In the louring, oppressive sky, thick with green clouds,

Neither sun nor moon was visible.

It was a land withered by age, lacking a single blade of grass.

The shaman's wife instinctively

Knew that she had to cross the river if she wanted to see her dead husband again.

But how on earth to cross a river where the water was high as a mountain and the current sharp as a blade, how to hazard her body in a river where gloomy lumps of rock were whirling like famished ghosts, oppressing her spirits.

Just then, a human form walked out of the hut...

No, crawled out.

It was a man who had neither arms nor legs, only a head and a torso.

His face was hideous as a wild boar, aged as a dead tree, cunning as a rat.

He introduced himself as Abakal. Abakal made bells and masks; he had been doing so for generations.

The masks he specialised in were those of a miracle-working bear, of iron clouds, of a storm of earth, of rain, and of a copper mirror,

Whoever wore the respective mask would instantly become a miracle-working bear, iron clouds, a storm of earth, rain, or a copper mirror.

People thought of him as a magician.

In his younger days, believing that there was nothing to which this magic could not be applied, he'd had the idea to make the death mask of a departed spirit. A mask that would give him the power to call the dead spirits back to this world.

One day he succeeded and, possessed by the spirit whom he had recalled, jumped into the river and lost all his limbs, becoming a cripple.

Legend has it that this river will one day dry up without warning

Exposing its bed of red stone; no one knows when that will happen, Abakal said.

Though I became a monster, though my body became one that can love no woman

and that no woman can love,

In spite of that, I still have the power to summon departed spirits with a mask, Abakal continued.

Abakal and the shaman's wife went into his hut.

Inside the hut, a space so cramped that two people filled it entirely,

Thick green light that leaked in through the gaps in the stone walls formed a transparent lattice between them.

On each wall of the hut hung masks which Abakal had made. There was the mask of an owl, the mask of an eagle, the mask of a bear, the mask of a wolf, the mask of a male goat.

Abakal spoke again: I am also able to translate what the dead spirits whisper to me into human language.

But no living human has listened to my words.

Please, the shaman's wife begged, tell them to me. I want to listen.

You will live with me in this hut, Abakal said, looking up at the shaman's wife from the floor.

You will live with me in this hut.

You will be my hands and my feet.

You will be my bed, my sleeping place.

You will bear six children of me.

The first child will be born blind, the second child a deaf-mute, the third child will be born without arms, the fourth will have no legs. And the fifth child will be born a leper, their whole body covered in boils. The sixth child will be a healthy girl.

You will love that child as your own eyes. And one day, the day red lightning strikes the earth, the day the mountains explode in a rain of fire and the river boils dry,

You will leave this hut;

You will dance lightly over the threshold without looking back; At that time you will not be alone.

You will leave this hut with that child hidden in your skirt.

You will leave me alone with my wretchedness.

So I will rain down curses on you.

Don't curse me, cried the shaman's wife, I promise I won't take your child.

What I am saying to you now is only what the departed spirits are whispering into my ears, Abakal answered.

From that day they lived together as woman and man.

According to Abakal's prophecy, they had six children, one after another.

The first child was blind, the second child was a deaf-mute, the third child had no arms, the fourth no legs. When the fifth child was born, the shaman's wife had to pick off with her hands the fly larvae which covered its entire body, which clung to the boils, and sucked the discharge from them, before she could see whether the thing she had given birth to was a pouch of wriggling maggots or a living baby.

The sixth child was a healthy, pretty daughter. The shaman's wife recalled the curse Abakal had spoken of, and asked him what sort of a curse it was.

If you leave me, this child will grow up and marry me in your place, he answered.

And so become my hands and my feet, my bed and my sleeping place.

And bear my children as blind, deaf and dumb, missing limbs, and afflicted with leprosy.

The shaman's wife was shocked. Surely that is too harsh a fate for such a pretty young child? she shouted. Think about it, when I myself first met you I was a very young woman, pretty as that child. But if I take this child away, won't that in fact save her from such a fate?

Look closely at my face, Abakal said, and something you do not yet know will rise up from the deep abyss of memory.

The shaman's wife gazed closely at his face,

And saw that this was the father she had never met,

Her flesh and blood father, who had abandoned her mother even before the child was born.

Abakal said, now you understand.

Since you have already taken that child and left me, I will take the child as a wife.

Just then, there was a roaring the like of which they had never heard before,

The world shook and flaming lumps of stone began to rain down onto the earth.

Red lightning struck the ground, the mountains exploded in a burst of fireworks, the water in the river gushed up to the sky and then boiled dry.

Uncovered in the blink of an eye, the riverbed was an endless expanse of dried earth, scattered with rocks sharp as spearheads.

Abakal's hut crumbled down around them.

Rocks tumbled onto Abakal's body as he lay on the ground.

He was being buried in a mountain of stones, screaming, dying. His face and torso became bloodied tatters. The offspring which had been born to them also became covered in blood. The filth and dark blood which covered their faces was like a sign that their existence was about to be erased.

So the shaman's wife knew that the time had come for her prophesied departure.

She knew it was time to dance lightly away from Abakal's hut, without looking back, as the words of the revelation had predicted.

So that is what she did.

Having made it through the heaps of sharp rocks littering the river bed, she arrived at the opposite bank and was immediately confronted by a huge bear. The bear knocked the shaman's wife to the ground with a single swipe, tore through her flesh with its teeth and swallowed her up.

The bear spat out the dregs, except for the soft meat and body fluids.

After being thus broken down and formed again, the shaman's wife was left as a terrifyingly aged hag.

Her womb had atrophied, and her breasts and stomach sagged down brutally. Her skin gave off a foul stench, her face was hollow as a corpse's, and her hair fell out.

Die, ugly beast, the shaman's wife muttered as she gazed at her own transparent body, but she couldn't recognise the thing she was addressing as herself.

Children appeared from the other side of the red hills and threw stones at her.

There were blind children, children who were deaf and dumb, children without arms or legs, children whose whole bodies were covered in boils.

The shaman's wife hobbled away as fast as she could.

When one of the stones struck her back it tore straight through the aged, pulpy flesh. Die, ugly beast, the children chorused at her back.

The children's voices rang out like the clear peal of a bell.

The shaman's wife walked the red wasteland for months without taking a single sip of water.

A well made of heaped-up stones materialised, but when she got closer it was a puddle of blood,

A pile of bread was visible on a distant tower, but when she got closer it was the carcass from a sky burial,

A heap of broken bones covered in reddish-black stains. The faint shape of mountains were strung along the far horizon,

But every time the shaman's wife got closer they would disappear as though erased.

The wasteland knew neither night nor day, and neither the sun nor the moon ever rose.

The wasteland only continued endlessly on,

In the form of caves and cliffs, hills of stones and thorn thickets, dried-up river beds and the broken stone images of gods.

Once she came face to face with an old hag who had suddenly appeared in the middle of the wasteland.

The shaman's wife asked the old woman who she was.

The old woman answered, I was Abakal's wife; because I loved the village shaman I starved my crippled husband Abakal to death, went to the shaman's house, and became his fifth wife.

We were very much in love. But our love couldn't last for long.

After our love was all done with I became a cow, as was predicted.

So I have to drag a plough through the stony fields until my flesh wears out.

And since I am now so old that it's completely worn out, with not even the form remaining,

No one, not even I myself, asks who I am.

And the old woman disappeared in a puff of smoke.

One day a huge white bird flew slowly over the shaman's wife's head, and as it moved away the shaman's wife was able to read the words written on its stomach.

Be happy, woman, your wish will be fulfilled,

In recompense for your worn-out flesh and your keenly-felt agony,

You will see your husband living again.

He will live again, he will continue his life in the world as before, but

He will not know you,

He will remember nothing of you,

You will have become an old woman,

But he will return as a beautiful young man, in spite of time,

And so will be unable to recognise you,

Ignorant of having been swallowed down into your lower half and brought back up again,

Of having passed through your blood and through your womb, emerging from your naked crotch,

And thus been restored to the light,

All while a drum was beaten,

And a female shaman dressed as a white bird danced,

And you will return to Abakal's house and see your lost flesh-and-blood daughter attending to the pleasures of Abakal's bed,

But your husband will live out his life with another wife.

In that case, what has my suffering amounted to? the shaman's wife thought, with her lump of a body that refused to die.

I who witnessed my husband's death

Did not hesitate

Did not look back

Crossed this river where all flesh-and-blood bodies inevitably become stinking corpse-figures;

I wanted only to bring my husband back from the dead; wasn't that in order to live with him again?

All the while I was searching for him, I saw his retreating figure as though he were in front of me.

I saw his heels beneath the hem of his robe.

At various times he was a rock I sat on,

He was my own head or stomach,

He was the stars in the night sky melting into drops of rain

And the open square of the dawn,

The stone image of a man standing alone in the centre of the square,

A train crossing the far horizon,

A red roofless tower used for sky burials,

Sometimes he was a wild cat that attacked me,

At certain moments he was even Abakal.

He was my eternal husband, my ancestor, my shaman.

But now he is one who has been resurrected, and there must be this distance between us.

Ah, this formless pain. Now my agony is even more cruel than when I witnessed my husband's death,

I suffer the nights through.

I suffer my life through.

I could never have imagined that there could be a greater suffering than accepting his death.

Who are you, you who are punishing me so cruelly?

I suppose after I die all the soft flesh of my body will be offered to the hawks as a sky burial.

So now please take this fate from me.

At that, a second white bird flew into view, covering the sky, and imparted to her the second revelation.

Daughter,

Since it is due to you that all the things of this world will ultimately come about or not,

You can both grieve at this knowledge, and be happy.

If you open your eyes right now, you will escape from this dream.

Your pain is understood,

And your leave-taking is complete.

You will wake from the dream, and at the same time you will enter another dream.

You will bid farewell to Abakal's life,

Bid farewell to the body Abakal's life left you with,

Forget what Abakal inflicted on you,

And you will no longer be Abakal's daughter-wife,

And through forgetting Abakal like this,

Because you left Abakal you will meet Abakal again,

And because you left Abakal you will begin a new life as Abakal's woman.

As you look on Abakal you will no longer question the meaning of suffering.

Your husband, who has fallen off the eternally-spinning wheel which you yourself still ride, stays in the realm of death.

People tear open the wall of the tent so as not to obstruct the spirit,

Making a threshold which the living cannot cross. His corpse is carried there.

You cry on the threshold.

His body is placed at the distant top of the tree of life.

His calm gaze is directed upwards, towards the hawks of the air who will harvest him.

He will speak without a voice.

'In my young days, I loved youth.

Only when I grew old and infirm, did I realise that I liked age and infirmity too.

And when I died, I found pleasure also in death.'

Objects will return to the place they were originally visible, the dead to hawks, human beings to Abakal.

Picture rising suddenly on a screen above the stage:
Enigma of a Farewell (Giorgio de Chirico, 1916)

Before the performance is due to start, I go the waiting room behind the stage and knock on the door. As soon as my mother opens the door, I tell her who I am. And then say what I've been wanting to say for a long time. "Do you mind me being here?" A three-quarter smile appears on my mother's face, yet she doesn't open the door fully to let me in. She explains the reason. "I'm afraid you're mistaken; it seems someone has told you a lie. I've never had a child. That is a fact, something it's absolutely impossible for me to be mistaken about." "But I've spent the last twenty years believing that you're my mother," I cry, quite shocked. "I even went all the way to Berlin to meet you, to meet my mother, because that's where I was told you were." "But I wasn't there, right?" my mother laughed softly. "People are mistaken now and then, it's not such a big deal. Whoever was telling you these things

must have confused me with someone else of the same name."
Indicating what looked vaguely like a chair and table at the rear
of the waiting room, my mother said, "As you know, I have to
give a performance now, so unfortunately there isn't time for
us to have a longer chat." She went over to the chair, sat down,
straightened up, and began to read the script out loud. Leaving the
door standing half open. I stand outside the door, listening to her
rehearsal voice ringing out in that small, dark, underground room
which, because I was unable to emerge from it—given that this
would have required me to enter it in the first place, which was
not permitted—suddenly reminds me of the womb. I wait for my
mother's voice to resonate inside my body and emerge through my
windpipe. I think of my father having once described a scenario
like this for me, predicting how it would turn out. Describing my
mother saying you're mistaken, I've never had a child. Occurrences
which are related before the fact are like a walking stick that
makes a path through the air. Constantly, throughout the course
of my life, my father describes. He whispers. He sings, and he
listens. He records. Pasting photographs in large notebooks with
yellowed covers. My father makes a scrapbook of picture postcards and tickets to readings, train tickets, payment slips and the
like, sketches a new type of beetle which he discovered while out
for a walk, describes the weather on a particular day, and inserts
diary entries in the form of brief memos here and there. Inside
it, I am the reading, the train ticket, the beetle, the payment. He,
who loved nature in its most seductive forms, inserts red poppies
and full-blown purple lupins between the pages of the notebook,
as well as tiny snakes that look like fish. He records the date on

which he discovered the lupins as the 8th of August 1990, the day I was born, and the place as 'one of the low hills of Seoul, around sunset.' He writes, the sun rises into the flat, milky sky, an otherwise empty expanse which has never before been filled with such a still, solitary light as floods it now. And then he goes away. I've lived in Seoul for twenty years and I still don't know where they are, these low hills where lupins bloom. And I've never met anyone who's seen them. I ask various people, but they all insist that no such place exists. There are some things which absolutely do not exist in the specific place that is Seoul; low hills where lupins bloom are one such thing, they say. But none of them can provide a convincing explanation as to why low hills where lupins bloom, of all things, are absent from Seoul, of all places. I am as ignorant of the manner of my father's death as I am of the texture of his life. His hometown, a place of early morning strolls through lupin hills, is not Seoul. The unfamiliar scenery that his gaze lighted upon will remain eternally unknowable for me. He encountered lupins directly, seeing them with his own two eyes. To him, nature is inherently good. Flowers come and go. People go to that place. He loves only the object-ness and will-less-ness of nature. I am a child neither planned nor wished for. My mother and father had no intention of becoming parents. One day each writes a letter to the other, hi, there's no need for us to ever meet again. They do not wish to live on through my body. They do not wish to know my body. But just as my father's legacy is the lupin he came across and placed in his notebook, just as my mother's is the voice she spent her life producing on stage, I too will be encountered and read through my involuntary parents, and this will eventually be all that remains of me; I find this oddly reassuring. They each go in opposite directions, but I think and feel what they think and feel. I touch what they touch. They gaze at me. I become a lupin, blooming on the low hills.

....

BAE SUAH was born in Seoul in 1965 and graduated from Ewha Women's University with a BA in Chemistry. After making her literary debut in 1993 with the short story "Highway with Green Apples," she has gone on to become one of the most highly acclaimed contemporary Korean authors and winner of the Hanguk Ilbo and Tongseo literary prizes. She has written five novels and more than ten short story collections, in addition to translating the works of German writers including W.G. Sebald, Franz Kafka, and Jenny Erpenbeck. *Nowhere to be Found*, her first work to be translated into English, was longlisted for a PEN Translation Prize and the Best Translated Book Award. Bae's novella *Nowhere to be Found*, her first work to be translated into English in 2015, was nominated for a PEN Translation Prize and the Best Translated Book Award, and Open Letter Books published her novel *A Greater Music* in 2016.

DEBORAH SMITH is a literary translator and founder of Tilted Axis, a nonprofit press based in London with a focus on fiction from Asia. She received a PhD in contemporary Korean literature at SOAS (University of London), and was awarded the Arts Foundation Award for Literary Translation in 2016. Her translations from the Korean include Han Kang's *Human Acts* and *The Vegetarian*, winner of the 2016 Man Booker International Prize, and two novels by Bae Suah: *A Greater Music* and *Recitation*, from Open Letter Books and Deep Vellum, respectively.

Thank you all
for your support.
We do this for you,
and could not do
it without you.

DEEP
VELLUM

DEAR READERS,

Deep Vellum Publishing is a 501c3 nonprofit literary arts organization founded in 2013 with a threefold mission: to publish international literature in English translation; to foster the art and craft of translation; and to build a more vibrant book culture in Dallas and beyond. We are dedicated to broadening cultural connections across the English-reading world by connecting readers, in new and creative ways, with the work of international authors. We strive for diversity in publishing authors from various languages, viewpoints, genders, sexual orientations, countries, continents, and literary styles, whose works provide lasting cultural value and build bridges with foreign cultures while expanding our understanding of how the world thinks, feels, and experiences the human condition.

Operating as a nonprofit means that we rely on the generosity of tax-deductible donations from individual donors, cultural organizations, government institutions, and foundations. Your donations provide the basis of our operational budget as we seek out and publish exciting literary works from around the globe and build a vibrant and active literary arts community both locally and within the global society. Deep Vellum offers multiple donor levels, including LIGA DE ORO ($5,000+) and LIGA DEL SIGLO ($1,000+). Donors at various levels receive personalized benefits for their donations, including books and Deep Vellum merchandise, invitations to special events, and recognition in each book and on our website.

In addition to donations, we rely on subscriptions from readers like you to provide an invaluable ongoing investment in Deep Vellum that demonstrates a commitment to our editorial vision and mission. Subscribers are the bedrock of our support as we grow the readership for these amazing works of literature from every corner of the world. The investment our subscribers make allows us to demonstrate to potential donors and bookstores alike the support and demand for Deep Vellum's literature across a broad readership and gives us the ability to grow our mission in ever-new, ever-innovative ways.

In partnership with our sister company and bookstore, Deep Vellum Books, located in the historic cultural district of Deep Ellum in central Dallas, we organize and host literary programming such as author readings, translator workshops, creative writing classes, spoken word performances, and interdisciplinary arts events for writers, translators, and artists from across the globe. Our goal is to enrich and connect the world through the power of the written and spoken word, and we have been recognized for our efforts by being named one of the "Five Small Presses Changing the Face of the Industry" by *Flavorwire* and honored as Dallas's Best Publisher by *D Magazine*.

If you would like to get involved with Deep Vellum as a donor, subscriber, or volunteer, please contact us at deepvellum.org. We would love to hear from you.

Thank you all. Enjoy reading.

Will Evans Founder & Publisher Deep Vellum Publishing

LIGA DE ORO ($5,000+)

Anonymous (2)

LIGA DEL SIGLO ($1,000+)

Allred Capital Management
Ben & Sharon Fountain
David Tomlinson & Kathryn Berry
Judy Pollock
Life in Deep Ellum
Loretta Siciliano
Lori Feathers
Mary Ann Thompson-Frenk
& Joshua Frenk
Matthew Rittmayer
Meriwether Evans
Pixel and Texel
Nick Storch
Social Venture Partners Dallas
Stephen Bullock

DONORS

Adam Rekerdres
Alan Shockley
AMr.it Dhir
Anonymous
Andrew Yorke
Anthony Messenger
Bob Appel
Bob & Katherine Penn
Brandon Childress
Brandon Kennedy
Caroline Casey
Charles Dee Mitchell
Charley Mitcherson
Cheryl Thompson
Christie Tull
Daniel J. Hale

Ed Nawotka
Rev. Elizabeth
 & Neil Moseley
Ester & Matt Harrison
Grace Kenney
Greg McConeghy
Jeff Waxman
JJ Italiano
Justin Childress
Kay Cattarulla
Kelly Falconer
Linda Nell Evans
Lissa Dunlay
Marian Schwartz
 & Reid Minot
Mark Haber

Mary Cline
Maynard Thomson
Michael Reklis
Mike Kaminsky
Mokhtar Ramadan
Nikki & Dennis Gibson
Olga Kislova
Patrick Kukucka
Richard Meyer
Steve Bullock
Suejean Kim
Susan Carp
Susan Ernst
Theater Jones
Tim Perttula
Tony Thomson

SUBSCRIBERS

Aldo Sanchez

Anita Tarar

Ben Fountain

Ben Nichols

Blair Bullock

Bradford Pearson

Charles Dee Mitchell

Chris Sweet

Christie Tull

Courtney Sheedy

David Christensen

David Travis

David Weinberger

Dori Boone-Costantino

Elaine Corwin

Farley Houston

Frank Garrett

Ghassan Fergiani

Guilty Dave Bristow

Horatiu Matei

James Tierney

Janine Allen

Jeanne Milazzo

Jeffrey Collins

Jessa Crispin

John O'Neill

John Schmerein

John Winkelman

Joshua Edwin

Kasie Henderson

Kimberly Alexander

Kristopher Phillips

Marcia Lynx Qualey

Margaret Terwey

Martha Gifford

Meaghan Corwin

Michael Elliott

Michael Wilson

Mies de Vries

Mike Kaminsky

Neal Chuang

Nick Oxford

Nicola Molinaro

Peter McCambridge

Stephanie Barr

Steven Kornajcik

Tim Kindseth

Tim Looney

Todd Jailer

Tony Messenger

Whitney Leader-Picone

Will Pepple

William Jarrell

AVAILABLE NOW FROM DEEP VELLUM

MICHÈLE AUDIN · *One Hundred Twenty-One Days*
translated by Christiana Hills · FRANCE

CARMEN BOULLOSA · *Texas: The Great Theft* · *Before*
translated by Samantha Schnee · translated by Peter Bush · MEXICO

LEILA S. CHUDORI · *Home*
translated by John H. McGlynn · INDONESIA

ALISA GANIEVA · *The Mountain and the Wall*
translated by Carol Apollonio · RUSSIA

ANNE GARRÉTA · *Sphinx*
translated by Emma Ramadan · FRANCE

JÓN GNARR · *The Indian* · *The Pirate*
translated by Lytton Smith· ICELAND

NOEMI JAFFE · *What are the Blind Men Dreaming?*
translated by Julia Sanches & Ellen Elias-Bursac · BRAZIL

JUNG YOUNG MOON · *Vaseline Buddha*
translated by Yewon Jung · SOUTH KOREA

FOUAD LAROUI · *The Curious Case of Dassoukine's Trousers*
translated by Emma Ramadan · MOROCCO

LINA MERUANE · *Seeing Red*
translated by Megan McDowell · CHILE

FISTON MWANZA MUJILA · *Tram 83*
translated by Roland Glasser · DEMOCRATIC REPUBLIC OF CONGO

ILJA LEONARD PFEIJFFER · *La Superba*
translated by Michele Hutchison · NETHERLANDS

RICARDO PIGLIA · *Target in the Night*
translated by Sergio Waisman · ARGENTINA

SERGIO PITOL · *The Art of Flight* · *The Journey*
translated by George Henson · MEXICO

MIKHAIL SHISHKIN · *Calligraphy Lesson: The Collected Stories*
translated by Marian Schwartz, Leo Shtutin,
Mariya Bashkatova, Sylvia Maizell · RUSSIA

SERHIY ZHADAN · *Voroshilovgrad*
translated by Reilly Costigan-Humes & Isaac Stackhouse Wheeler · UKRAINE

COMING FALL/SPRING 2016–2017 FROM DEEP VELLUM

CARMEN BOULLOSA · *Heavens on Earth*
translated by Shelby Vincent · MEXICO

ANANDA DEVI · *Eve Out of Her Ruins*
translated by Jeffrey Zuckerman · MAURITIUS

JÓN GNARR · *The Outlaw*
translated by Lytton Smith· ICELAND

CLAUDIA SALAZAR JIMÉNEZ · *Blood of the Dawn*
translated by Elizabeth Bryer · PERU

JOSEFINE KLOUGART · *Of Darkness*
translated by Martin Aitken · DENMARK

SERGIO PITOL · *The Magician of Vienna*
translated by George Henson · MEXICO

EDUARDO RABASA · *A Zero-Sum Game*
translated by Christina MacSweeney · MEXICO

BAE SUAH · *Recitation*
translated by Deborah Smith · SOUTH KOREA

JUAN RULFO · *The Golden Cockerel & Other Writings*
translated by Douglas J. Weatherford · MEXICO

ANNE GARRÉTA · *Not One Day*
translated by Emma Ramadan · FRANCE

YANICK LAHENS · *Moonbath*
translated by Emily Gogolak · HAITI

DEEP VELLUM